The Dismaying Discovery

It was bad enough that Gillian had gone riding without a groom. It was even worse that her garb verged on impropriety. But worst of all was the man who discovered her napping in a forest nook.

"Do you make it a habit of lying about unattended on the property of scarcely known gentlemen?" the Marquess of Clare asked. "What would Rockingham think of his future bride? Or don't you want to wed?"

"Why are you not married, my lord?" Gillian replied tartly. "Because you've not a loyal bone in your body?"

"Precisely." Clare arched a mocking eyebrow. "Leg shackles are damnedly confining for a man. But for you, it is the ticket to wealth and social standing."

Gillian had had enough. She tugged on her horse's reins to lead it to a rock that could be used as a mounting block. Before she reached it, Clare caught her by the waist and turned her toward him.

"What?" she gasped.

"I am only helping you to leave," he murmured.

If so, he was doing a singularly bad job of it. . . .

D0054454

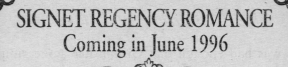

The Irish Rake

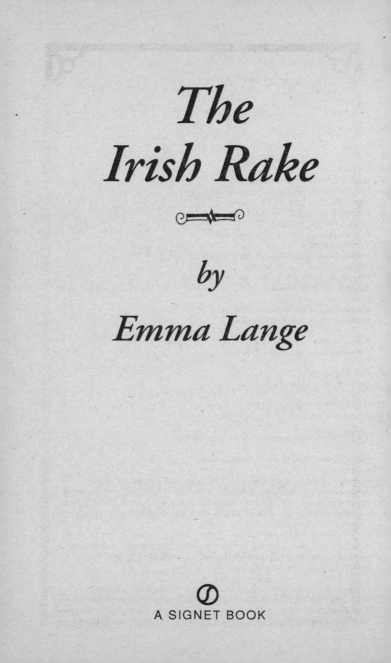

by

Emma Lange

A SIGNET BOOK

SIGNET
Published by the Penguin Group
Penguin Books USA Inc., 375 Hudson Street,
New York, New York 10014, U.S.A.
Penguin Books Ltd, 27 Wrights Lane,
London W8 5TZ, England
Penguin Books Australia Ltd, Ringwood,
Victoria, Australia
Penguin Books Canada Ltd, 10 Alcorn Avenue,
Toronto, Ontario, Canada M4V 3B2
Penguin Books (N.Z.) Ltd, 182–190 Wairau Road,
Auckland 10, New Zealand

Penguin Books Ltd, Registered Offices:
Harmondsworth, Middlesex, England

First published by Signet, an imprint of Dutton Signet,
a division of Penguin Books USA Inc.

First Printing, May, 1996
10 9 8 7 6 5 4 3 2 1

Chapter 1

The Marquess of Clare saw her first from the window of an inn. She and two other girls of similar, scarcely tried age were below him upon the lawn that was the small inn's principal draw, for it sloped to a picturesque, sun-dappled stream over which a fleet of majestic swans held sway.

Lazy from lovemaking with the woman still dozing in the bed behind him, Clare had strolled to the window simply to test the weather and had idly noted the two girls, who so resembled every other fresh-faced, moderately pretty English girl of about seventeen or eighteen that his eye had moved on to the river. She stood there, throwing bread scraps to the swans. Standing with her back to him, clad in a sturdy carriage dress that concealed her figure, she looked scarcely different from the other two girls. He'd have glanced away, back to the bed, perhaps, but she did an unexpected thing. One of the larger swans had appropriated a piece of bread she'd intended for a gosling. When the old swan did the same thing a second time, the girl availed herself of a nearby stick and thwacked him with it not once but twice, despite a shrilly aggressive response from the old swan.

Clare chuckled.

The other two girls cried out in alarm. The third girl, the fearless one, turned around. And Clare's lazily amused expression changed. She was not moderately pretty, or even pretty. True, she was a girl yet. Perhaps she had made her come-out, but Clare did not think she could have had more than one Season. Yet, the pure, fine-drawn bones of her face would have made her beautiful were she in leading strings or an old harridan. From a pleasantly broad brow her face narrowed to a firm chin. Her only slightly tilted nose was straight and slender, and though he could not see the color of her eyes, he could see they were well spaced and wide. Her eyebrows were delicate arches, distinctly darker than the tawny curls escaping from the edge of her bonnet. She was laughing, perhaps at the antics of the swan now waddling indignantly away. Clare would have studied her mouth—would have with most women—for it was full, and like the rest of her features, pleasingly formed, but the effects of her laughing smile distracted him. Her smile lit her face, filling it with such warmth and charm, he felt something more than the usual desire for a beautiful woman stir in him. Perhaps it was a desire to smile with her.

He did not. Wearing naught but a pair of unfastened breeches, his naked shoulders propped against the window, his mistress of the moment in the bed behind him, Clare felt ages older than the girl, his innocence too long lost to smile with her no matter how lovely her face or luminous her smile.

"Now, I wonder what it is that has kept you out of bed, Jason," purred the woman whom he had thought in bed still. Lady Caroline Castlemont, wife of a gouty, if wealthy, earl, wrapped her arms around Clare's sleek waist. "What are you watching so intently?"

"Innocence at play, Caro mia," he drawled, failing to remove his attention from the girl on the lawn despite the soft press of the countess's breasts against his bared back.

"Innocence! How very dull, Jason, and I might add, not at all in your style." Lady Castlemont fanned her fingers across his bare stomach. It was hard and flat, and she might have explored lower, but some twinge of curiosity prompted her to look over her lover's shoulder, whereupon she gave a very dif-

ferent cry. "Good, God! Emily and Betts Wade! Blast! What
are they doing here?"

"Feeding the swans?" Clare inquired, glancing blandly over
his shoulder.

"Such humor, Jason!" Lady Castlemont grabbed a sheet
from the bed and wrapped it around herself before she returned to peer over his shoulder again. "And the silly twits are
not feeding the swans. I don't doubt, they are too frightened.
Gillian Edwards is the girl feeding them, but I am no happier
to see her!"

Jason Devereux, Marquess of Clare, flicked his gaze from
the slender young goddess only a half story below him to his
mistress. Lady Castlemont, glancing up, saw the quizzical lift
of one of his dark eyebrows. "She knows me! Oh, lud, but not
half so well as the other two! They are Hetty's girls. La! I
knew it!" she hissed suddenly diverted by a movement on the
lawn below. "Hetty is with them."

"Surely that is not too surprising," Clare observed, looking
outside again, though not at Caroline's cousins or their
mother. Gillian Edwards. It was a suitable name for it was as
English as she looked. "Young ladies do not travel about un-
escorted, and the most likely person to escort them is generally
a mother."

His voice was deep and lazy and carried just the hint of an
Irish lilt. Normally it turned Lady Castlemont to liquid, but not
just then. "It is all very well for you to act unmoved, my lord
of Clare! What is the worst that can happen to you if we are
discovered? Castlemont would scarcely challenge you to a
duel, for he knows as well as anyone the fate of the others who
have fought you! Oh, perhaps you would be received in fewer
homes than you are now, but as you are scarcely received
now, and do not care, I cannot think you will mind much,
while I . . ."

When she theatrically clapped her hand to her ample
bosom, Clare laughed out loud. "While you will thrive as al-

ways, I don't doubt, Caro." He was black-haired with dark
eyes and a dark, chiseled face. Although he was not classically
handsome, his smile had made women melt for him since he
was a boy. So when he smiled, even half mockingly, Lady
Caroline Castlemont forgot the worst of her pique.

"Barbarian," she purred, rubbing herself against him.

Clare shrugged the well-made shoulders that were, admit-
tedly, another element in his appeal for women. "I like to think
of myself as a realist, Caro my dear, and realistically I can see
no need for excitement. Do you truly believe Castlemont has
not heard any gossip to do with you?"

She hesitated a moment, not certain whether Clare referred
to gossip about the two of them, or gossip about her and some
other lover. There had been several, if none other so intriguing. In the end, she shrugged the uncertainty away, for the answer was the same in either case. "Castlemont may have heard
a whisper or two, but he has his own pleasures and does not
begrudge me mine so long as I am discreet. To have my own
cousin discover me with you, however, would not please
him."

"Then, you have no need for worry, Caro mia. Simply avoid
inviting your cousins to our room. Though I would never object, you understand."

He flashed her another smile, and if Clare was thinking of
the Sassenach-looking girl with the Sassenach-sounding name,
Lady Castlemont could not know it. "You are a devil, Jason!
And I don't doubt that if they did come, you would see it as
your obligation to entertain them. Lud! They'd probably never
leave."

Clare accepted the compliment with a lazy bow that made
Lady Castlemont hit at him, but her playful mood only lasted
until she caught a movement on the lawn below. Then her
pretty face fell. "But, Jason, don't you see? They will not be
obliged to come to our room in order to know I am here with a
man other than my husband. Their groomsmen are bound to

meet my groomsmen in the stables, and they know each other. Mine have visited Roundley House for years!"

"Calm yourself, Caro." Jason lightly flicked her chin with his finger. "Your groomsmen are not to return for another hour. You chose this particular inn because it is close enough to Salisbury that they'd have something to do and yet is far enough away from the town that no one you know would ever think to come here."

"Well, it is off the road Hetty should be using!" Lady Castlemont tossed her head, embarrassed at having forgotten in her consternation the leave she'd given her groomsmen. "The road from London to Somerset travels west out of Salisbury, not south."

"Perhaps the Wades are about to pay you a visit, then, Caro. Arley Hall is south of us, is it not?"

"It is, but they cannot be coming to visit me!" Lady Castlemont's bottom lip jutted forward as she frowned. She was accustomed to getting her way, and having her cousins arrive at the inn where she was trysting with her current lover was a distinctly unwanted occurrence. "Hetty knows better than to pay unannounced calls."

"Betts! Stop running and the silly thing won't chase you."

The voice was light, even, and pleasant. Clare glanced out the window, sure it belonged to Gillian Edwards. It did. The younger of Caroline's cousins was trying to escape a belligerent swan. As it chased her about the lawn, her exertions and shrieks elicited derisive laughter from her sister, and the sound advice from Miss Edwards.

"Ah! I have it!" Lady Castlemont clapped her hands together. "Betts is in school at Sherborne! It is only a few miles away, and they must have brought her here for an outing."

"If she chose the spot, she must have a taste for fear. Now she has taken to a chair."

Following his gaze, Lady Castlemont giggled. The youngest Wade girl had clambered into a chair and was standing on tiptoe crying to be delivered while the swan hissed viciously at her. As they watched, Gillian Edwards got up from the table where she and the others had taken seats, and by merely lifting a stick at the swan, sent the ill-tempered thing running into the water with a squawk. Laughing, her face alight with the sheer absurdity of the situation, she then helped Betts Wade down from her ineffective perch.

"She is not for you, Jason."

Clare had not realized Caroline was watching him. He'd been that lost in the Sassenach girl. Still, he found a lopsided smile. "And why not, Caro mia? Because I have no taste for inexperienced chits more innocent than interesting? Or because she looks so English, I feel half moved to throw up the window sash and recite the Bard's famous lines about 'this little England' to her?"

Lady Castlemont's smile did not quite reach her famous sapphire eyes. "I had forgotten you've little use for anything English, but for Englishmen's wives, of course. Yet there are two other reasons why she is not for you, and I find I will be pleased to inform you of them, for you have spent entirely too much time looking out the window at her. One"—she slid a long, manicured finger down the smooth muscles of his arm—"Miss Edwards will be your neighbor when you are ensconced at Beechfield Hall. Yes," she said to Clare's look of surprise. "Her uncle and guardian, Lord Albemarle, owns Moreham Park, the estate that marches with Beechfield. And second"—she caressed the same muscles with two fingers—"should you decide you might not object to debauching your nearest neighbor's innocent ward, Miss Edwards is all but betrothed to my brother. Lionel will be going to Hetty's soon, ostensibly to make a cousinly visit and to hunt, but in fact, he will continue to pay his addresses to Miss Edwards. If all goes as it ought, I suspect he will invite her to Mother and Father's for Christmas, when he will ask her to marry him. So you see, my darling, she has already been claimed by a . . . what do you call us?"

"Fools?" Clare queried with a straight face.

Immediately Caroline struck him, making him laugh, but when she tried to tug him toward the bed, his laughter faded. "I cannot, Caro. You will recall that my reason for traveling to the west is to meet with Lely's counselor at Beechfield Hall tomorrow morning, and if I am to keep the appointment, I must be off now while the weather holds."

"But Hetty and the girls will see you!"

"And what do you believe they will think, if they do see me, which is not at all certain, if I leave by the front of the inn?" That you are the most handsome devil they've ever seen, Lady Castlemont thought, but had the discretion not to blurt. When she remained silent, Clare shrugged. "You see? They are not likely to look at me and say, 'Of course, it is Clare! He must be with our cousin, Caroline.' "

"But what of me?" she demanded, her voice rising as he shrugged into his shirt.

"I warned you yesterday when I must leave, Caro."

He wasn't even looking at her but rummaging about the room for his boots. She stamped her foot. "But my groomsmen will not return for another hour! Surely one piece of property is not so important to you as I am."

"I thought that you desperately wished to meet me at that same property when you pay your duty visit to your Wade cousins next month." His voice was muffled, for one boot had landed under the bed. "If I do not go," he continued, straightening, "I will forfeit the property, and alas, you, Caro my dear, will be obliged to sleep without me when you next visit Somerset. I know I, at least, would be desolate." With his boots in his hand, his coat thrown carelessly over his shoulder, and his shirt half undone, he looked utterly disreputable. And more desirable than any man Lady Castlemont had ever seen. When he flashed a smile at her, her knees actually went weak.

"Come, kiss me farewell, Caro mia, so that I shall have something to remember you by."

She kissed him fervently, hoping to distract him, but quite soon, Lady Castlemont stood alone, staring at the doorway Clare had filled, her pale hand on her mouth, stifling a futile plea for him to bring his sleek, powerful body back to her arms.

Chapter 2

"Oh, Gilly, here he comes again! Stop him! Please!"

"Betts, you need only whack him with a stick yourself. He will cease to torment you when he knows he will suffer for it."

By then Gillian had no need even to rise from the table set beneath one of the massive shade trees on the inn's lawn, and despite her own good-natured advice, she rescued the younger girl by waving her handy stick in the direction of the swan.

"You are shockingly missish, Betts!" The elder of the Wade sisters, Emily, called out as her younger sister retreated from the stream to a seat beside Gillian. "I vow the young men in London will eat you alive when you make your come-out."

"You don't look the worse for wear, Em, and you are no braver than I am!" Betts shot back, much bolder with a sister than an unreasonable animal. "I recall when Gilly had to rescue you from that dog that had not a tooth in its head. And the young men in town will not eat me alive! Will they, Gilly?"

It was a lovely golden fall day. Gillian looked up from the stream meandering along nearly at their feet to smile amusedly. "I doubt they will, Betts. I have not read any recent reports of cannibalism in England."

Despite herself Betts laughed. "La, I wish I could have had my come-out this Season with you, Gilly. I'd have felt ever so much braver just waiting for you to say something like that.

And now, while I must languish another year at Miss Millington's, you are both nearly as good as married!"

Emily Wade gave her sister a smug look, but Gillian's brow lifted slightly. "Emily is betrothed to Lord Alnwick, true, Betts, but I am not betrothed."

"Cousin Lionel is distinctly attached to you, Gilly! Em wrote to tell me!"

"Your cousin and I have known each for some years, and he was kind enough to ease my path in town, but we are not betrothed."

"Cousin Lionel did more than ease your path, Gilly!" said Emily. "He was very particular in his attentions, driving you in the Park, dancing with you at every ball, and calling upon you nearly every day. Lud! Though I am loathe to admit it, I think Betts is in the right for once. You are all but betrothed to Lionel Townshend, Viscount Rockingham and future Earl of Becquith."

"Perhaps we should not say so!" Betts exclaimed before Gillian could decide exactly how she wished to reply. "Sally Rivers believes that if you say something will happen before it does, you may actually prevent it from happening!"

"Sally Rivers is a nodcock fool, Betts!" Emily rolled her hazel eyes to the heavens. "You cannot be listening to her. Assure me!"

"I listen to whom I please! In this instance, however, I only meant to explain why Gilly might not wish to say she and cousin Lionel are as good as wed."

"As the old saying goes: there is many a slip between cup and lip," Gillian remarked agreeably, and then, before either of the other girls could say more about the viscount, calmly changed the subject to Emily's betrothal and betrothed, subjects upon which the other girl could speak for hours.

Emily had just gotten to how Lord Alnwick had gone down on one of his knees to propose to her, when Mrs. Wade came sailing out from the inn to announce for the second time that they must go. Betts immediately burst into tears, but her mother was accustomed to dealing with the emotional outbursts of schoolgirls and handing her youngest daughter a handkerchief, merely warned Betts that unless she dried her tears, she would have a deplorably red nose when she returned to Miss Millington's Academy.

Gillian accompanied the younger girl to the necessary room to help her repair her appearance, and when they emerged the host of the inn informed them that Mrs. Wade and Miss Wade had gone already to their waiting carriage. Thanking him, the two girls left the inn with Betts in the lead. About halfway across the empty yard, the sound of a horse coming quickly around the corner of the inn prompted Gillian to glance over her shoulder to see if she and Betts might be in the rider's way.

Had they been, the horse could have done them damage. It was a powerful chestnut stallion and restive. As Gillian ran an admiring eye over the animal, noting how its coat gleamed in the afternoon sun, the stallion tossed its head and rolled its eyes, unnerved by the unexpected sight of a pair of young ladies.

Yet Gillian never feared that the stallion might elude the rider's control. He sat his mount with such negligent ease, controlling it so effortlessly yet completely, that Gillian looked up at him, half smiling in admiration.

And caught her breath. She had had no idea he was looking at her. But he was, and openly, almost as if he knew her.

He did not. There was absolutely no question of their ever having met. An unsteady bubble of laughter welled up in Gillian at the thought that she might, somehow, have forgotten the man. His features were roughly chiseled and striking beneath thick soot-black hair, while his shoulders were well fashioned and his body fine and lean. Most particularly, though, she knew she would never ever have forgotten his eyes. As dark as his black hair, they gleamed with a dancing, somehow intriguing light.

Or perhaps it was a mesmerizing light, Gillian thought when she realized with something akin to bewilderment that her eyes were still fixed upon his. Nor did she seem able to pull her gaze free. For a half moment, she even thought he would smile down at her while she stared up so openly, unacceptably at him.

But then Betts glanced over her shoulder and, seeing the stranger, gasped in awe. At once, Gillian jerked her gaze from the man, and sliding her arm under the younger girl's elbow, hastily urged Betts toward the waiting carriage, while the man on his chestnut stallion passed without further ado behind them and turned down the road to the north.

In the carriage, settled at last beside Betts on the seat that faced backward, Gillian glanced cautiously at Mrs. Wade and Emily. But both ladies were quite distracted, for while her friend was leaning forward to look out the window in the direction the stranger had taken, Mrs. Wade was shaking Emily's arm and admonishing her not to act in so vulgar a manner.

A sidelong look at Betts assured Gillian that she, too, was ignoring her mother in favor of following the stranger. Further, when he had passed out of sight and both girls had subsided back into the carriage, Gillian saw they were flushed enough that her own warm cheeks could not be thought remarkable.

"Who is he, Mama?" Emily demanded, her hazel eyes sparkling with excitement. "You know him. I know you do! You are wearing 'that' look. Is he a rake? Is he? He is striking enough!"

"Emily! Where is your composure! Where are your manners! La, if your grandmother were to hear you . . ."

"But, Mama!" It was Betts, looking quite as avidly interested as her sister. "We only want to know who he is! Tell us what you know!"

Gillian said nothing. She was as noted for her composure as the Wade girls were for their excitability, but just then, she felt entirely discomposed. Never in her life had she exchanged such a look with a stranger. It was not done. Yet she had done it, and though the exchange had lasted no more than a minute, her heart was still racing.

"Oh, very well!" Mrs. Wade threw up her hands in the face of her daughters' badgering. "I suppose you will have to know something of him. Lud, I cannot think what he was doing at this inn. The road to Chicksgrove is north of us, but that is his destination, I vow."

"That man is going to Chicksgrove!" Emily exclaimed, her words and her tone perfectly echoing the astonishment both Betts and Gillian felt at the news that the stranger's destination was their own village in Somerset.

Mrs. Wade nodded rather reluctantly. "Yes. He is the Marquess of Clare . . ."

"He is a marquess!" cried Betts.

"It is an Irish title," Mrs. Wade countered, frowning, "and he is not for you, Betts. However striking he may be, Clare is not received in the best company. His father was English, it is true. Though only a distant cousin of the Devereux's in Ireland, he inherited the title as the Irish branch had no sons, but Clare's mother was native Irish."

Both her daughters drew in scandalized breaths. Everyone knew the native Irish were little better than barbarians. They lived beyond the Pale, the English section of Ireland, and the phrase had already come to mean beyond civilized society.

"But why is he coming to Chicksgrove?" Emily asked impatiently.

"Because," her mother announced half vexedly, "he owns Beechfield Hall now."

"Beechfield? How can that be? Why on earth would Lord Lely sell to him?"

"Lord Lely did not sell. He gamed with Lord Clare, though the man has the luck of the devil, and promptly lost Beechfield to him."

"He wagered one of his estates?" Emily looked quite as shocked as her mother thought she ought to, but Betts' interest was not with the loser in the game.

"Is Lord Clare a gamester then, Mama?"

"I have never heard anyone suggest that he cheats, if that is what you are asking, Betts, but Clare does live off gaming. His Irish estate brings him nothing. It is too poor, and debt-ridden besides, and so, as I understand it, if he is to eat, he must game. They do say he never games against green boys," Mrs. Wade added, almost reluctantly. "But still, he wins far more often than he loses."

"And he is coming to live in Chicksgrove!" Her eyes taking on a rather dreamy look, Emily sank back against the thick squabs of her father's coach.

Her mother frowned at her. "I daresay he will not stay long in our backwater. And you will think no more about him, Em. He's a rogue, governed by rules of his own making. Lud, he's dueled at least twice and . . . well . . ." She seemed to think better of what she had been going to relate and shrugged. "Well, what I mean to say is if he has not compromised a well-bred girl to date, that is not to say he will not take an interest in innocence in the future, if he has the opportunity. Think of Alnwick, my girl."

"I will, Mama! I adore Matthew! Now, now, do not shake your head at me. Alnwick gave me leave to address him by his name, but that is my point, don't you see? He is such a dear, I would never stray. Nonetheless, you must admit it is exciting to have a titled, Irish rake living so close to us. Lud, he will be your closest neighbor, Gilly, for Moreham Park marches with Beechfield!"

Gillian's mouth curved on the instant. "That is true, yet somehow or other I cannot imagine—how was it you described him, Em? A titled Irish rake? Well, I doubt such a man will come frequently to Moreham to take tea with either Aunt Margaret or Uncle Arthur."

Even Mrs. Wade laughed. Gillian's guardian, Lord Albemarle was a thorough countryman who was known far and wide, first for his absorption with his estate, and second for his dislike of all things "dandyish" or "townish," while his sister, Lady Sutton, Gillian's aunt, was known equally far and wide for being a stickler of the highest order.

Still chuckling, Mrs. Wade shook her head. "No," she agreed. "I can scarce imagine Clare sitting down to tea with your Aunt Margaret. And as to what he might find to say to Albemarle! La, Gilly! While my girls make much of nothing, you are steady as usual!"

But Gillian knew she was not at all steady as usual. Merely knowing the man would live so close made her heart race again.

Chapter 3

Water flowed swiftly through a gutter-like ditch beside the lane, for it had rained each of the three days since Gillian and Mrs. Wade and Emily had returned from visiting Betts, and when Gillian reached a smaller lane turning off to the right, she had to raise her voice to be heard by the large dog loping before her.

"Come, Delhi! We go a different way today." The wolfhound turned and cocked its head as if it questioned her intent. Aware of a change in the rhythm of her heartbeat, Gillian called again, "Come. The Wythy may be too high for us to reach the island."

It might have been the truth, though why she thought she had to give any reason to a dog, Gillian did not know. Perhaps she had fairly shouted the words for the sake of Mrs. Jennings, who was hanging her laundry on the line. The tenant farmer's wife waved, and Gillian returned the greeting.

Mrs. Jennings did not look the least suspicious, of course. And why should she? "I don't intend to meet him, Delhi," Gillian muttered to her companion as their lane turned upward. "Grabbist Hill is on Uncle Arthur's side of the Wythy. I mean only to look for him. After all, it isn't often I've the opportunity to observe a rake and a gamester even from afar." Some note in her voice caused the wolfhound to raise his dark head and glance back at her. "Do you think my curiosity very bad, Delhi?" she asked. "He is Irish like you, and possesses similar dark, rugged good looks." The dog gave a friendly bark, never breaking stride, and then returned, its tail wagging rhythmically, to the task of sniffing the new lane they traveled. Gillian chuckled. "There! I do believe I have your permission to spy, Delhi. I will confess I suspected his similarities to you might appeal. They evidently do to me. I have not thought of much else these last three rainy days."

At the top of the hill, Gillian reined in, while Delhi charged into the bushes. A placid, willow-hung river, the Wythy curved around the bottom of the hill. The near bank belonged to Gillian's uncle, but the far bank was the border of the property the Marquess of Clare had won at cards. From her vantage point, Gillian could survey most of Beechfield; even in the distance she could see the high chimneys of the hall itself. She saw as well a man driving a cart along a lane; another two men stacked hay in a nearby field; and a group of men were reaping standing hay farther away. But there was no one riding a chestnut stallion.

She had not really expected to see him. "It was only a possibility," she confided to Delhi when the dog returned to her. "Something to enliven a gloomy day." Gillian glanced to the sky that was still leaden with clouds, aware she felt a not dissimilar heaviness of spirit. "Perhaps I miss the social flurry of the Season more than I thought." Glancing at Delhi, seated on his haunches now, looking at her, Gillian grimaced faintly. But she said no more about the Season. Abruptly, after one last look across to the neighboring estate, she turned her horse down another lane that led directly to the Wythy. She rode along it for almost half an hour, but still caught no sight of the man whose black eyes had had the mystifying power to seize and hold her fast.

Nor did Gillian see him the next day or the next. After a fourth day of riding the boundary of the two properties, she sighed, looking down at the dog that had been her faithful companion for the ten years she had been in England. "It would seem I told Emily nothing less than the truth when I said that proximity to him would mean little, Delhi. It appears the marquess has either abandoned his new property or prefers the house to riding out on his estate." The words, "It's likely for the best," she did not speak, though they did dance in her mind. To banish them, she said quickly, "Shall we visit Mrs. Wright? She'll provide us diversion from the Irish rake."

Delhi barked. A clever dog, he recognized the name of the person at whose house he received a treat whenever he visited. Gillian grinned at him, and setting her mare to a canter, came in a little while to a quaint stone cottage, almost entirely covered on one side by a heavy growth of ivy.

When Gillian opened the gate in the hedge that surrounded the cottage, Delhi bounded toward the front door, giving a series of happy, deep barks.

"Well an' look who's come to visit," a round, apple-cheeked maid laughed when she opened the door in response to those barks. "There's a good boy! So well mannered, ye are, Delhi." Patting the dog, who had sat down to wait for his mistress, she smiled at Gillian and bobbed a suggestion of a curtsy. "I wish ye'd come an' train my boys to be as good as Delhi here, Miss Gillian. It's not in 'em to wait quiet like at a door so far as I know."

She shook her head, and Gillian laughed. "How is your mistress today, Maddie? Is she receiving?"

"Oh, aye, Miss Gillian. Mrs. Wright has a visitor already, but he's not to stay long." Giggling, she added on a half whisper, "More's the pity! But go along in, and I'll fetch the tea tray. Come, Delhi. I do believe I saw a bone somewhere or other. We'll . . ."

Gillian divested herself of her hat and rather absently patted her hair into place as she proceeded the few paces down the hallway to Mrs. Wright's parlor. The widow would have heard Delhi's bark, as well as Gillian's entrance, but still she knocked at the door, and awaiting a summons to enter, caught the faint scent of sandalwood drifting on the air.

They had that exotic scent in common, she and Mrs. Wright, for they had not only lived in India but left it together. Mrs. Wright's husband, a sergeant in the British army, had been taken by the same fever that had taken Gillian's parents, and so it had been the widow, who had escorted Gillian to Moreham Park. Out of gratitude, Lord Albemarle had offered the garrulous, warmhearted woman the free use of one of his cottages for the rest of her life. Living on a modest pension and with most of her family only fifteen miles away in Dunster, Mrs. Wright had been only too delighted to accept the baron's offer with the result that she had enjoyed regular visits from Gillian over the years, despite their very different social stations.

"Well, here you are, my girl, come to enliven this parade of gray days!" Mrs. Wright cried when Gillian entered the small, perpetually overheated parlor. "Not like India, is it, where the sun is a bright angry eye in the sky?"

"And most everyone complains how hot it is," Gillian said with a chuckle as she leaned down to give Mrs. Wright's cheek a kiss.

Mrs. Wright threw back her head and laughed heartily. " 'Tis the human way, is it not? To complain about weather, but I am forgetting my manners more than even I usually do! Gilly, I've a guest. 'Tis our new neighbor, the Marquess of Clare." Availing herself of the walking stick at her side, she gestured from Gillian to the far side of the room. "My lord, this is my landlord's niece, Miss Gillian Edwards."

Gillian had not thought again of the visitor Maddie had mentioned. Mrs. Wright often had callers. She'd two sisters and their children living in Dunster, and old friends from her army days frequently called. Never for a moment had Gillian considered that *he* might be Mrs. Wright's visitor.

To her dismay, her heart began to hammer in her chest, and

she found it necessary to grip the back of Mrs. Wright's over-stuffed chair. She was that uncertain that her knees would support her as she dropped into the requisite curtsy.

"My lord."

Her voice had come out a little low, but mercifully it was steady. Her eyes, however, she could not control. They skimmed up over his long black boots and tight buckskins to his blue riding coat and the shoulders that caused it to hang so well. She remarked his height as she surveyed him, for he was taller than she had realized, but at the center of her thoughts was the understanding that she must meet his eyes, if only briefly. And impersonally, of course. Yet, despite her thorough understanding of courteous behavior, Gillian could not bring herself to run the risk his black eyes represented to her, now that she was unexpectedly face-to-face with the reputed rake. Hazily, she took in an impression of a strong chin, of a mouth neither too full nor too thin, but well-defined, of a lean, strong jaw, and of thick wavy black hair. She noticed his ear, too. Absurdly Gillian's gaze became fixed upon that perfectly unexceptional feature, noting in passing that it was well formed. Nor did it bear a gold earring as his rather piratical appearance made her fancy there might be.

"This is a pleasure, Miss Edwards. You are the second neighbor I have had the honor of meeting, Mrs. Wright being the first."

Gillian watched his ear turn away from her, as he, evidently, looked to acknowledge Mrs. Wright. Clearly Lord Clare did not remember her from the inn yard. Though she had thought of little but him, his quite impersonal and entirely commonplace remark proved that he'd forgotten her after only three days.

"Sit down, child. Sit down!" Mrs. Wright shook her walking stick in the direction of a wing chair near the marquess, but Gillian slipped into an uncomfortable, straight-backed seat immediately next to her hostess. "That's better." Mrs. Wright nodded in approval, though she gave Gillian a sharp look. The wing chair was the one her young visitor usually chose. "Lord Clare has acquired Beechfield from Lord Lely, which cannot but be an improvement in my estimation. I take liberty to warn you, my lord, you'd best be on the lookout for that rapscallion agent of old Lely's. The tenants all say he's naught but a thief."

Though Mrs. Wright continued to enlighten Lord Clare about the agent few in Chicksgrove trusted, Gillian scarcely heard her. She tried to compose herself, but her blood was pounding distractingly in her ears. He was notorious. He was a rake and a gamester. He had given her a lengthy, glinting, quite improper look in that inn yard! And she had returned it.

She shot a glance his way from the corner of her eye. He filled the wing chair, his head easily topping the back, though she felt dwarfed by the mate that was her usual chair. His elbows extended beyond the arms, and his well-muscled legs stretched some feet forward onto Mrs. Wright's Indian rug. His boots were mud spattered, but Gillian could tell from the quality of the leather that they were excellent, expensive boots. He did well at cards, it seemed.

The thought reminded her how disreputable he was. Ought she to go? It was a rhetorical question. Wild horses could not have pulled Gillian away, though the dutiful answer she gave the image of her aunt that appeared briefly in her mind was that she could not distress poor, semi-invalid Mrs. Wright by snubbing her guest.

He was looking at her. No. She was being absurd. Just as she had been of far less real interest to him in that inn yard than she had thought, so now she was imagining that he looked at her. Still, slowly, while Mrs. Wright fussed with a spaniel that had just come to yapping life at her feet, Gillian allowed her head to turn.

And met his eyes. He *had* been looking at her. He had . . . and he did remember her. Her heart slammed against her chest. His eyes were just as she had recalled them, black and gleaming. Only now, there was more in them; there was recognition. Without saying a word, he told her that he remembered her. Even that he remembered her very well, and for some reason, the knowledge brought heat to her cheeks.

"Well, now that Neddie's settled, I shall say that I think it is very fitting that Lord Clare's first acquaintances should be the two of us, Gilly."

"Oh? How is that ma'am?" Gillian hoped she had not jerked when Mrs. Wright said her name. She might well have. She had been right to be wary. Gazing into his eyes, she had almost completely forgotten herself again.

"Well, we are both foreigners to Somerset, just as he is. I know, I know," the older woman went on, waving a heavy hand. "I was born no more than ten miles from Chicksgrove, but my years abroad have set me apart from my old fellows as surely as if I had been born elsewhere."

"Where were you born, then, Miss Edwards, if not in Somerset?"

His voice was low and masculine, with a hint of a lilt but no more than that, and it was tinged, she thought, with amusement. And why should he not be all but laughing? She was behaving like a goose of a schoolgirl.

Clasping her hands tightly in her lap, Gillian forced herself to look composedly at the man who was, after all, not a pirate as she had privately imagined when she had envisioned that gold ring in his ear. Unfortunately she discovered that the reason it had been so hard for her to look at him directly in the first place had had nothing to do with his reputation, but everything in the world to do with his unnervingly striking looks. Before Gillian knew it, as if they'd a will of their own, her lashes shielded her eyes, and though she tried to take comfort in the knowledge that looking down in that demure way was what a well-bred young lady was expected to do, she felt again a silly green girl. "I was born in India, my lord, in Calcutta."

"Gillian and I returned to England together," Mrs. Wright told the marquess with a fond smile for Gillian. "And we have stood by each other ever since. Why, we've even shared a dish of curry, though Maddie was scandalized just by the smell of it."

"Now then, I weren't any such thing!" Maddie protested as she entered the room. Carrying the tea tray to a table beside Mrs. Wright, she gave her employer a superior look. "If you wants to be burnin' your tongue and young Miss Gilly's, too, then it's none of my affair."

"No, indeed, it isn't, but still you wrinkled that nose of yours! I ought to have made you eat a bite. It would have done you a world of good to taste something unusual."

"Not me!" Maddie cried, looking horrified. " 'Twould be the death of me stomach to eat such heathen foods."

Gillian was trying not to smile outright, a battle she often fought when she came to Mrs. Wright's, for her hostess almost invariably squabbled with her maid. Curious as to how an accomplished rake and gamester would view such goings on, she shot Lord Clare a glance. Only to find again that he was watching her, which discovery could well have sent her gaze flying from his, particularly as his eyes were lit with amusement. But his half smile and the gleam in his eyes were rather different now. She understood somehow that he was laughing with her, sharing her amusement, and she felt her own mouth lift further in response.

Gillian lost all sense of how long the rapport lasted, though of course it was undoubtedly only a moment. It did not take Maddie an endless amount of time to set down the tea tray and arrange its contents to Mrs. Wright's liking. Still, to Gillian it seemed a very long time that she—gently reared, upstanding Gillian Edwards—smiled into the dark, too-compelling eyes of the Marquess of Clare, the Irish rake who looked at once entirely out of place in the small, overstuffed, overheated parlor of a sergeant's widow and yet completely at his ease there.

The moment ended when Maddie withdrew, for Clare looked to Mrs. Wright and rose. "You will have to excuse me from tea, Mrs. Wright. I came only to beg your pardon about the sheep and must be on my way now."

"I'm that sorry to hear it!" Mrs. Wright proclaimed forthrightly. "In all, I think I am grateful to your sheep for blundering into my garden. What are a few flowers to a visit from a man like you, eh, my lord?"

Gillian could not keep from smiling at her hostess's frankness. Clare, she noted, was not thrown the least off his stride by the praise. He laughed, his smile flashing very white in contrast to the darkness of his hair and eyes. "The pleasure was mine, ma'am, I assure you, and I promise I shall be back for more of your insights into matters at Beechfield."

"You are a flatterer!" Mrs. Wright said delightedly, and beamed when the marquess lifted her hand to his lips. "And you're every inch the rake you look, too, I don't doubt! Come again soon!"

"I will, ma'am. You have my word on it." He turned then to Gillian, but did not kiss her hand, as she had half expected, or hoped, perhaps, that he would do. He only inclined his head rather lazily. "Good afternoon, Miss Edwards. It has been a privilege."

And that was that. Perhaps he gave her a smile, she could not be quite certain, for the smile he had worn had been faint and seemed more directed at some amusement of his own than at her. Then he was already striding to the door almost before she could murmur her own quite commonplace adieu.

After Clare's departure, Mrs. Wright held forth on the sheep that had gotten out of one of his fields and crossed the Wythy at the last of the three bridges in the vicinity of Chicksgrove in order to trot, for no discernible reason, directly to Mrs.

Wright's garden. Gillian nodded now and again, but found herself only half listening to her hostess.

Lord Clare's departure had left her oddly deflated. She had just begun to feel a little comfortable in his presence when he had taken his leave. And now . . . but what had she expected: that he would invite her and her aunt to tea at Beechfield, if she somehow managed an initial encounter with him? In fact, it was highly improbable that they would even lay eyes on one another again. As Mrs. Wright was observing just then, a disreputable rake would not likely linger long in their quiet little corner of the country.

Chapter 4

Jason spurred his stallion, setting the chestnut to a canter. He could hear a dog barking with what seemed to be urgency somewhere ahead, and he welcomed the distraction. He had been surveying the gently undulating land he now owned. And managed.

That was the vexation, not the orderly, fertile land with its thick stacks of hay and fat sheep and abundant orchards. He had fired the accursed agent, Murdock. All the perfectly sound reasons he'd had came to his mind: the man had been a rotter—the sort to cringe before his masters but kick his inferiors—lazy, incompetent, and not least, the thief Mrs. Wright had named him. Jason had taken an implacable dislike to him on sight and would not have paid him another penny in salary, had Murdock been the last agent on earth.

Still. He had not intended to remain in remote, dull, if beautiful, Somerset beyond Caroline's visit a month hence. Until then he had thought to while away much of his time with Darnley, Staunton, and Oversby. They were to come in a few days, bringing women. Darnley had mentioned opera dancers. Or perhaps actresses. Their professions did not matter; were, indeed, much the same, for both provided the women pursuing them the opportunity to display their charms for prospective supporters.

What would Bexton think of his female guests? An unholy gleam lit Jason's dark eyes as he contemplated the reaction of the starchy butler who had served Lord Lely's family for decades only to find himself now in the employ of an Irishman. Never mind that Jason was half English with the not insignificant title of marquess. For Bexton, as for most Englishmen, Jason's native Irish mother canceled out any respect that might be accorded him on account of the former two points. The knowledge had once affected Jason. He'd taken pleasure in besting—whether with his fists or his mind—the English puppies who had thought to sneer at him at school. Later he had taken equal pleasure in winning those grown prigs' money for Conmarra and wooing their wives to his bed. The duels had merely been a part of the whole, though he could not say he had not enjoyed sighting down his pistol and watching the no-longer-so-arrogant cuckold at the other end and squirm a bit.

He was older now, though. He had seen enough prejudice on the Irish side to realize prejudice was not a wholly English sin, and then, too, with time his skin had simply grown thicker. Bexton had kept Beechfield Hall and its staff in excellent order, though his employer, Lely, had visited only once every year or two. Jason respected that kind of dedication to duty and had no intention of turning the man off, though, recalling Darnley and the opera dancers, he could not but admit—that gleam in his eye again—that he was not so aged and reasonable that he would not find a bit of fun in tweaking the butler's lofty nose.

And what did it matter if he stayed beyond the month on which he'd planned? Lely, or his father, had put down some excellent brandy. He'd persuade Darnley to stay and help him drink it while he managed the estate and looked about for a suitable agent. When he had one, he'd return to town and its pleasures as he had planned. Eventually, when he had found a buyer who would meet his price, he would sell Beechfield and send, as he always did, the major part of winnings back to Ireland, to Liam working away at Conmarra. The rest? Well, he had expenses of his own, among them the little house in Brook Street and whomever he chose to occupy it.

Smiling faintly, he glanced across the Wythy to Lord Albemarle's land. *She* most certainly would not occupy that house in Brook Street. Indeed, she would be quite wasted there. Though she was more than beautiful enough for the position of mistress, she had been trained for a wife's role.

What would she think when she heard, as she was bound to do in so small a community, of the Cyprians brought to Beechfield for his pleasure? She would, of course, be shocked to the pretty tips of her toes, and that was just as well. Censorious, she would be a great deal less likely to look at him with heated interest.

That heat, that awareness of him as a man, had sizzled in her eyes for no longer than a second. Jason doubted she had even been aware of it. She was too innocent, too inexperienced, as well as bred not even to recognize so unseemly a response. But that peculiarly charged excitement had flashed in her eyes, nonetheless, when finally, after seating herself as far from him as possible in that spine-torturing, high-backed chair, she had, all unexpecting, met his eyes.

He was too experienced not to recognize her interest in him as a male, but even had he been a green boy he would have known that he affected her in some way. There had been too much color staining her fair, silky smooth skin for him not to know. Though in Miss Edwards's case, it was likely that her blush had been produced by more than uncertainty at being in company with a stranger. Hugh Wade's wife would have warned her that he was a disreputable stranger.

The world of the upper ten thousand of English society was exactly that, a small world of ten thousand, and he was as well-known within it as were the eligible bachelors. After all, mothers had to know from whom to protect their daughters.

Yet, Jason half smiled again, though she had to know he was to be avoided, she had not turned on her heel and fled

Mrs. Wright's parlor. She'd at least a little taste for adventure. He smiled again at the thought, then recalled the odd, almost companionable moment when they'd shared their amusement at Mrs. Wright's relations with her maid. She had then, in addition to some sense of adventure, another admirable trait, a sense of humor.

None of that, of course, was to mention the gray eyes that had sparkled with that humor. He had seen they were gray when he had ridden by her in the inn yard, but it was not until he was able to see her eyes unshadowed by the brim of a bonnet that he'd received their full impact. They were the gray of a mist, and as changeable, going from the darker gray of a rain to the light, luminous gray of mist caught in sunshine. And all the while set off by the lashes that were, as he had expected, darker than hair that was the color of a fawn's coat.

She was a beauty, a thoroughly Sassenach one, tawny-haired and gray-eyed. And though thoroughly innocent, begging not to be. He could seduce her without half trying.

"Bloody hell," Jason swore aloud. "Bloody, bloody hell."

He could not remember the last time he had exerted himself to resist temptation. Particularly feminine temptation. And yet he was not such a rogue that he would seduce a young innocent girl, even a beautiful, receptive, Sassenach girl.

Jason did not realize he was scowling until, suddenly, his mouth twitched. What a very pitiful lad he was, indeed, moaning over one noble act, when his resolution would never be tested. He would never see the girl again. Certainly her guardians would not be inviting him to tea to throw him together with Miss Edwards. Even were they rustics, they would learn from Hetty Wade he was no candidate for marriage. Nor was he, for he had not the least interest in domesticity. He had not been bred for the faithful life, likely, but neither had he any need to leg-shackle himself. Liam, good Liam, had the succession at Conmarra safely in hand, which left Jason free to please himself. And if the price of that freedom was resisting one girl he would never see?

Jason laughed aloud. He was a pitiful lad, indeed.

But he was on something of a mission. The barking sounded much louder now and came, as far as he could tell, from a hill just ahead of him where there had once been a stone quarry.

The quarry had been abandoned long before. Trees and bushes grew out of the exposed rocks, but Jason found that a well-worn path wound up the hill. It led him by dozens of smaller excavations, probably dug by local men needing stones for their fences. One or two of the excavations looked as if they had fallen in on themselves, or perhaps had hit a natural fissure in the rock, for they were dark enough to indicate they were dangerously deep.

He was close now, nearing the top of the hill. The dog was just ahead and had to be a huge thing, judging from the depth and power of its bark. Rounding a thick group of birch trees, Jason saw how right he was. Beside a low bramble bush stood an enormous, grizzled Irish wolfhound. Jason's brow lifted. The animal was clearly valuable and someone's pet, but he was not left to puzzle long. Riding forward only a few steps, he saw the mare and recognized her as the same mount that had been standing before Mrs. Wright's gate when he had left her and Miss Gillian Edwards to their tea.

A sudden frown lowering his brow, Jason spurred his stallion forward. Predictably the chestnut reacted to the mare, but Jason held him steady, and soon had him tied securely to another low limb. The dog ceased barking to look toward him, and then in an oddly communicative gesture tossed his head, as if to say, "Come here!"

Jason did not need the urging. Spared the dog's noise, he could hear Gillian Edwards's voice. "Listen to me, Davy! You will be all right, if you hold tight to your ledge. You must be brave and guide me, for I am going to come down the rope to you."

Rounding the bushes, Jason saw her on her knees bending over a narrow, exceedingly dark hole. "What in the devil?"

At the sound of his voice, Gillian started in surprise. For just a moment when their eyes met that same warm and feminine light flared in her eyes, but it was gone almost before he remarked it to be replaced by a look of passionate relief.

"Lord Clare! Thank God Delhi's incessant barking brought you! Young Davy Jennings has gotten himself into the worst scrape. He has fallen onto a thin ledge down in this shaft. I have tried to lower this rope to him, but there is another ledge above him that interferes, and I am afraid the only way to rescue him is to go after him."

Jason took in the rope, the nearby sapling to which it was tied, and the knot he could see at a distance was slipshod enough to have gotten her killed. "Why in the name of God did you not fetch some help?" he barked at her, glowering.

She blinked those wide gray eyes, diverted. "Well . . . I did not believe there was time. The ledge is slippery."

"And yet you'd time to fetch a rope! Or do you make it a habit to ride with one?"

Her expression turned decidedly cool. "It was Davy who brought the rope. His cousins dared him to go down into the shaft to retrieve a sovereign they dropped, but partway down he slipped, lost the rope, and only just managed to break his fall on the ledge. Now, my lord, have you other questions I may answer while the boy slips from the ledge to his doom? Or shall we get on with what must be done?"

Distracted by her other attributes, Jason had half forgotten the spine she had displayed with the aggressive swan at the inn. Before he could think better of it, he flicked her rather stubborn chin with a gloved finger. "We'll save the boy, now I am satisfied you are not a complete fool."

Her gray eyes flashed wide. Jason judged that though his remark might have displeased her, it was his touch that had startled her. If so, he was not chagrined. By God, she needed to learn that consequences would follow the sort of heated, if brief, looks she had given him. Men were not, in general, angels, and if she went around flashing those eyes at other men of whom she knew little more than their names, she'd end up suffering consequences considerably worse than a flick on the chin.

Ignoring her start of surprise, Jason knelt down beside Gillian to peer into the black depths of the shaft. When his eyes had adjusted to the dark, he made out a young boy huddled upon a very narrow ledge. Even from above, Jason could see he was shaking with fear. "Davy?" he called in a calm but authoritative voice. "I am Lord Clare. You need have no fear. I will check the knot you tied first, and then I will come down for you. Do you understand?"

After a moment a very faint, very high, "Yes, m'lord," floated up to them.

It took Jason a moment to retie the boy's inexpert knot, and another to tie the end of the rope around his own waist. Coming back to the pit, he shrugged out of his coat and looked to Gillian. She had been speaking softly to the boy, but now she glanced up at him, awaiting direction.

He threw his coat across a convenient bush. "I am going to go down to Davy's left, because there is a bit of ledge there for me to stand upon."

She nodded. "I shall try to guide you."

"Only with your voice. If you lean over too far, you will block my light. Go to that side." He pointed to the spot where he wanted her. "From there you should be able to see without obstructing my view. And chin up, girl. I've known men who would make this climb for amusement."

She stared at him a moment, uncertain whether to believe him. Jason gave her a swift smile to convince her, yet when she rose, she murmured softly, "I take leave to doubt you, my lord, but thank you for trying to assure me. And good luck to you."

Jason nodded, half smiling, for she had, in all, not merely clear gray eyes, but clear seeing ones as well, then catching up the rope, began to lower himself over the side of the shaft. It was as well he had Gillian to direct him. The moment he reached the shadows, he was half blinded by the dark.

"Move two steps to your right, Lord Clare," she called down. "Yes, there, that's good."

Hand over hand, feeling with the toes of his boots to find a purchase on the damp rocks, Jason made his way to the boy. He'd further to go than he realized. From above he had judged the ledge to be no more than ten feet down, but he'd been deceived. The boy was a good fifteen to twenty feet down in the darkness.

A stone came loose, tumbling down, and Jason heard a frightened sniffle below him. "You are doing splendidly, Davy," he said, keeping his voice low. "I am sorry if that rock hit you, but there won't be many more."

"Still farther right, Lord Clare," Gillian called down.

Looking down between his feet, Jason saw he was in danger of stepping on the boy. "Stay where you are, Davy. It won't be much longer now."

When he had found the ledge with his foot, Jason braced himself against it, and looked down at Davy. The child regarded him with wide, frightened eyes. "We've almost done it now, lad. I am going to straddle you and then lift you with one hand, but you must help. As soon as you can, I want you to wrap your arms around my neck, and then your legs around my waist. Will you do it?"

Davy had pressed himself tightly back against the damp side of the shaft. "Y-y-yes, m'lord," he whispered.

Jason carefully inched along the thin, slippery rock ledge, maneuvered one leg over the boy's head, then lowered himself a step below the ledge. The position was awkward, but his legs were long enough to manage the stance. When his waist was at the level of the boy's head, he reached down and caught

Davy's arm. "Now I am going to lift you toward me. Push up with your legs, if you can."

He was young. No more than six or seven and terrified, but with a grown man directly in front of him, speaking calmly, Davy found the courage to move when directed to do so. Pushing up, as if to stand, he soon was high enough to wrap his arms around the marquess's neck. At once, Jason pulled himself up to stand on the ledge, a position that relieved pressure on the rope that was of uncertain stoutness.

"Now then," he smiled encouragingly, "wrap your legs around my waist, and we'll be off."

With the boy clinging to him like a limpet, Jason began his ascent. Above him, he could hear Gillian running around the edge of the shaft to meet them, but he concentrated most of his thoughts on pulling up, one hand over the other, while his feet sought out the largest and stablest rocks for support.

When Jason neared the top, Gillian reached down and plucked young Davy off him, lifting the boy to safety. She did not forget the rescuer, however. When she had set Davy down, she caught Jason's arm and helped him scramble the last few feet out of the pit and away from danger.

"My thanks, Miss Edwards." Resting on his knees, breathing hard, he nodded to her, then looked to the boy. "Are you all right but for the fright you took, Davy?"

The boy jerked his head in a negative motion, and Jason realized he had his hand clasped tightly to his knee. Gillian was no slower to understand. "Did you hurt your knee, Davy?" she asked, gently lifting his hand away. He had scraped it on the ledge, and there was a considerable amount of blood to be seen. Without the least flinching, she withdrew a handkerchief from her sleeve and wiped the wound to inspect it.

"It is not a deep cut, Davy. After it is washed, I think we'll find there is no need even to call upon Dr. Hogwood. But the first thing we must do is get you home." She looked up at Jason. "And thank Lord Clare. Can you do that, Davy?"

"Thank you, Lord Clare" came the response in a tiny voice.

Jason nodded. "I am glad to have been of service to a boy so brave, though I do hope he has learned not to be so foolish as to descend into a dark shaft again."

It was a question, though made as a statement. When Davy nodded with convincing fervency, Jason smiled his approval. "Well then, if Miss Edwards will lift you up to me, I shall get you home to your mother."

As Davy was able to stand, Gillian had no difficulty lifting him up when Jason had mounted the stallion and the removal to the boy's home was accomplished easily enough. Indeed, the closer they got to his home, the more Davy seemed to throw off his frightening experience, and by the time they reached the Jennings's modest home, accompanied by Gillian and her dog, Davy was sitting straight and quite proud before the marquess.

Not caring a great deal for the maternal fuss Mrs. Jennings made first over her son and then over him, Jason soon excused himself, pleading unspecified and in all illusory business.

Gillian followed him out of the tenants' house, waving her adieus, too.

"You can find your way back to the bridge, my lord?" she asked, for they had had to turn down two lanes after crossing the Wythy.

"Yes." Jason raked his eyes over her. Her riding costume was wrinkled and grass-stained, and her bonnet was slightly askew, but she did not look much the worse for wear. Far from it, in fact, she looked as tempting as a just-ripened peach, and his eyes narrowed.

"My lord, I wish to thank you very much for your assistance." Gillian was studying the limb of a nearby tree, quite unaware of the change in Jason's expression. "Had you not come to Davy's aid, he might have been killed . . . and I as well. I am sure my uncle would wish to thank you, himself, if you would care to come to Moreham Park for tea."

"I would not in the least care to come." Her eyes flew to his. He held her gaze, his own eyes gleaming with a mocking light. "A word to the wise, Miss Edwards: I am not now nor ever will be a candidate for domestication. I hope I have made myself clear?"

Though she did not speak a word in response, Jason mounted his stallion satisfied that young Miss Edwards had understood him very well. Rosy color had surged from her neck to her hairline as her mouth parted in shock at his rudeness. Yet embarrassment had not been the only emotion she betrayed. Rather against his will, the memory he carried with him as he rode away was not of that blush half so much as the indignant and sorely tempting heat that had flashed vividly in her gray eyes.

Chapter 5

"Well, Gilly, were the Wade ladies beside themselves to know every detail of our new neighbor's rescue of the Jennings lad?"

Gillian gave her uncle a wry smile. "They were, though they knew a bit already, of course. I don't doubt half the homes around Chicksgrove had the gist of the story by yesterday, one day after."

Her uncle gave a great laugh. "Or by evening of the day. But just think, Gilly, a stranger, who has won a rich estate at cards, comes to our sleepy backwater, and what should be his first act in Chicksgrove? Why, he plays the hero!"

Lord Albemarle chuckled richly again, but he did not bother to inquire as to what had interested the Wade ladies. The conversation of females, even though he dearly loved one of the females involved, held as little interest for him as the finer points of tilling a field might for Gillian.

As they rode toward Chicksgrove, a comfortable silence settled between them. Albemarle frowned abstractedly, doubtless thinking of the conversation he had had with Mr. Wade, which left Gillian to follow her own thoughts, whether she wanted to do so or not.

And she did not much. The exchange at Roundley House had been nerve-wracking. Lud, she had had to keep so much back while appearing to tell all, she felt exhausted. And worse, a sly-boots.

Even the simplest question had been fraught with pitfalls and evasions. "Did he only give his name or did he say he owns Beechfield now?" Emily had asked, her eyes dancing with interest for even so minor a detail.

Gillian had murmured something vague about how they'd not had the time to go into particulars, though, of course, the honest answer would have been to say he had had no time to present himself, that Mrs. Wright had already presented him to Gillian, but no one knew of that meeting, because she had not thought there was any reason to send her aunt into vapors by reporting it. The omission had seemed quite innocent at the time. Gillian truly had believed she would never see Lord Clare again.

By the time the second difficult question came, Gillian was forewarned, but not, as it turned out, to much effect. Given her interest in details, it was not surprising that Emily should innocently want to know what sort of clothes Lord Clare had worn, yet Gillian had had no answer for her friend except the vague excuse that her alarm for Davy had prevented her from remarking much of Lord Clare's dress other than that he had been dressed for riding.

And even that excuse had come after a split second of rattled silence, for while she had struggled mightily to recall what Lord Clare had worn, all she'd been able to think of was the moment when he had shrugged out of his coat and stood before her in only his shirt.

The action in itself had been unremarkable. The coat had fit too tightly across his shoulders to allow him the unrestricted movement he needed to bring Davy out of the shaft. It was the effect upon her that had not been at all unremarkable.

Despite her distress for Davy, Gillian had caught her breath for the veriest second. She had no brothers, and her uncle, though he proclaimed himself a thorough rustic, never went about without his coat. Sheltered as she had been, Gillian had not been prepared for the sight of a man dressed in nothing more than a soft lawn shirt tucked into the waist of his breeches. Nor, certainly, for the oddly liquid fluttering she'd experienced.

She ought to have kept her eyes on his face, granting him that courtesy, and yet her eyes had flicked down over him, even fastening for a split second, she was horrified to admit, just where the shirt disappeared into the breeches that hung low on his hips.

Riding along beside her uncle, Gillian closed her eyes a long moment. Worse, she had not stopped there. No well-bred young lady should remark that a man had legs. She should not even mention them to herself, and yet, she . . . she had brazenly let her eyes travel further down over Clare's legs, a near stranger's long, booted legs!

Gillian bit her lip. She knew to the inch how to behave. Her aunt had instilled decorum in her. More, she was known for her composure, her good sense, her levelheadedness.

And he . . . he had known how he affected her!

"I am not a candidate for domestication, Miss Edwards."

She shut her eyes against the sting of those words and the mocking look that had accompanied them. And only saw more clearly those black eyes that had read her so clearly. She had, indeed, been calculating that given his good deed on behalf of one of her uncle's tenants, she could gain him an invitation to her aunt's drawing room . . . and after the one visit . . . she had not thought that far ahead, and yet he had presumed to guess she intended repeated invitations. *Domestication.* She would rather have liked to hiss at him for that condescending—and deuced premature—rejection.

Yet, despite that mortifying, infuriating parting, still, it had been all Gillian could do not to leap to Clare's defense at the Wades, when Mrs. Wade had remarked breezily, after Gillian had described Clare's brave rescue, "La, I confess I would not have expected the marquess would exert himself so on behalf of a stranger's child." Gillian had had to bite her tongue against the impulse to inquire cuttingly whether it was because his mother had been native Irish that Mrs. Wade had thought Lord Clare might leave a young, helpless boy to slip to his doom; or if it was Lord Clare's fondness for gaming and women that had led Mrs. Wade to her assumption. Gillian did believe she'd a strong sense of fair play, but she could imagine rather too well what Clare would say, were he to learn of her impulse to defend him. The mere thought kept her face warm.

"Jove, Gilly, we've reached Chicksgrove already! 'Twas a short trip, indeed." To Gillian the ride had seemed to take hours, but as she had no desire to explain why, she merely observed aloud that her uncle had seemed to be deep in thought. " 'Twas to do with the Wythy," he said. "The river needs ditching badly. With all the dead limbs in the stream, we could have a flood after one rain, but clearing it takes a devilish amount of work, and I was putting my mind to thinking who might do what. I thank you for allowing me to think my thoughts, Gilly. You're a deuced restful female, not like some I know who are forever pestering a man with some silly nonsense or other!"

When her uncle's broad face drew down into a deep, wonderful scowl, it was all Gillian could do to stifle a laugh. She knew he was thinking of his sister, her Aunt Margaret, whom he had been obliged to bring to live with him, when Gillian had arrived on his doorstep. Her uncle was her official guardian, but a bachelor of well over forty years at the time her parents had died, he'd not had the faintest notion what to do with an eight-year-old girl, and so, had turned to his sister, Lady Sutton, a widow with no children of her own. She had thought it by the Almighty's design that she was free to return to her girlhood home and raise her youngest brother's daughter, but the rub was that the Almighty had created brother and sister like oil and water. They agreed on nothing but their devotion to Gillian. While Lady Sutton had been born careful about the properties, acting the gently reared noblewoman even as a little girl, Lord Albemarle had never given a fig about polite courtesies or playing the gallant. He liked his food and drink, his horses, his dogs, and his land, and he liked them all with great energy and enthusiasm.

He was not, however, such a rustic as to leave his niece to scramble down from her mare without assistance when they reached Chicksgrove. Lord Albemarle was not so lost to the proprieties as that, but no sooner did he have her safely on the ground than, glancing over the neck of her mare, he gave a shout and plunged away from Gillian without another thought.

"Ho there! Lord Clare, I believe!"

After a moment's stunned, disbelieving hesitation, Gillian turned slowly to find Clare was, indeed, there, stepping out of Mrs. Green's sundries' shop. It seemed too prosaic an activity for him. Mrs. Green was a spare, elderly widow, whose goods, it was often said in Chicksgrove, were as old and musty as she. What would an Irish rake have bought there. Tobacco? Did he smoke a pipe?

No. Somehow Clare did not look like a pipe fancier to Gillian. He looked too untamed.

Perhaps it was his black hair gleaming in the sun that made him seem so. He ought to have been wearing a hat. Even her uncle wore one. And in their section of Somerset, while there were a good many brunettes, there was no one with hair as black as crow's wing. Nor, of a certainty, was there anyone in Chicksgrove, or its surroundings, with a face quite so sharply chiseled, or eyes so unrelievedly black. Gillian imagined she was not the only one who could imagine him with a gold earring gleaming in his ear.

Mrs. Green was peering out her window, watching Lord Albemarle greet the newcomer. Trying to see Clare through Mrs. Green's eyes, Gillian noted that untamed air about him had naught to do with his riding clothes. His dark green coat and his buckskins were remarkable only because they were of better cut and quality than the ordinary. Which was, no doubt, why they fit him so well. The coat hugged his fine shoulders without a crease, and the buckskins outlined his long legs in a way that would have looked ludicrous on her far heavier uncle. In all then, Mrs. Green would think him elegantly dressed, though Gillian thought even a country widow would categorize his elegance as of the offhand variety. There was nothing of the dandy about Clare. He was too assured, and if he did bother himself to glance at his cheval glass after he dressed, Gillian guessed he would only do it to be certain his valet had not made a fuss of his neck cloth.

Gillian's heart seemed to stop when she realized her uncle was leading Clare across to her. For a moment she hesitated, uncertain what to do, or more accurately, what she wanted to do, for she knew full well that her aunt would have admonished her to slip quietly into the nearest shop until her uncle had concluded his business with the Irish rake. But she waited too long to decide, or perhaps, just long enough.

Before she could avoid meeting the rake in plain view of half of Chicksgrove, before she could escape his black, knowing eyes, Gillian's uncle called out to her.

"Gilly, my girl!" Lord Albemarle's voice boomed out loud enough to be heard by everyone within a mile. "I've met the marquess, our new neighbor! Allow me to present my niece, sir," the baron went on, then caught himself. "But you know her, of course! Saved that boy, Billy, with her! It was a brave thing you did, my lord, and I am beholden to you!"

"It was Davy Jennings, Lord Clare rescued, Uncle Arthur. And as you say, we have met. How do you do, my lord?"

On the off chance that she would meet him again, Gillian had practiced a composed, even slightly cool tone. Repeatedly. And she met Clare's gaze as steadily as she had sworn to herself she would. It helped that she had balled her hand into a tight fist in the folds of her skirt, particularly when she found that quite as she had anticipated, Clare's dark gaze was faintly amused. Her chin lifted without any prompting.

The gleam appeared to deepen. "Miss Edwards. I trust you are well this afternoon."

"Oh, quite well, my lord." And then some devil in Gillian prompted her to add, as she petted Delhi, sitting at her side, "My dog and I have been the very picture of domesticated bliss these last days."

Clare may have laughed. It sounded more as if he coughed, but Lord Albemarle shouted, "Domesticated!" so loudly, Gillian was never certain how Clare had responded. "Why, of course, Delhi's domesticated!" her uncle roared on. "Great God, even Margaret will tolerate him! I gave the hound to Gilly, don't you know," he announced to Clare. "Thought she should have a pup after . . . well . . . any child should have a dog! And not one of those absurd rugs, Margaret favors. Can't abide 'em! They yap and get underfoot and are not good for a farthing! No, indeed, I'd not see Gilly saddled with one of those addled things! Might as well give her a mouse."

Quite despite everything, Gillian could feel the corners of her mouth lifting. Her uncle was regarding Lord Clare almost belligerently, demanding a response, and Gillian could not but imagine that the marquess must think he had encountered a madman. Absurd rugs, indeed, and of course, he would not know who Margaret was.

If he did think Lord Albemarle mad, however, Lord Clare did not show it. "I quite approve your choice, sir, for it was the wolfhound that summoned me to Miss Edwards's aid on Quarry Hill."

For which perfect reply, Lord Albemarle gave him such an approving pound on the back a lesser man would have stumbled. Lord Clare merely resettled his shoulders and seemed to bite back a smile.

Gillian, more to her chagrin than not, wished he had looked to her to share that humor, but already her uncle was directing the marquess's attention down Chicksgrove's narrow High Street. "The White Horse has the best ale in the west country,

Lord Clare. Come have a pint with me, and we'll discuss this business with the Wythy. Lud, I am glad you'd the sense to turn off that rapscallion agent Lely had the poor judgment to employ! I never could abide the man! Come along with us, Gilly. You'll not mind listening to our men's talk, and I know you've a fondness for Mrs. Addams's tarts."

Gillian could easily guess her aunt's reaction to her uncle's proposal. And she knew all too well Clare's thoughts on the subject of her taking tea with him. Yet, the alternatives—poking about in Mrs. Green's shop or visiting Mary Beswick, the vicar's daughter—were entertainments she had experienced hundreds of times before. Therefore, Gillian placed her hand on her uncle's arm and allowed him to sweep her off to the White Horse, where Mr. Addams bustled forward to show them into the private room they always took, and brought, along with two tankards of ale for the men and tea and tarts for Gillian, a dish of milk for Delhi.

"Now as to this business about clearing and ditching the Wythy, Clare!" Lord Albemarle plunked his tankard of ale on the table and leaned forward, full of vigor and enthusiasm for his project. "If the work's not done now, the stream will flood and the fields on either side will be untillable swamps when spring arrives. I've been doing the work with my own men these last several years, but I would greatly appreciate assistance, if you could see your way to sparing a few of your men. Wade means to do his part. He's the lower section . . ."

Clare lounged back in his chair, listening, his legs stretched out casually before him. Once or twice he asked a question. Gillian followed the conversation, and knew as well every time Clare took a swallow of ale, or when he crossed or uncrossed his ankles, or when Delhi trotted to him to be petted, but though she followed his every move, she kept her gaze firmly trained on the window behind her uncle. She would not look at Clare. She mistrusted those knowing black eyes of his too much. Even were she to glance at him through her lashes, she thought he would know. And so have another reason to believe she'd developed an interest in him. A schoolgirl's, starstruck interest he no doubt thought.

Abruptly, almost in mid-word, Lord Albemarle heaved himself to his feet. "I'll just call out to Addams for another round of ale, eh, Clare? I work up a thirst when I'm deep in discussion. How about you, Gilly, girl? Will you have more tarts or tea?"

"No, thank you, Uncle," she said, but in a rather faint voice, for he was proceeding to the door even as she spoke, and leaving her, when he disappeared into the hallway, his voice booming, quite alone with Clare.

Her gaze shot to the marquess before she could think better of it. At the discovery that Clare was regarding her rather lazily, Gillian could feel herself begin to blush and promptly straightened her spine. He could reject her company. It was his privilege, but by God she was determined he would not do so because he thought her a witless fool.

She lifted her teacup and glanced at him over the rim. "You sounded quite the confirmed rustic, speaking with my uncle, my lord. After your contention at our last meeting, I confess I am surprised."

When she saw a gleam light his eyes, it felt to Gillian as if her blood suddenly began to fly through her veins. It was a dizzying, but not unpleasant feeling.

"Perhaps there is something peculiar in the air here in Somerset, Miss Edwards."

"Do you think so? I wonder what aside from your own unexpected interest in the Wythy would lead you to that conclusion, my lord?"

Clare had taken up the box of matches, Lord Albemarle had tossed onto the table. Gillian watched his long fingers idly toy with the box. "I hope you will not take offense, Miss Edwards, but your uncle strikes me as somewhat eccentric, almost as eccentric, indeed, as Mrs. Wright, and it seemed natural to me to wonder, if there might not be something in the air around Chicksgrove that produces eccentricity."

He said it so solemnly, Gillian required a moment to understand that he was teasing her. She laughed then, her face lighting. "Do you fear for yourself, my lord?" she asked.

She put the question to him in the same teasing spirit as that in which he had addressed her, but Clare's mood seemed to have changed. As he studied Gillian a moment, his expression grew somehow guarded. "There are circumstances in which every thinking man should fear for himself, Miss Edwards," he said, all the amusement quite gone from his eyes.

Gillian had no idea why the game he had started no longer pleased him, but even had she found the courage to question him, she was not to be given the time. Though she wanted an explanation of his last remark, and with an urgency that was out of all proportion to the issue, her uncle charged back into the room, looking distracted.

"There's a fellow asking for you outside, Clare. Heard him speaking to Addams at the door. I'd hazard that's his carriage there."

As the room's window looked onto the inn yard, Clare had only to glance over his shoulder. "Ah, it is Lord Darnley, a friend," he said, rising. "I shall have to take my leave now, Lord Albemarle, but I shall be pleased to do whatever you like in relation to the Wythy. Simply send me a note over, if you wish. Miss Edwards, I hope you will excuse me."

His eyes met hers as he gave her a faint bow, but Gillian could not be certain his expression had really softened, as she thought for a moment. He was gone too soon.

When the door closed behind him, Gillian thought the room unbearably empty. Lord Albemarle, though, slapped the table heartily. "A damned fine fellow, eh, Gilly? He's not one of those town dandies who don't care a thing about his land. He can't be, or he'd not have rid himself of that leech, Murdock."

Out the window, Gillian could see Clare walking with another fashionably dressed gentleman of fair coloring. When they reached a gleaming black carriage, the door opened and two women leaned out, giggling. They were beautiful women, but arrayed in overbright dresses that were cut as low as evening gowns at the neckline. One of them coyly drew her fingers across the bosom she displayed, then held her hand out to Clare. He kissed it, palm up.

"Oh, yes," Gillian muttered, her jaw tight, "he's a very fine fellow, indeed, Uncle. Very fine."

Chapter 6

"I vow, brother, you have proven me right again!" Gillian's Aunt Margaret gave Lord Albemarle a withering look across the dinner table. She had just learned with whom Gillian and her uncle had taken tea that afternoon in Chicksgrove. "You lack even a semblance of wit! How could you have presented Gillian to a man of his reputation?"

"Curse your sharp tongue, Margaret! I am no dandy with naught to do but listen to gossip! What would I know of his reputation? To me he appeared a reasonable fellow. 'Tis Lely, who should have the black reputation. He's the one who hired the worst agent imaginable and gave the knave a free hand to do naught!" Lord Albemarle paused long enough to finish his gooseberry tart, wolfing the last piece down before he looked up to stab his sister with another scowl. "And I did not present Gillian to him! He assisted her, if you will remember, in the rescue of the Jennings boy! Foul rogue that he is!" Throwing down his napkin, Lord Albemarle thrust back his chair and stomped from the room.

Lady Sutton sent a quivering look after him. "Men can be so unpleasantly loud, and none more so than my ruffian of a brother! But, Gilly, my child, I must know if this Lord Clare offended you in any way."

A clear and forceful image of Clare saluting the palm of the woman in the carriage formed in Gillian's mind, and she took the time to wipe her mouth with her napkin before she replied.

Her aunt had not inquired about anything she might have over-seen, but about the marquess's manners with her. "No, Aunt," she answered that question truthfully. "He was courteous, but in all said little to me. You know Uncle Arthur. The conversation was all of the Wythy: in spate, in drought, and in be-tween." Gillian summoned a smile. "Truly, no harm was done."

"This time, Gilly," Lady Sutton corrected firmly. "In future, however, you must rigorously avoid the man's company. Men like your uncle never understand these matters. If a gentleman rides well or listens to him prose on about ditching or some other pedestrian matter, Arthur considers him unexceptional, but this . . . Irishman is not received in proper society, Gilly. Lud, if you had been seen with him in town, your reputation could be quite, quite ruined!"

Gillian reminded her aunt she had not been in London, but little Chicksgrove, where everyone had been making al-lowances for her Uncle Arthur since he was born. "If there were questions about our meeting, they'd have had to do with whether the new lord at Beechfield will do his part to maintain the river."

It pleased Gillian that her aunt's expression eased, for be-neath Lady Sutton's starchy exterior beat a heart that was de-voted to her niece. That said, however, Gillian felt, despite her fondness for her aunt, something of the same prickle of rebel-lion she had felt when discussing Clare with Mrs. Wade. Whatever rumor said of the marquess, what Gillian knew of him since his arrival in Chicksgrove deserved applause. He had put himself in danger to aid a tenant's child; treated a sergeant's widow with grace and gallantry; and tolerated her eccentric uncle with good humor. What purpose, she found herself wondering, did the rules of society serve if they caused such a man to be excluded from most drawing rooms, but al-lowed welcome to be given to fops who would have refused to

descend that shaft on Quarry Hill for no better reason than a
reluctance to ruin their boots?

And as to the one indisputable count against him, the
women in the carriage, Gillian and Emily had discussed
women like that—doxies, they were called—with the other
girls at Miss Millington's. From those whispered and rather
avid discussions, Gillian had gathered that many respectable
gentlemen enjoyed the favors of such women. Some of the
girls had even maintained that they would want their own hus-
bands to discharge their "intimate needs" with "that sort," for
then they would be spared the embarrassment of attending to
their marital duties themselves.

Gillian did not share the sentiment. Optimistically she reasoned that a man's embrace could not be *so* terrible, for if it
were, there would surely not be so many children in the world.

"Gilly, I vow, you are not attending to me!"

Gillian looked up with a start. Her aunt was frowning formi-
dably as well she might be, given that her niece's thoughts had
begun with championing the marquess and proceeded to an
optimistic—even faintly excited—consideration of marital duties.

"I do beg your pardon, Aunt Margaret. I was just thinking
of, ah, marriage. Emily was positively giddy today, for she
had received a letter from Lord Alnwick."

Gillian winced at the thought that she was becoming exceedingly adept at not quite lying, but she was to be paid back
a bit by the subject her aunt raised.

"And had the Wades word from Lord Rockingham, my
dear? Do they know yet, when he will arrive at Roundley
House?"

"No, Aunt. Lord Rockingham had not sent word as to when,
precisely, he will visit."

"Well, I know you must be impatient, but he will come
soon. Fox season opens in a fortnight, after all."

"Oh, yes. Lord Rockingham is very much a sportsman."

Gillian changed the subject then, inquiring after her aunt's progress with her embroidery, for Lady Sutton had recently commenced on a difficult project, and they did not further discuss either Lord Clare or Lord Rockingham's impending visit to Somerset.

The subject of Lord Rockingham's visit to his cousins was reopened a few days later, however, when Emily came to visit at Moreham Park, bearing a letter from the young man in which the viscount fixed the day of his arrival for the second of November, the day before the first hunt. Unfortunately he was obliged to add that he could stay only a few days at that time, for the Duke of Bedford, the father of a close friend, had invited him to shoot pheasant on his estate in Cornwall.

"Cousin Lionel does say he will return for Mama's ball, however," Emily assured Gillian sympathetically, referring to the ball her mother gave every year for those of their circle who came to the west country in the late fall for hunting and shooting.

"But that is excellent news!" Lady Sutton cast a pleased look at her niece. "I had feared that if Lord Rockingham came for hunting at the first of the month, he would not be able to stay for the ball. I don't doubt you are delighted, Gilly. Now, you shall have a handsome partner for the opening quadrille."

"And one who does not mangle my toes," Gillian observed humorously. "Is Lord Alnwick coming, too, Em? Has he written to say?"

"He has, and he cannot come then! I would be inconsolable, but his mother has invited us to visit them in Kent after Christmas. We may stay as long as a fortnight!"

It required some two hours for Emily and Lady Sutton to exhaust the subject of the ball, the company the Wades expected at the end of the next month, and the kind of hostess Lord Alnwick's widowed mother would prove to be. Gillian commented from time to time, mostly humorously, and laughed when she should, but as soon as Emily took her leave, returning home in her father's carriage with her abigail beside her, Gillian donned a riding habit and made her way to the stables, Delhi at her side.

She could not have remained indoors. Her uncle's house had seemed to close in on her at the first mention of Rockingham.

She knew she felt nothing more monumental than a green girl's nerves. Surely many girls on the verge of betrothal felt the same wild impulse to flee. The next step was irrevocable. For all of her life she would be married to Lionel Townshend, Lord Rockingham.

Delhi barked, and glancing to him, Gillian realized they had reached the lane that wound up Grabbist Hill. She had turned that way so often of late, her wolfhound questioned her intended destination.

"No, Delhi," she called out, keeping a straight course. "We go to our island. It's solitude I need today, not the sight of our rake-hell neighbor. Besides, he is likely occupied," she added, though with little emotion, for it was not Clare and his doxies who filled her mind that day, but the Viscount Rockingham.

Everyone assumed she would marry the best catch of the Season, as well they might, for Rockingham was wealthy, titled, and exceedingly handsome. For that matter, Gillian had enjoyed his company. He had eased her way in the strange and not altogether appealing territory of London during the Season, not to mention keeping at bay the bewildering hordes of young men who had besieged her almost from the first.

She was grateful, but . . . but it seemed to her as if her life were being decided before she knew what she wanted, and for all that the viscount was unexceptional company, she was not certain she wanted to live all her life as his wife. Gillian had only to think how he had greeted her, when he had first come to call upon her in town to be reminded that their sensibilities were not always the same.

"Everyone is lauding you as a Diamond of the First Water,

Miss Edwards," he had said with the utmost seriousness as he bowed over her hand. "My sincerest congratulations to you." Gillian had known him since he was twelve, and privately considering the appellation ridiculous—for it seemed to her to be based upon nothing but looks, and she had met beautiful girls at Miss Millington's who were stultifyingly dull—she had tried to joke with him. But Rockingham had gone stiff and even a trifle sulky when she had laughed at the praise she had received, and at him for taking it so seriously.

He had gone on later, after she had soothed him, to say something about being delighted to call himself her childhood friend, as he hoped the prior acquaintance would give him an advantage over her other admirers, *but*—and Gillian marked how often "but" seemed to arise in regard to Rockingham— what she knew of him as a child, from his visits to his Wade cousins, was not entirely in the young viscount's favor. He had been handsome enough even then that Mary Beswick, the vicar's daughter, had half swooned over him, and he had been most charming at times, but Gillian recalled other times when he had failed to get his way, or when he had lost at some game. Then Rockingham had sulked not unlike he had, when she had teased him in town about caring what others dubbed her.

Would he always care so much for what others thought? Could he take pleasure in anything so unsung as her island? Gillian glanced moodily across the Wythy as her mare picked its way across the shallows to the little island that had long been her refuge. Would Rockingham even come to see it, if no one of distinction were about to mark him visiting it? Great God! She was being as unfair as she could possibly be. The viscount had been good company in town, nor was her aunt any sort of fool. Gillian bit her lip. Lady Sutton favored the future Earl of Becquith to such a degree, she'd said that if Gillian married him, she would consider her life's work well

done. It was, in all, though she knew her aunt had not intended
it as such, an exceedingly burdensome statement.

   Jason allowed the gelding he had chosen for his mount that
day to pick its way along the bank. He had not selected his
stallion, because he carried a fishing pole and fish basket.
They had been his excuse to leave the hall. Not that he had
needed any excuse with his guests. The men were the kind of
friends who accepted he would do what he wished when he
pleased, and the women were paid to accommodate not question. It was for himself he had needed a reason to leave the
revels at Beechfield.
   Had he ever grown weary of debauchery before? Surely he
had, though he could not, offhand, think when. It was not the
women. They were as seductive and accommodating as Darnley had promised. Perhaps they were not great wits, and one
could occasionally catch the broad, flat accents of the less-
educated classes beneath their studied tones, but when had a
coarse accent and relatively vacant mind put him off?
   It all seemed to go hand in hand. He scowled, as if he saw a
tangible connection between his sudden longing for fresh air
untainted by strong perfume and his firing of that damned
agent—not to mention his dutiful agreement to assist Albemarle in clearing the Wythy. Next he knew, he'd be thinking
of spending Christmas in the country, burning yule logs, and
taking Gillian Edwards to his bed.
   Jason laughed then. At least he'd not undergone so complete a transformation that he could not recognize any of his
thoughts.
   Not, of course, that he would take her to his bed. It was
merely a game to think of stroking that creamy skin of hers.
Or to imagine the rosy flush that would rise on her cheeks.
And the way her gray eyes would light, almost as if she were
laughing except the light would be hotter. . . . It was all a
game.

A frustrating game, though, that he must school himself to forgo. He'd be in Bedlam soon, if he did not. If his luck was in, he'd never see the chit again. But he would have a basket of fish. That was why he had come: to fish, not to brood moodily upon a girl a decade younger than him.

And in timely fashion, the gelding came to a halt on a rocky bank from which Jason could cast his line upriver into a deep pool. At the river's edge, however, Jason saw the island just downstream. Starchy Bexton had mentioned it, saying the fishing was good from there, and more to Jason's interest, the island appeared unapproachable. His guests had boisterously teased that they might come after him, to observe him at his "country" pursuits, but they would never think to find him there.

It was her dog, Jason saw first. Delhi came bounding to meet him, tail wagging as if in greeting, and perhaps it was a greeting, for the wolfhound failed to bark, only ran energetically at Jason, then turned and bounded back down a narrow path into dense woods. Following, telling himself, he couldn't be certain she was there, or if she were, that she was not hurt. He found her lying on a rock beside a pool, a straw bonnet covering her face, and her skirts lying an inch or so above ankles that looked trim even clad in half boots.

Sleeping Beauty, waiting for Prince Charming. His jaw tightened. She'd gotten the wolf, instead, the little fool. Great God! Where was her groom, or her chaperon, or someone of the army of protectors with whom well-bred girls were surrounded? Or did she want him to take her? Had she come to display herself for him? The skirt of her habit had settled slightly between her legs. He could see the slender length of them; could see the outline of her thighs round and firm, and if he looked . . .

In his most biting voice, Jason broke the silence of the glade. "Good afternoon, Miss Edwards."

Given another situation, another time and place, another

woman, an available woman, he might have smiled at the way she jumped. Her hat fell forgotten to the ground and her hair had either never been tied back with a ribbon, or had been untied. Jason flicked narrowed eyes over the loose, tawny mass spilling across her shoulder then pinned her with dark, decidedly unfriendly eyes.

"Do you make it a habit of lying about unattended on the property of scarcely known gentlemen, Miss Edwards?" She gaped, staring at him blankly with wide, still rather sleepy gray eyes, as if she were not certain she was not dreaming. Her cheeks were flushed from sleep. He'd known how she would look when she awakened: creamy skin, touched with pale rose, begging for stroking. "Damn it!" he railed, before she could drag her muddled thoughts together and make some reply. "Where are your aunt and uncle? Where is your groom? What sort of rearing have you had?"

That brought her fully awake. Her gaze focused and her shoulders straightened. "I have had an impeccable rearing, sir; certainly a finer one than yours, I'd say, given your manners! And I always come here. This is *my* place."

"Bexton said it was mine," he replied, only too happy to bicker with her. She frowned, trying to place Bexton. "My butler," he informed her curtly.

"Oh, yes." She'd been, then, to Beechfield Hall when Lely had owned it. She would not be going there now it was the residence of an Irish rake. She'd only be lying around on his property looking like a tousled angel. She frowned and pushed a long strand of silky, fawn's-coat-colored hair off her cheek. "I have always thought this was Uncle Arthur's island. No one has ever come here but me."

"Bexton has, it would seem, or some acquaintance of his. He told me the fishing was excellent here."

Her gaze shifted to the fishing rod and the basket he held, and as if the sight of the prosaic fishing equipment confirmed Jason's claim, she flushed. "I see," she said softly, avoiding his gaze. "Well, I, ah, am sorry to have put you out. I didn't know. . . ." Her voice was muffled because she'd bent to retrieve her bonnet. She made no attempt to put it on or right the disorder of her hair, but turned away to go to her mare with the bonnet dangling from her fingers. "I hope you'll excuse me for trespassing."

There was no fire to it. To the contrary, she sounded so flat, she made him feel like a tyrant. "Stop." She slowed but did not stop until she had picked up her mare's reins. Turning halfway around, she flicked a glance toward Jason, but looked away the moment their eyes met. "I've an unsteady temper," he bit out.

"I have noticed it before," she murmured, just loudly enough for him to hear. "But as it would seem I have no right to be here, you have the right to complain at not finding the privacy you expected. I will just . . ."

Before he could consider what he should do, Jason threw his leg over the gelding and leapt lightly to the ground, shedding the fishing equipment without a second thought as he strode toward her.

"I did not mean to overset you," he said, his tone more curt than apologetic. "I did not think you so missish."

"You did not overset me!"

Jason almost smiled. At least there was a spark of the old fire in evidence again. "What subdued your mood, then, if not me?"

Her eyes widened a fraction. Perhaps she was surprised by his interest in her mood. Perhaps she thought his interest presumptuous. There was no question it was idiotic. In the end, she tore her gaze away and shrugged. "You woke me, my lord. No more."

"Not willing to trust your secrets to me, Miss Edwards? Very proper of you, perhaps, but I find it difficult to resist a challenge. And so I will guess that it is not being able to sit by my pool and cast sheep's eyes at me while I fish that has subdued you."

If he had meant to taunt her into a show of spirit, Jason succeeded, and if he had meant to anger her so she betrayed the source of low spirits, he succeeded there, too.

"You had nothing to do with my mood, my lord! Nothing at all! If I was subdued, it was because . . . because I have learned that a certain gentleman of whom I am fond will not be staying in Somerset so long as I had expected!"

That would be Rockingham, Caroline's brother. Jason had rather forgotten the puppy.

"What is the problem, Miss Edwards? Are you too spirited for him?"

For a half second he thought her eyes darkened, but he must have misjudged her response, for in the next moment, her eyes were hot with indignation and she was going on the offense, "Why are *you* not married, my lord? Because you've not a loyal bone in your body?"

"Precisely." Jason arched a mocking eyebrow at her, knowing he'd cut the ground she considered lethal out from under her. "Leg shackles are damnably confining for a man. But you, Miss Edwards, are a woman. And for women, a leg shackle is a far different matter. It is the ticket to wealth and social standing. Little wonder you were subdued."

He did not cow her. Jason had to give the little gray-eyed Sassenach that, when she gave him a scornful look.

"You have overlooked entirely one of the principal reasons to marry, my lord, but I am not surprised. Likely you are too absorbed with your own pleasures to care about children. However, in one thing you are right. I would be ruined for any respectable marriage, were I discovered here with you. And as *I* do wish to marry, I shall take my leave of you. Enjoy *your* island. It is . . ."

Either unable to or unwilling to put into words what the island was to her, she swung around and tugged on the mare's reins to lead it to a rock. Before she reached her improvised mounting block, however, Jason caught her by the waist and turned her.

"What?" she gasped on a yelp, and struck at his hand with her fist.

But Jason was aware of little except that beneath his hands he felt no stiff stays, only a slender, willow-supple waist. "I am only helping you to leave," he murmured and lifted her, obliging her to catch frantically at his shoulders to steady herself.

He had betrayed all his instincts by touching her. Now he could not seem to divest himself of her, but held her so her soft, generous mouth was only inches from his. The moment drew out as Jason fought with himself. She made no further protest. Indeed, her lips parted a little. Her fingers, though, were digging into his shoulders and she had caught her breath while her eyes had gone wide. She was afraid, he realized finally—perhaps of her response to him, for she was an innocent, untried girl, and he was half bullying her.

Jason placed Gillian on the mare very carefully and stepped back so she was out of reach. "I have admitted already that I've an uncertain temper, Miss Edwards. I apologize for making you bear the brunt of it, and you may be assured, I'll not deny you this island. It is yours. Come whenever you like."

He expected she would go with no more than a murmur of thanks, her tail tucked between her legs. But she did not, and it made him feel the oddest pang, when she managed even to give him a smile, albeit an unsteady one. "It is your island, my lord. I could not accept such a gift." Her smile turned distinctly wry. "It would be most improper."

Then she used her heels on the mare, and Delhi came charging out of the bushes to lope after her. Jason watched them go, half wanting to wring the dog's neck, for the dratted animal had quite missed the wolf in the glade, while it sniffed after nothing in the bushes. But the other half of him wanted to applaud. Perhaps she was a green girl, but she had spirit and wit. Rockingham would be as fortunate as a married man could be.

Chapter 7

"**F**inally the vicar has relinquished you, Miss Edwards! I feared I would soon be obliged, for the sake of his soul you understand, to remind him of the Christian ideal of charity, he seemed so set upon keeping you for himself."

Lord Rockingham smiled. And Gillian had proof how long three months could be. She had half forgotten what a charming smile he had. A dimple showed on his right cheek.

When the viscount had arrived at Roundley House with his friend, the Earl of Bolton, earlier that afternoon, Mrs. Wade had gotten up an impromptu dinner party, inviting the vicar, Mr. Beswick, and his wife and daughter in addition to the party from Moreham Park.

"I have scarcely been able to say a word to you, and I very much wish to tell you what a distinct pleasure it is to see you, Miss Edwards. You entirely deserve the distinction, Diamond of the First Water, though I know you think the phrase half absurd."

His dimple flashed again, giving Gillian further cause to upbraid herself for having been unfair to him. If Rockingham had once been displeased because she did not share his respect for that particular title, he could laugh now over the difference. Perhaps he had changed. Or perhaps her perception had. Gillian knew for a certainty it was possible for perceptions to change and in only a little time. When Rockingham had first bowed over her hand in Mrs. Wade's drawing room that evening, it had flashed through Gillian's mind that the viscount was too handsome. She had never thought so before. As children, when Mary Beswick had gone into rapturous sighs over how beautiful he was, Gillian had quite agreed, but just for a little earlier that evening, she had wondered if his refined good looks were not dangerously close to pretty. Now, nearly two hours later, she had become accustomed to his looks again. Or had defeated the image of a stronger-featured face. Gillian cut off the thought instantly. There could be no comparing the men, for the viscount had honorable intentions toward her, while the marquess had . . . no intentions at all. And besides, slender as he was, Rockingham would have looked odd with features more forcefully fashioned.

"I do hope you understand about my going on to Cornwall for a little," Rockingham was saying. "You remember Lord Greville, I think? Yes, well the Duke of Bedford is his father, and when the two of them got up this idea of a shooting party, I could not refuse. One simply does not refuse His Grace, you know."

"I do understand, of course." Gillian made a mental grimace, directed at herself not Rockingham. She was being unfair again, examining his every remark for flaws. Who was she to say she would have refused the duke to stay with the man she wished to wed? She had never met Bedford and could not say with any certainty that he was not as daunting as Rockingham made him out to be. "I am sure it must be very beautiful in Cornwall in the fall."

"The shooting is excellent," Rockingham replied enthusiastically, if not quite to the point. "His Grace has marvelous gamekeepers, and the birds are always plentiful."

He went on for a little about the good sport he anticipated, then Gillian turned the subject to his mother, who had suffered an inflammation of the lungs that had kept her at her husband's seat, Chevely, during the Season.

"How is your mother, my lord? I hope she is feeling better now."

"I am very pleased to report that Mama is much improved. She was even able to go up to town for the Little Season for the come-out of my cousin, Clarissa Dumont. The two of them insisted that I be on hand to play Clarissa's escort. Fortunately Bolton and Greville were in town, so I was not bored to tears, but I could not get away as soon as I would have wished."

His regretful look gave Gillian to understand that if he could have gotten away, he would have come to her. She could not help herself then; she thought of what she would have missed: a stinging lecture from a thorough rake on her failings in the area of comportment, and the same rake's notice, sardonically conveyed, that he preferred doxies to a wife. Nor was any of that to mention the feel of his hands about her waist as he lifted her effortlessly onto her mare. Had she leaned forward even an inch . . .

"Mama is most eager to see you again, Miss Edwards. She had not met you since you were a child, and with all of her friends going on about you so, she is thoroughly intrigued. It is my great hope that she will feel up to having you and your aunt and uncle to Chevely for Christmas. I tell you this in confidence, you understand, for I do not wish to say anything to your aunt until Mama knows her strength. She has only just returned to Chevely from town, you see."

"I quite understand, my lord, and I hope for her sake that she finds she did not overdo. I recall her as very beautiful and gracious."

Rockingham smiled, understandably pleased. "She is both, and she will approve of you, Miss Edwards. I know it, though I cannot always say I believed as much."

"No?" Gillian regarded him in some surprise. "Why did you have doubts, my lord?"

"In truth?" When she nodded, intrigued now, Rockingham shook his head. "When we were younger, you were always going on in such an approving way about India, praising the strange birds there, the odd food, and the women's outlandish dress . . . You even told that dreadful tale of the man you saw killed in the bazaar. Do you remember?"

"Yes, of course." Gillian laughed. "The sins of my youth have come back to haunt me! I believe I had only just met you, and as you were four years my elder, I could not think how to impress you but to tell you my most bizarre story. Alas, you were more disgusted than impressed, and it was Emily who wanted to know all the details."

"I recall." The smile with which Rockingham had met the revelation that Gillian had wished to impress him when she was eight faded as he glanced down the table in the direction of his cousin. "Emily was a shatterbrain as a child, and though I am devoted to her as her cousin, you understand, I cannot say she has changed much over the years. Egad, look how she is rattling on witlessly now. Poor Bolton! She is talking his ear off."

Gillian changed the subject, asking after Rockingham's sister, Lady Castlemont, for had she not, she'd have had to observe that her friend chattered in that particular way only when she was nervous. Of all Rockingham's old school friends, Bolton was Gillian's very least favorite.

Whatever wealth Lord Bolton's family might once have possessed had long since been lost, leaving the earl a hanger-on of sorts, who curried favor with a few wealthy old school friends by employing a malicious, spiteful tongue to cut down everyone else. And he particularly liked to employ his sly, disparaging wit on people who were too kind to strike back. Gillian thought Emily a heroine for accepting the duty of sitting by him.

She told Emily as much after dinner, when the ladies had adjourned to the drawing room, and she and Emily and Mary Beswick had found seats some distance from the elder ladies, who had chosen to sit by the fire. Emily gave a long suffering sigh in response and remarked half wearily that though she must consider her cousin loyal for standing by Bolton, she wished Lionel would stand by him some place other than Roundley House. "But," she went on, gaining spirit, "the beastly man's not worth another moment of our time, particularly as Mary has the most exciting story! She and her father were driving to a parishioner's house, Gilly, and just guess who should ride by them. Lord Clare! And he stopped to speak."

"Well, my father did hail him," Miss Beswick said, for she was a rather literal person.

Emily waved off the qualification. "Never mind that, Mary, tell us everything he said. And how he looked!"

At that question, Mary Beswick flushed, and Gillian found herself in the grip of a need to shake the quiet, rather plain girl and demand why she turned rosy red at the thought of Clare. But of course he had not said or done anything to make Mary blush. She was merely shy at being thrust onto center stage.

"He was dressed quite well in fine riding clothes . . ."

"No, no!" Emily bounced sharply. "I mean how did he look? Did you think him handsome?"

"Oh, yes! Very." Miss Beswick looked shyly from Emily to Gillian. "You know how I have always thought Lord Rockingham so very handsome, Gilly, and so I know you will not be offended when I say that in my opinion Lord Clare quite rivals the viscount. They are different, to be sure," she added in a rush, as if she truly feared she might have hurt Gillian. "Lord Rockingham is so fair and . . . well, angelic in his good looks, while Clare is dark and . . ."

"Devilishly handsome!" Emily finished off, laughing.

Mary Beswick rarely giggled, but she did then. Gillian pasted something more like a grimace on her face, finding it impossible to smile lightheartedly about Clare, given the odd ache she had carried around inside her since their meeting on the island. Sheep's eyes . . . he had been wrong in his guess there. She'd been dispirited by the thought that a future with Rockingham seemed so set, but . . . she would not have objected to sitting by the pool with Clare while he fished. He was different from anyone she had ever known, and could have entertained her for hours with all he had seen. Clare had not had any patience for her and her inexperience though . . . except for that one instant when he had begun to lift her onto her mare. She had thought for a stunning moment that he might kiss her. Rockingham had not ever kissed her, and she had felt so uncertain, so untried that she had been afraid. But not afraid enough to break away from him. No, she had stayed there clinging to him mutely, half fearful, but half excited, too. And then in the twinkling of an eye the moment was over, and she was atop her mare, feeling only a sense of loss.

if she had presented a temptation to him, and she was not certain she had, she had also proven resistible. He disliked leg shackles and sheep eyes in too hearty and equal a measure to give in to any desire to kiss her. And she must listen to herself and cease dreaming about what might have been! God help her, but she had returned to the island twice only to leave when she found he was as good as his word and not there!

As Mary and Emily could talk for hours without noticing that she was abstracted, Gillian was relieved when the gentlemen joined the ladies early in the drawing room. She needed distraction and Rockingham presented it nicely, with his golden hair and sapphire blue eyes.

Smiling charmingly at all three young ladies he bowed gallantly. "Lord Bolton and I are, indeed, lucky to have three such lovely young ladies to entertain us. That is I trust you will not object if we join you? You do look as if, while you were free of us, you had a devilish pleasant coze." It was the most unexceptional of remarks but Emily, thinking of her description of Lord Clare, went into a fit of giggles, causing her cousin's pleasant mood to cool. He eyed her askance as he took a seat by Gillian. "Evidently being buried here in the west country all fall without any entertainment to speak of has rendered you giddy, cousin, for I cannot think I said anything quite that amusing."

Gillian was not surprised to see Emily bristle in her turn. The cousins had ever squabbled on occasion. What Gillian could not have expected was the reply Emily would think to make.

"I vow, Cousin Lionel, you consider us nothing but country rustics here in Somerset, yet we have not been so lacking in amusement as you like to think! How could we be with a reputed rake not only living here but riding about the country assisting Miss Edwards to save overly adventuresome boys!"

"What?" Lord Rockingham turned his very blue eyes from his cousin to Gillian. She marked that the charming, golden-boy dimple had not reappeared. Quite the opposite, he was frowning ever so slightly, though he had not heard the story.

"There was only one boy. Your dear cousin likes to exaggerate," Gillian said, giving Emily an amused look and deliberately denying Rockingham an explanation. The possessiveness his frown implied annoyed her.

"Well, do you not wish to make a story of it, Gilly?" Emily demanded, nearly bouncing with impatience.

Gillian managed a laugh. "I think the person most eager to tell the story must be the storyteller, and I am certain all here would agree that you are nearly beside yourself in your eagerness to tell it, my dear friend."

Entirely pleased, Emily shot her cousin an arch look. "Do you know of the Marquess of Clare, Cousin Lionel?"

"I have met the marquess, yes, but what . . ."

"But he won Beechfield Hall from Lord Lely in a game of cards!"

"Clare is living at Beechfield?" Rockingham stared at his cousin with undisguised surprise, gratifying Emily immensely.

"Yes! He even has a small party visiting him. Papa went to

call and said Lord Darnley is there, and Lord Staunton, and Mr. Oversby."

The young woman drew breath as if she were going to add something, but Rockingham addressed Gillian first in a markedly stiffer voice. "Lord Clare's reputation is scarcely spotless, Miss Edwards. Exactly how was it you came to meet the man?"

If she had not cared for the suggestion of displeasure in his frown, Gillian found she resented the outright suspicion in his tone rather more. Yet she quelled the impulse to advise him how little she liked being called to account for herself as if she were a child, and before her friends, too. The less she made of Clare, she decided, the sooner they would move on to another subject.

"Do you recall my dog, Delhi, my lord?" She was not surprised when Rockingham nodded. Few people forgot her wolfhound. "It was his insistent barking that alerted both Lord Clare and me, riding respectively on opposite sides of the Wythy, to the plight of a young boy who had gotten into difficulties in one of the many shafts on Quarry Hill. I could not get a rope to the boy as there was a ledge in the way, and so Lord Clare climbed into the shaft and brought the boy out."

"It was very good of him to put himself to such trouble!" Miss Beswick asserted with some feeling. "The boy was only a tenant's son, and I believe a good many gentlemen would have left the effort, and the danger, of rescuing him to his father."

There was a moment's oddly pregnant silence as the members of the little group digested Miss Beswick's rather breathless defense of the marquess.

Then Lord Bolton spoke. "The boy was a tenant's son, you say, Miss, ah, Beswick?" When Mary Beswick responded affirmatively, flushing furiously, the young earl nodded with exaggerated ennui. "Ah, well then," he drawled, giving a dismissive wave of a pale, small, impeccably kempt hand, "I shouldn't say that Clare stooped to any great effort. After all, he is nearly upon a tenant's level himself."

While Mary gasped, Rockingham laughed and Bolton allowed himself a sly smirk. Gillian curled her hand into a fist in her lap. She did not believe for one moment that Bolton would have dared speak such insulting words had Clare been present. He wished to ingratiate himself with Rockingham, or perhaps more precisely with Rockingham's deep pockets, and he had.

Gillian deliberately caught the fop's pale eyes. She had resisted defending Clare before Mrs. Wade and her aunt, but Bolton had gone too far. "No man stoops to bravery, Lord Bolton," she said quietly but distinctly. "He either is brave and resourceful or he is not. Lord Clare was both in this instance, and so fortunately a young boy lives." Whatever his financial straits, Bolton was an earl, she a mere girl. Rockingham moved sharply beside her as if he meant to remonstrate with her for speaking so forcefully, and in challenge, yet, of his friend, but Gillian turned to fix Rockingham with the same steady look. "What do you think, my lord?" she asked, levelly before he could speak. "Is Mary right? Would most gentlemen have thought Davy so far beneath them that they'd have left him to his fate?"

Rockingham was not well pleased to have been put to a test of sorts and so publicly. The corners of his mouth had turned down in a way Gillian recognized from his childhood, but in all he had little choice as to his answer, and he gave it, albeit stiffly. "I cannot speak for other gentlemen, Miss Edwards, but I would not leave anyone to his death, if the situation were truly so serious."

Gillian inclined her head. "I am reassured to know I have not misjudged you, my lord."

It was a fraught moment, and might have become more so, had the silence been allowed to draw out. But Emily addressed Lord Bolton. "I hope there is not bad blood between you and Lord Clare, my lord?" she asked quite seriously.

It seemed to Gillian that the dandy looked oddly unsettled for a moment, but if so, he recovered himself quickly enough to sound utterly bored when he replied, "Why no, Miss Wade. In truth, I scarcely know the man. But why do you ask, pray?"

"Well, you see, as I was just going to say to Miss Edwards and Miss Beswick before you joined us, when Papa went to Beechfield yesterday, he learned that Squire Throckmorton has invited Lord Clare and his guests to join the hunt tomorrow."

Chapter 8

Squire Throckmorton's manor house was not so large as the houses at Beechfield and Moreham Park, but the old brick stable yard behind the house held the twenty or more people gathered there comfortably enough. Gillian had always enjoyed the time just before a hunt when her rising excitement at the prospect of the full-out, challenging, perhaps even dangerous, ride she would soon have matched the excited pandemonium in the squire's stable yard. In their pens, the hounds yelped eagerly, while the hunters, and those who had come to see them off, milled about the yard, shouting greetings at one another and warming themselves against the crisp November air with steaming mugs of hot punch. When Squire Throckmorton, the master of the hunt, passed by, they yelled out boisterously to ask when his huntsman would signal that the fox was drawn. Accustomed to their boisterous impatience, the squire invariably responded with the inarguable logic that the time would come when it came and meanwhile sent another tray of the potent punch their way.

Standing on a small terrace that separated the house from the yard, Gillian took in all the swirl of noise and color, but the scene she usually enjoyed to the full was the merest background that day. Her pulses had leapt so when Emily had announced that Clare was to join the hunt, she had had to take refuge behind her teacup to hide the sudden flush in her cheeks. Yet she had had an even more intense reaction when she had seen him earlier that morning. When she had first stepped out of the Throckmorton's house onto the terrace; her eyes had found Clare immediately, though he was standing on the far side of the stable yard. Rockingham had been just behind her with Lady Sutton, but when Gillian had caught sight of the marquess leaning comfortably against a paddock fence, looking tall and fit and lean, his hair gleaming blue-black in the sun, her pulses had raced so, she had actually forgotten her audience. With all her might she had willed Clare to look her way, though she could not have said what she'd have liked him to do then: give her to understand with a look that he had come to the hunt to see her? Of course he had not come on her account, and he did not magically sense her presence, either. Before anything at all could happen, Rockingham came up beside Gillian and taking her arm, jolted her into recalling the world around her.

Clare had come to the hunt to provide his guests entertainment. Or one of his guests. Lord Staunton and Mr. Oversby had evidently elected to stay at Beechfield, but Gillian recognized Lord Darnley from the time he had met Clare in Chicksgrove. Close to the marquess in height, he had a cheerful smile he used to good effect, for the serving girls with their trays full of steaming mugs were never far from the pair. Rakes, both.

But their popularity with the serving maids did nothing to discredit them in the eyes of many of the gentlemen present. Whatever Mrs. Wade might think of Clare, Mr. Wade, upon seeing him, had proceeded straight across the yard to join him and Lord Darnley. Her uncle had gravitated to their group, too, drawn along with a good many of the other hunters by the bursts of male laughter that could be heard from time to time.

Gillian watched the group from the corner of her eye, no more. Rockingham had recalled her to where she was, and she was grateful to him. She could scarcely believe she had forgotten even her aunt. And on whose account? A man who had warned her off of him.

"Miss Gillian! Miss Gillian! I am to hunt today! Papa said I could. Andrew is going to watch out for me. Are you riding, too? Will you see me blooded?"

Gillian laughed aloud. It was the first good humor she had felt since she had walked onto the terrace, seen Clare, and stared so witlessly.

"So you are old enough to have a dab of fox's blood brushed on your cheeks after the hunt are you, Robin?" She ruffled Squire Throckmorton's youngest son's auburn hair. "Well, I am confident you will fare better than I. I feared I would swoon when your father approached me with the bushy foxtail he used to brush my cheeks."

"What did you do, Miss Gillian?" the young boy demanded earnestly.

"Why, I clung to your brother, of course," Gillian said, nodding to Andrew Throckmorton, the squire's eldest son, who stood behind his younger brother. "He was steady as a rock and kept me on my feet, as I am certain he will do for you."

"Is that what happened?" Andrew Throckmorton scratched his head as a grin edged up the corners of his mouth. "I thought it was the other way about. I thought I was clinging to you, Miss Gillian."

"Likely you were, Andrew!" young Robin cried. "You have ever sung Miss . . ."

"Miss Edwards," Rockingham cut into young Robin's speech without seeming aware he interrupted. "Would you care for a taste of punch? Your uncle insisted earlier you must have at least a swallow, but I must warn you I consider it quite potent for a lady."

"Squire Throckmorton's punch is a tradition, my lord," Gillian replied, and aware of everyone about them, kept her tone good-humored. "The punch is for good luck, which Robin will need also. Just take a sip," she advised the young boy as she handed him the mug, "or as the viscount warned, you'll not be able to sit your horse."

Robin manfully took a swallow, but made a comical face as the potent brew burned his throat. "It takes getting used to," Gillian told him with a laugh. "And now the mug goes to your brother." Andrew Throckmorton was a gangly young man with a rather homely face, but they were old friends, for being of an age, he and Emily and Gillian and Mary Beswick had played together as children. "There's to the first hunt of the season, Andrew! May we have bang up rides!"

Gillian smiled broadly again and did not allow herself to consider that Rockingham likely would not approve either the cant she'd used or her familiarity with Mr. Throckmorton. She was grateful to the viscount for wresting her attention from Clare before she made a fool of herself, but she was not so grateful that she wished him to hover over her all day and wear a miffed expression if she so much as smiled at an old friend.

"Your pose is indolent, Jason, my lad, but now we've a half moment alone, I shall advise you that your gaze—when it roves in the direction of that terrace—is not indolent at all. And giving you away, it gives me insight into your newfound affinity for the country. But I cannot, in all, fault you. Indeed, had I known a girl with her looks was on the marriage mart this Season, I might have lowered myself to Almack's."

Jason shot an amused look at his friend. "Somehow I doubt even Miss Edwards could persuade you to stoop to marriage, Dar. As to my stay in the country, however, the length will be determined by how quickly I am able to find an agent who is both honest and competent."

"Ah, and so you wish me to believe that you did not come apurpose today to admire the incandescent beauty attired in a burgundy hunting costume?"

"Well, she did not advise me she would be wearing the burgundy, no," Jason replied, but so blandly that it was a moment before Darnley threw back his head and laughed aloud. Before his friend could crow, "I knew it!" however, Jason added dryly, "And if you will recall, Dar, it was you who wished to come to the hunt, because you thought it would an amusing lark to insinuate ourselves among my respectable neighbors."

"Poor squire!" Lord Darnley exclaimed, diverted for the moment. "Not only is he improbably thin—really I have never seen a thin squire in my life—but he is too much the rustic to know the least bit of town gossip with the result that he invited us fresh from our . . . friends . . . to hunt with the good, up-standing people of Chicksgrove, of whom one," the viscount added on an accusing sigh, "I discover by the merest chance is a truly rare beauty."

She was that, actually, in a burgundy habit trimmed with black braid. The rich color combined with the brisk air, made her skin appear to glow. Or perhaps it was her mood that set her alight. She had recovered her spirits since Jason had last encountered her. Completely. The smile she bestowed upon Throckmorton's youngest son was radiant, and remained so as she laughed and handed a steaming mug of punch on to Throckmorton's eldest son, a pup who looked as if he would fall down and worship her, if she asked it of him.

"You could at least have warned me about her, Jason. I'd have made certain to wear my best boots."

Seeing Darnley was not inclined to drop the subject of Miss Edwards, Jason shrugged. "The price of her charms is marriage, Dar. I'd no notion you were ready to settle into respectability quite yet. Forgive me, if I mistook your mood."

"Hmm, well, I would not go so far as to say I am prepared to settle into respectability. Even repeating the phrase makes me feel dull. No, I was thinking along other lines, actually. In my knowledgeable opinion, she would make a splendid mistress after she has been married a year or two."

When his friend did not answer at once, Darnley glanced at him. Jason's expression was unreadable, but he did incline his head in the direction of the terrace. "A satisfactory mistress requires a satisfactory husband, and it does not look to me as if Rockingham will be particularly complacent."

Darnley's brow lifted. "Well, by Jove, it is Rockingham hovering about her like a self-important rooster! I should have recognized Caroline's rather priggish brother. I did see the poisonous Bolton earlier. You recall him. I think you administered some rough justice to him once after he was particularly rude to an Irish serving maid in that gaming hell near the docks." When Jason simply ignored the reference to a night just as well forgotten, Darnley looked again to the terrace and immediately chuckled. "Great God, I would say you do have the right of it, Jason! The boy is even bristling at that thin, homely chap who's the spitting image of the squire. Jove, that is playing dog in the manger seriously."

Miss Edwards did not seem to object to the viscount's possessiveness, though. She was smiling vividly when she looked from Throckmorton to him. And by her own account she had been saddened when she learned he would not remain long in Somerset. That Rockingham should appeal to her was not surprising. He looked the epitome of the English nobleman, with his pretty features illuminated by the sun and his blond hair slightly ruffled by the breeze. Perhaps he had asked for her. Perhaps knowing the viscount would hover about her for the rest of her life had made her buoyant.

"Egad, Lady Sutton has brought forth a smile for the viscount! Has she some connection to . . . Miss Edwards, I believe you did say her name was?"

"Yes, Lady Sutton is the girl's aunt. Do you know her?"

"I do, actually. She was a friend of my mother's. And a stickler of sticklers, I can tell you. It's as well you favor your freedom, Jason."

Darnley said it so lugubriously Jason laughed. "I take it Lady Sutton would not favor me over young Rockingham?"

"Never," his friend replied, giving no quarter. "She is not the sort to look beyond your Irish factor, and of course, everyone believes you are next to penniless, though what the gossips think you have done with your winnings over the years, I cannot fathom."

"High-living and doxies," Jason remarked, though absently. He was watching Rockingham place a gloved hand upon the small of Gillian's back and noting an unreasonable reaction in himself.

Lord Darnley was not so distracted. "Your reputation with women is yet another reason Lady Sutton will not likely look with favor upon you. No, dear boy," he went on, in mock seriousness, "in my judgment you will remain a happy libertine yet a while longer. You see, for you to have Miss Edwards, Rockingham would not only have to marry her, but to obligingly die soon afterward. Then, perhaps, you could console his grieving widow."

"I am well and truly doomed in that case," Jason remarked wryly, unable to resist Darnley's absurdity, "for the viscount appears to be in the pink of health."

If Rockingham was healthy, he was not some hour or so after the hunt began entirely hale. The huntsman had drawn a fleet, active fox that had run the riders over hill and dale. Jason rode abreast of Darnley and Albemarle with Gillian a bit ahead to their left, and Rockingham just behind her. There had been several fences already, some more difficult than others, but Gillian had sailed over them all with ease. Still, the fence ahead looked difficult enough to give Jason concern. Not only would they take it going up a hill, but it was a wide hedge fence. Several mounts balked before it, but Gillian's mare went over nicely.

Rockingham's hunter was not so fortunate. A rear hoof caught the hedge, causing it to stumble badly and throw the viscount. He was not hurt. Looking back over his shoulder, Jason saw the young man get to his feet, but Rockingham was without a mount. Even then the riderless horse could be seen galloping away from the noise of the hunt.

It was impossible to say whether Gillian knew. By the time Jason was satisfied that the young man was not hurt and looked to her, she was concentrating on the next obstacle, a stream narrow enough to take at a jump.

Two or three miles farther on, the hounds plunged into a thick woods, forcing the riders to fan out to find their way through the undergrowth. Jason saw Albemarle and Darnley hie off to his right, but he kept his mount in line with Gillian's. Several other riders veered to the right as well, perhaps in the belief that Albemarle knew the land. Jason thought the idea credible and considered shouting to Gillian to suggest it, when her horse suddenly pulled up.

"What is it?" he called out, slowing, though his hunter tossed its head in protest.

She glanced to him briefly, her expression set. "My mare is limping. She may have pulled a tendon, or may have caught a stone in her hoof."

Jason directed his mount to her, though Gillian had not asked for his assistance. Indeed, by the time he reached her, she had jumped down from the saddle and was trying to see to the mare herself. When she lifted the horse's back leg to examine the hoof, however, the mare sidestepped, avoiding her. Despite her difficulty, Gillian ignored Jason even after he had dismounted.

"Allow me," he said, his tone as ironic as the look he gave her.

"The others have gone on, my lord," she said with no trace to be found of the vivid smile she had earlier bestowed upon every male on the terrace. "And as you have pointed out before, I should not be alone with you. When I have tied her reins to a branch, I can look after Clover myself. Thank you."

"Don't be a fool. You are in a difficult spot. And Rockingham will not obligingly appear to help you, either. He fell." She had not known. Her eyes went wide with unfeigned surprise, and Jason added curtly, "He was not hurt, but his mount ran off." His eyes trained on her, Jason stepped forward, forcing Gillian to move out of his way, unless she wanted to fight him physically. Beneath the mare's shoe, he found a stone lodged so tightly, he could not remove it. Dropping the mare's leg, he straightened and met Gillian's eyes. "Are you betrothed to Rockingham yet?"

She stiffened instantly. "My relations with the Viscount Rockingham are none of your affair, my lord. What of my mare? May I ride her now?"

"So, you are not betrothed yet," Jason guessed, his eyes narrowing as he fought an urge to pull her into his arms and show her why she would be a fool to accept a man as priggish and passionless as Rockingham had been bred to be.

At his look, a faint line of color rose on her cheeks, yet she thrust up her chin and held his gaze. "I do not care to repeat myself, Lord Clare. Now, either you tell me the condition of my mare, or I shall take her reins and lead her through the woods until I find another person who will help me."

He might as well have been that goose she'd thrashed at the inn near Salisbury. She had indeed regained the spirit she had so conspicuously lacked during their encounter on the island. Because she expected Rockingham to ask for her?

"You may not ride your mare. I could not remove the stone she picked up. You will have to ride pillion behind me."

Her gaze fell from his abruptly. Too abruptly. And vivid color washed her cheeks. Had she not wanted to ride behind him, had she been determined not to, she'd have looked him in the eye and said so. A fierce, entirely unexpected and not much welcomed heat swept him. She wanted to ride close behind him. The hot blush in her cheeks proclaimed it, just as her averted eyes spoke of dismay at her own desire.

By the devil, he ought to make them both walk. But Jason knew he would not make them trudge for miles, and that though he knew that teasing them both with such closeness was playing with fire.

"Come on then," he said angrily, for he was angry and with each of them. If he was nearing thirty and should have little interest in an innocent Sassenach chit ten years his junior, she was, as she well knew, all but betrothed to a man, who had every interest in marriage, not to mention the approval of her family. "I'll mount first and give you a hand up. Devil it! I'll not eat you alive!" he snapped with no fairness at all, when she did not follow him immediately.

Not surprisingly, she took umbrage. Her eyes flashed hotly. "I beg to differ there, my lord! Your temper and your mercurial moods bite indeed! I did not cause Clover to go lame to burden you!"

But she was a burden, though it was none of her doing that she was so desirable. She could not help the spirit and warmth that lit her quite perfect features, any more than she could be held responsible for the shimmering misty-gray of her eyes.

"No, you did not," he allowed at last, but he had stood looking down into her eyes too long. His gaze had softened.

And she knew it full well. There was no trace of frustration or resentment in her eyes now. They had gone a smokier, deeper gray. Then her soft lips parted slightly.

Abruptly, before he lost the will to do it, Jason broke the spell, turning sharply away from her to sweep up her mare's reins then mount his hunter. She did not know what she asked for with those parted lips and those wide gray eyes. She was intrigued by him. Perhaps she had never been kissed by anyone. Certainly she had never been kissed by a rake, and he had noted before she did not lack for some sense of adventure. She wanted to taste the forbidden.

Devil take her! The forbidden was very much tempted to comply with her wishes, only he knew all too well how trying it would be to stop after one taste.

His mouth a taut line, Jason held out his hand to her. He'd left the stirrup free for her, and she made use of it, slipping her foot into it as she took his hand and pulled herself onto the back of his mount. The hunter sidestepped, protesting the added burden, though she was a light one. Too light, Jason thought grimly. Though he fought an unaccustomed surge of protectiveness, he could not rid himself of the thought that she was too light and slender to take stone fences and pound through streams as full of rocks as water.

"I am ready now, my lord."

Her voice, God help him, was husky enough to set his blood coursing through his veins.

"You will fall off, holding only to the saddle." Strain made his voice harsh and his temper snappish. "I grant you this is not an ideal situation, but there is no point in making it more difficult with green-girl missishness. You will not reach your uncle intact, unless you hold onto me. Now, let us get on with it."

Jason was being entirely and completely unfair again, but he'd be damned if he would apologize. He had already warned her his temper was not the most placid, and he could not imagine anything likely to try it more sorely than the prospect of riding an as yet unknown number of miles with Gillian's arms wrapped tightly around him.

Chapter 9

Clare was right, Gillian realized. The low saddle gave her next to nothing to grip. Awkwardly straddling the horse, her skirts edging halfway up her boots, she felt herself slipping sideways and caught Clare at the waist just before she fell.

He set the hunter to a trot. Had he walked the horse until they reached her uncle, they might have been obliged to ride together all day. Gillian did understand, but with every move of its hindquarters, the horse still threatened to unseat her. Easily, too easily she could imagine the expression on Clare's face were she to fall. He would be looking down on her, an eyebrow raised . . . abruptly she threw off her reluctance to embrace him and wrapped her arms about him, holding herself close to him of necessity.

Gillian might have laughed then, had she been capable of anything so light as laughter. Necessity was the least of it, the excuse. She ought to have been dismayed by such proximity to a man who had told her more than once how little interest he had in allying himself with her honorably. She ought to have been, but her heart was pounding in her chest.

She held her hands palm flush against his stomach. The feel of him took her by surprise. The only other man she had ridden pillion behind had been her uncle. Lord Albemarle's downy stomach had not prepared her for Clare's. She could feel his muscles working beneath her hand. The sensation made Gillian bite her lip. And for a time, she was aware of naught but the ripple of his hard muscles, and the agile, lean strength they implied.

But his back was so close before her it heated her, though they were separated by the low barrier of his saddle. After a little, she took in how easily he held his back straight; and how it tapered from his broad shoulders to the waist that was narrow and firm beneath her arms. Slowly Gillian's eyes traveled up Clare's back and came to rest upon his dark hair. She had not noticed before, but his hair curled naturally at the nape of his neck. The fingers Gillian held over his stomach tensed, as she fought an almost irresistible urge to brush them through that unexpected boyish curl.

She tried to imagine what expression he wore. She feared that at the least she was flushed. But Clare? Was his mouth tight with impatience? Curved sardonically? She knew there was no humor glinting in his eyes. From the moment he had stopped to help her, though he had done so at his own insistence, he had seemed as much angry as anything.

Except for that one silent exchange just before they had mounted the hunter. For that one moment, his dark gaze had softened. She did not know why he had momentarily softened so, nor even how she had responded. She had been too lost in the subtle shifting of his expression, lost in the dark, gleaming eyes that had suddenly, miraculously, gentled.

Gillian closed her eyes, holding that one look in her mind. She had wanted something like it since she had walked onto the Throckmorton's terrace; had even stared at him, silently willing him to look at her until Rockingham had stepped up beside her and recalled her to reality, not the least of which was that Clare had warned her against developing an interest in him. She had not listened, though. When he had ridden up to her in the woods, she had had to work so hard not to betray how glad she was that it was he who had come to her aid, she had been almost angry with him.

Yet, as matters had turned out, she had gotten even more

than she had hoped for. She had him all to herself for a little at least. And he could not see her, if she did make sheep eyes at him. Carefully, lest Clare notice, Gillian tilted her head forward until her lips brushed against his back. The superfine of his coat felt soft and smooth, and she wanted to lay her forehead against him, but his voice suddenly shot her out of her reveries.

"Be damned." Gillian went rigidly straight even before Jason drew up and twisted to face her, and at the look in his eyes, she sat straighter still. His black eyes were glittering with emotion. Anger, she thought. But perhaps not only anger, for something in that hot light made her blood thud with an odd heaviness in her veins. "Shall we get down here, Miss Edwards? Shall I compromise you in a pile of autumn leaves? Now?"

He had a gift for making her face flame. Perhaps she ought to have become accustomed to his cutting tongue, but to Gillian it seemed quite the opposite had happened. She suffered more acutely every time. Angry with him, and frustrated with herself as well, she lifted her chin and gave him a stubborn look, refusing to dignify his scathing questions with an answer.

"Ah, I see"—Clare's eyebrow arched in a way certain to keep the telling stain of embarrassment high on her cheeks—"you've only silence for an answer. You are fortunate I do not take it for assent. Doubly so indeed, as you will realize if you will clear your mind of the not-so-innocent-by-half thoughts clouding it. Do you hear the squire's hounds now? If I am not mistaken, they have run the fox to ground not more than a quarter mile away, and if you have a care for your reputation, not to mention my self-control, you will sit very straight and very properly until we reach them. Do you understand?

The question was evidently rhetorical. Clare urged the hunter to a start before Gillian had quite digested his previous remark. She had strained his self-control? How? But she knew. She had known from that first look he'd given her in the inn yard that he was not unaffected by her. That was not to say that she believed his self-control was so thin that he might leap off the horse and press himself upon her there and then. But he wanted to.

Excitement spiraled inside her as Clare spurred the hunter to a faster pace. He wanted her!

He wanted her . . . and the doxies awaiting him at Beechfield. An image of the women in the carriage came to her mind quite uninvited, and Gillian very nearly balled her hand into a fist to strike a cruel blow at the hard stomach beneath her hand.

And how would he respond when she explained why she had hit him? Give her one of those derisive looks and inquire—sardonically, of course—if he had given her the least reason to believe she was the only woman of interest to him. Nothing would come of the fact that he found her attractive. After the hunt, he would ride back to his doxies. Merrily no doubt.

Her chest tightened. He would ride out of her life after that, sooner or later. Perhaps there was some attraction between them—stronger on her side than his, she thought—but that was all there was: an inexplicable, intangible attraction that would never be acted upon. She'd an impulse to grasp his coat in her fist and hold him.

As surely as Clare would have resisted any attempt on Gillian's part to restrain him, he rode steadily on toward the baying hounds, and all too soon they emerged into a clearing alive with hunters and hounds. Instantly Gillian snatched her arms away from him, catching him lightly at his sides to hold herself in place, though as she did it, she braced herself for a mocking remark, something to the effect that he was relieved to know she had some concern for her reputation. But Clare responded to her jerky, guilty movement with dead silence.

When Gillian peered around his shoulder, she saw several

of the hunters turn toward them. Her uncle, usually in the middle of the excitement at the end, was on the edge of the crowd, but he did not turn their way. If he had meant to be on the lookout for her, Lord Albermarle had become distracted—likely, Gillian thought, by the bloodying ceremony following Robin Throckmorton's first hunt.

Clare made straight for the baron, and after a shout went up from the group, signaling the end of the ceremony, Albemarle turned and rode forward at once.

"Gilly, girl? Did you suffer a mishap?"

She mustered a smile, still leaning out to look around Clare. "No, Uncle Arthur. I am quite fine. Clover pulled up lame, and Lord Clare kindly stopped to help me."

Lord Albemarle looked from his niece to Clare, a shrewd, even penetrating gleam in his eye. Clare returned the look with a steadiness that prompted Albemarle to give an abrupt nod of his head. "I am in your debt, then, sir. I was just coming to look for Gilly myself."

"I am glad I could help," Clare responded, speaking for the first time since he had demanded of Gillian whether she wanted him to take her in the woods. Now his tone was emotionless.

A horseman moved apart from the rest of the hunters, catching Gillian's attention momentarily. Lord Bolton stared at her and Clare. But only for a moment, then he turned his mount in the direction of Chicksgrove and rode away.

It occurred to Gillian that he would report her arrival with Clare to Rockingham, but she could not bring herself to care. Having dismounted, her uncle had come to lift her down.

"Come on, then, lass," he said, and there was nothing for it but to allow herself to be plucked away from the marquess. "Thank you again, Clare." Lord Albemarle gave him an amiable wave.

"It was nothing, sir." Clare inclined his head, and Gillian sensed that he meant to leave without even looking to her. Immediately she stepped forward, forcing his gaze to her. "Thank you, my lord." She wanted to keep him, though she guessed he was impatient to leave, and added almost at random, "I am grateful I was not obliged to walk."

He did not smile or flatter her with some nonsense about it having been a pleasure to help her. Not at all. "Miss Edwards" was all he said, and curtly his jaw hard-set, though his eyes, dark and unreadable now, did not immediately lift from hers.

Indeed, it was Lord Albemarle who ended the moment. Having remounted, he held his hand out to Gillian. "Now then, Gilly girl, take my hand and I shall pull you up," he said, at which Clare backed his hunter away and left Gillian to her uncle without another word. "You'll want to see Master Robin, or rather, he will be beside himself to see you. He had a grand first hunt. But I am sorry for you, lass. Did Clover pick up a stone?"

Gillian answered her uncle and satisfied the curiosity of Squire Throckmorton and the other hunters in a manner that was evidently unexceptional, for no one looked at her askance.

That did not happen until she reached the Throckmortons'. Her uncle rode directly to the stable yard in order to see to the mare's hoof as soon as possible, and even before Gillian had dismounted, Emily came hastening out to the yard, as if she had been watching for them. Miss Wade did not eye Gillian askance, it was true, but she did regard her friend with such excited interest brimming in her eyes that Gillian no longer had to wonder if Lord Bolton would report what he had seen.

"Were you really alone with Lord Clare?" Emily demanded, her eyes dancing as she tugged Gillian away from Lord Albemarle. "Bolton rode posthaste to report the news! And I must warn you, Gilly, Cousin Lionel was not well pleased." Emily rolled her eyes. "It is all masculine pique, of course! Cousin Lionel took a fall himself, and then to learn that Lord Clare, the absolutely most intriguing man I have ever seen, should have been the one to stop for you . . . well! Of course he is jealous!" Emily giggled with every evidence of delight. "I vow the experience cannot but do Lionel a great deal of good!"

Despite everything, Gillian smiled. "And just why is that, Em?"

"Why? Because like most men, he is in the habit of taking ladies for granted! But, Gilly, I did not hurry out only to warn you of Cousin Lionel's uncertain mood. You should know that Lady Sutton was not well pleased, either. She did not say anything, of course! You know how collected Lady Sutton is, but I know her, and I thought it wise to warn you that she is waiting upstairs in Mrs. Throckmorton's guest room—where by the by there is hot water for you."

"You are the best of friends, Em, to prepare me for my reception, but in truth, Clare's conduct was quite blameless."

Gillian met her friend's eyes without hesitation, for she considered her statement to be, in all the essentials, the truth. And it was as well she did believe it, for she was to be obliged to repeat the assertion twice more that afternoon, just as Emily had warned her.

When Gillian entered Mrs. Throckmorton's guest room, Lady Sutton stood, facing the door, her back rigidly straight and her sharp nose lifted, as if she were scenting for scandal.

"You did not suffer injury during your ride, did you, Gillian?"

At once the feeling of ill-usage that had built in Gillian as she mounted Mrs. Throckmorton's stairs receded. Most would think Lady Sutton the kind to ask first what had happened in regards to Clare. "No, Aunt Margaret. Clover pulled up with a stone in her shoe, and Lord Clare stopped to take me up behind him."

"Arthur did not come back for you?"

This question was put in a somewhat more querulous tone, and Gillian tried to spare her uncle a scolding. "The field of hunters was quite large today. Uncle Arthur would not necessarily have missed me."

"Because he was too absorbed with being the first to the fox," her aunt declared in a tone that did not invite contradiction. "Albemarle has no sense at all!"

It was not the time for Gillian to point out that her uncle regularly triumphed over her at chess. Instead she went to the heart of the matter. "I know that Lord Clare has a regrettable reputation, Aunt Margaret, but however justified the gossip may be with me today, I vow to you, he was quite honorable."

Lady Sutton's spine seemed to give a fraction with relief, but she was not entirely soothed. "It is the second time he has offered you assistance. People may well talk, Gillian."

"If they do, it will be because they are either bored or malicious," Gillian said, thinking specifically of Bolton. "Anyone who is fair, however, will understand the necessity behind both encounters. Davy Jennings might have lost his life had Lord Clare not heard Delhi barking, and today I would have had to walk miles without his assistance."

Gillian held her aunt's regard with a clear, determined gaze. Whatever her own wayward impulses, Clare had resisted them. She would not have resisted had he embraced her in the woods and . . . but he had not done anything of the sort, though he had known very well what she would have allowed. Even wanted.

Before her aunt could make a reply, Gillian added with more emotion, "Should he have passed me by, Aunt Margaret? Surely you would not have wanted that?"

"No, of course not," Lady Sutton declared in her decisive way. "Indeed, I am grateful to Lord Clare for helping you. Still, I do not think it should be surprising that I would wish almost any other gentleman had to come to your aid. His reputation is most unfortunate, as you know; but, too, he is . . . he is, I cannot but be aware, a man of potent appeal."

Gillian's eyes flared with surprise, at which her aunt nodded sharply. "I believe in seeing things as they are, my dear, and I would be a fool not to see that Lord Clare is exceedingly compelling. It is my experience that rakes often are, lamentably; and though I know you to be a girl of good sense, Gillian, I know as well that you have little experience of men. You have been in his company more than once now, and for that reason I consider it my duty to impress upon you that Lord Clare is a man of loose morals by everyone's account. Such a man is rarely interested in marriage, Gillian, and Lord Clare, in particular, has evidenced no desire to ally himself honorably with a girl of good family. I daresay that from his point of view, he has no need to marry. He cares nothing for his estate. He cannot, for he seldom returns to Ireland from what I understand. And if he cares naught for his patrimony, then he has no reason to desire an heir. What cares he, if a cousin inherits? Or a perfect stranger, for that matter? Perhaps he even believes his land is better off without him. No, my dear, he is not of our sort, and would bring to any girl who associates with him only pain. Do you understand me, my dear?"

"Yes, Aunt," Gillian said, and she did. How could she not as Clare himself had taken pains to tell her much the same thing? She wondered what her aunt would say to that information, but did not feel the least temptation to enlighten Lady Sutton. In fact, she suddenly felt weary of everything to do with the marquess, and hoping her aunt was done, crossed to the stand on which stood a bowl and pitcher. "I hope the water is warm. Emily advised me that I've a smudge of dirt on my cheek."

"Emily was teasing you as usual, my dear," Lady Sutton remarked. "But I do think it advisable for you to make yourself as presentable as possible."

Gillian caught a considering note in her aunt's voice and glanced inquiringly at her over the cloth she had wet. Lady Sutton took a deep breath, uncharacteristically seeming to weigh her words. "I believe I must add a word about Lord

Rockingham, my dear," she said after a moment. "I do not know if you are aware of it, but the viscount suffered the indignity of a fall, and if that were not test enough for his pride, he subsequently learned that his fall had caused him to miss the opportunity to offer you assistance. He was most dismayed, and I hope you will deal with him forbearingly, when you see him below." Lady Sutton's expression turned a trifle wry. "It is my experience that gentlemen can be rather more fragile than is generally imagined, on their part at least, but in all he is a fine young man, of an excellent family, Gillian, and will make you a proper husband, one you can trust never to do you dishonor."

Gillian buried her face in the washcloth. Her aunt might as well have said Clare would betray his wife, if he were for some unforeseen reason to take one. She did not dispute the point. She had nothing but intuition to support the belief that if he married, Clare would only marry a woman he had no desire to betray.

When Gillian and Lady Sutton descended from Mrs. Throckmorton's guest room, Emily came hurrying into the hallway to announce that her cousin had gone into the library. "Cousin Lionel did not send me to tell you, but I think he would benefit from speaking with you, Gilly, if Lady Sutton will give her permission."

When Lady Sutton nodded, Gillian went off to the library. The door was open, and she left it so when she entered, not caring to be faulted twice in one day for being alone with a gentleman.

Standing before one of the bookcases, Rockingham appeared to be perusing a book, but he was not so lost in his reading that he did not hear her footstep. Snapping the book shut, he looked to the door, then gave Gillian a small, formal, unsmiling bow. "Miss Edwards, I am relieved to see you look well. Alas, the hunt was not quite satisfactory for either of us."

Gillian made herself smile. "Indeed, it was not, my lord. My aunt told me of your fall. I am most sorry. You do not appear harmed, however?"

"No. I suffered no more than a bruise to my pride. Fortunately when my horse ran off, I encountered a helpful farmer, who saved me a long walk . . . as you, too, found a helping hand, I understand."

He looked away from Gillian then, but too late to hide the flash of vexation in his eyes. She studied his profile, taking in the drooping, rather sulky set of his mouth, and had to remind herself forcibly that her aunt thought him a fine young man worthy of forbearance. Had she not, Gillian might have succumbed to a rather sharp desire to remind the viscount that there were no formal—or informal—agreements between them.

"Yes, I did." Keeping her voice light, she went on to name the source of Rockingham's displeasure, acting on the theory that the more open she was, the less it could be suspected she had aught to hide. "It was Lord Clare who stopped to help me, and I am as grateful to him as you no doubt are to your farmer. In truth, though, I cannot say the marquess was well pleased to have had to pull up in the middle of the hunt. He did not say a great deal, but he did save me a long walk."

"I regret that I could not have been the one to assist you." Rockingham's nostrils were flared slightly, yet somehow he reminded Gillian of nothing so much as a little boy about to sweep up his toy soldiers and go home.

She could almost imagine herself patting him consolingly upon the shoulder. She could not, however, imagine herself giving him to believe that she, too, regretted he had not been the one to stop for her. The lie simply stuck in her throat. Tipping her head slightly, she remarked instead, "Well, my lord, you may assist me now and on a rather urgent matter, too."

When an eager light dawned, along with surprise, in his eyes, Gillian knew she had gotten by the sticky moment. If he had wished her to second his lament, he was diverted now.

"What may I do for you, Miss Edwards? I should be eternally grateful if I could perform some service for you."

"You may save me from the danger of starvation, my lord, for though I should not admit it, perhaps, as young ladies should not possess anything so vulgar as an appetite, I will admit to you alone that I am almost painfully sharp set at this moment."

Rockingham was pleased by her teasing. His dimple appeared. "It would be an honor to save you from such a dreadful fate, Miss Edwards."

Clare did not come between Gillian and Rockingham again that day. He was not in the dining room when they entered, having returned to Beechfield and the doxies, quite as Gillian had expected.

Chapter 10

Gillian tapped her toc impatiently against the floor, the latest edition of *Godey's Ladies' Journal* lying unread in her lap, then suddenly she tensed, leaning forward to listen to some sound in the distance. Yes! She leapt from her chair, tossing the journal carelessly aside, and made for the entry hall. When she saw her uncle there, she affected surprise.

"Why, it is you, Uncle Arthur! I am expecting Emily and Lord Rockingham. She is to fetch me for a visit to Mary Beswick in Chicksgrove, while he may, if he's the time, stop to bid us adieu."

The baron's laugh boomed out heartily. "I am sorry to disappoint you, Gilly girl, but 'tis only me!"

As it was, in truth, he, not Emily or Rockingham, she had been awaiting with growing impatience, Gillian could say with perfect sincerity, "But I am not the least disappointed, Uncle Emily will come in time. But where have you been so early in the day? From your boots, I would judge you have ridden a good way."

Lord Albemarle glanced down at his boots, and promptly uttered a rueful oath. "You'll pardon my language, I hope, Gilly," he said, speaking the rote phrase he used every time he cursed, "But, Jove! If Margaret sees the mud on these boots, she will have my head! Nor will it matter that I have made a mess of myself playing the good Samaritan, helping Jack Thompson after half his sheep took it into their heads to escape their pens in the night and go wandering about the parish."

"Did you find them all?" Gillian inquired, though her mind was less on the tenant's sheep than on her uncle's principal errand that morning and how to bring the conversation around to it.

"I confess I cannot say." Lord Albemarle subsided into a chair and held up his leg to allow a footman to extricate him from the thickly caked boots. "After an hour in the morning chill, I made an excuse to escape."

Gillian laughed. "And what excuse did you use?"

"I said I had to see Clare, may the Lord have mercy upon me."

In his stocking feet, the baron rose to make his way to the sanctity of his study. Falling into step beside him, Gillian put a great deal of effort into asking her next question as offhandedly as if they were speaking still about one of her uncle's tenants rather than the very man about whom Gillian had been waiting impatiently to ask all morning. In the several days since the hunt, she had not seen or heard of Clare, though she had gone to the island twice and once to visit Mrs. Wright.

"Did you not go to see Lord Clare, then, Uncle?"

"Oh, aye." Lord Albemarle nodded heartily. "I did, but before I encountered Thompson. Nonetheless, I am hopeful that God will not consider mine an unforgivable lie. The day is cold and damp for an old man's bones, and besides, I sent along two of my own men to replace the one of me."

They were fast approaching the library, beyond which Gillian had no reason to walk with Albemarle. If she was to learn what she wanted to know, it seemed she would have to ask outright.

"I should think Mr. Thompson would be pleased to have two men for one, Uncle Arthur, but how was Lord Clare? Will he ride in the hunt on Saturday?"

"I had hoped he would! You know how I like to have good

riders in the field, but he'll not be with us this time. He has gone."

Gillian was not prepared. Her step faltered. He was gone. With no warning. She could not quite accept it. How could he go . . . but what had he owed her? Nothing, of course, not even a farewell.

She was aware of an ache welling up in her. The pain took Gillian aback. She had not realized quite how deeply she had become interested in the Marquess of Clare. What had she expected to happen? Before she could answer herself, another thought imposed itself. She did not have to ask with whom he had gone. She was suddenly imagining Lord Darnley and the women he had brought to Somerset laughing gaily as they rode along in a carriage with Clare.

Gillian tightened her fist in the folds of her skirt, welcoming the feel of her nails biting into the soft flesh of her palm. It was obviously for the best that Clare had gone. At the very least she would now be spared wondering when he would leave Somerset. Or whether he would exert himself to bid her adieu.

"I am sorry you were disappointed, Uncle Arthur." Her voice was too unsteady, and immediately she asked something mundane. "Does this mean you will have to stand the full expense of clearing the Wythy, then?"

Albemarle shook his head forcefully. "Nay, nay. I had heard that Gray, off near Bridgewater, had let his excellent agent, Willet, go because he was obliged to give the position to a cousin. Deuced shame to my mind! Willet's as good as they come, and the cousin's highest recommendation is his family connection."

Before her uncle could launch into a recital of all the reasons to avoid hiring family relations, Gillian asked, "And so you recommended this Willet to Clare?"

"Aye, I did. Talked to him at Throckmorton's last week and by damned if Clare didn't go along the next day and hire the fellow! Deuced quick work, but as I said, Willet's a good man. We settled the business about the Wythy. Clare left him a free hand, you see, and in possession of an interesting bit of information, I might add." Lord Albemarle grinned. He was deep into his fifties, yet to Gillian her uncle looked like nothing so much as a mischievous boy, and she could not but give him a fond smile.

"I trust Mr. Willet proved no match for you, uncle, and that you gained that bit of information."

Lord Albemarle's grin only deepened. "In truth, there was no game in it. Though Willet's a good man, he's a shop-keeper's son, unaccustomed to brandy. I'd only to see he had a dram or two, and he was soon confiding that Clare means to put a full half of the rents back into the estate. It's a sum greater than most owners can afford, but that was the least of the interesting news, Willet had. Like everyone, I assumed Clare would use the rents from Beechfield for his own living, but quite to the contrary. He's left instructions with Willet to send most on to Ireland, to his estate there, Conmarra, it's named. Ha!" Lord Albemarle's exclamation was full of satisfaction. "And Margaret maintains he cares naught for his inheritance! Well, though he may not care to live on it—and I grant he can be faulted for that—it is obvious he has not forgotten his land or his people entirely. She's too deuced quick to judge a fellow for the worst!"

As Gillian suspected her uncle was referring as much to his sister's judgment of him as of Clare, she did not respond. Nor did there seem any reason. He was gone. What did it matter if he were more responsible about his Irish property than most realized?

Certainly he was not so concerned over his land that he wished to leg-shackle himself in order to produce an heir. No, instead he had chosen to go racketing about the countryside with his friends and their doxies. On her reading of *that* aspect of his character, her aunt had been entirely right.

"Ah, well, I suppose it does not matter much that he's not quite the ramshackle fellow Margaret thought him," Lord Albemarle observed, giving voice to Gillian's very thoughts. "I doubt we shall see him again. He has not advised the staff at Beechfield that he would return, only told them to keep the house in order, and it's Willet's opinion that Clare means to sell."

He would never return to Somerset. While she had been thinking of him the last few days almost more than she dared admit even to herself, he had been preparing to leave Somerset forever. As she had known all along he would, it was absurd that she should feel bereft. She was a green girl, he a rake. They had met by chance a few times. Nothing more.

After taking leave of her uncle, Gillian went into the library and sank more than sat down in a chair, staring before her, seeing not the wall lined with leather-bound books, but a pair of dark eyes and a dark head. For a fleeting moment she saw those dark eyes softened as they had been in the woods the day of the hunt, but as suddenly as that memory had arisen, Gillian squeezed her eyes tightly shut to rout it.

It really was for the best that he had gone, she told herself. So long as he was near, she would tantalize herself with the hope that "something" might happen. But what? That . . . he might fall in love with her? Gillian let her head fall back against the chair. Surely she had not been so foolish as to hope for that. He had warned her himself! And in truth she allowed after a little that she could not say precisely what she had hoped might happen. She had not gotten so far as to hope for anything specific. She had just wanted to go on seeing what might come.

New sounds of activity drifted from the entryway to Gillian. Rockingham. He and Bolton were to leave that morning, and at the farewell dinner Mrs. Wade had given the night before, the viscount had asked Lady Sutton if he might stop by Moreham Park to bid her and her niece a final adieu.

Gillian rose slowly, feeling numb. She had little desire to entertain the viscount, even to bid him farewell, and the difference in her attitude regarding the departure of Clare on the one hand against Rockingham's on the other was not lost on her. True, the viscount was not leaving forever. He was to return in only a few weeks, but . . .

Gillian heard the rapid approach of footsteps almost with relief. It was not the time to make a final judgment concerning Rockingham. She would have time aplenty while he was away to think clearly about him, and about her aunt's hopes in regards to him. More time than she had wanted . . . but it was certainly not the time to think of Clare, either.

"Miss Gilly." It was one of the maids, peeping into the library.

"Yes, Maude? Has Miss Wade come?"

The girl bobbed her head. "She has, Miss Gilly, and the viscount, too! I was tellin' me mum yesterday that there's no fairer gentleman than his lordship. I know it's daft to say such a thing, but he could be an angel, he could!" Though Lady Sutton ran a strict household and idle chatter on the part of servants was not encouraged, Gillian was not taken aback by Maude's disclosure. The young maid was her age, and as Maude's mother worked in the kitchens, the two of them had grown up together.

"The viscount is handsome, Maude. I quite agree, and just so you'll not feel daft, I shall tell you that Miss Beswick also considers that his looks are angelic. Did Padgett show our visitors to the south drawing room?"

"Yes, Miss Gilly. The sun's good there before luncheon, you know, and he sent Rose for Lady Sutton."

Having reminded herself of the mistress of the house, Maude hurried away. Her rushed departure had nothing to do with a fear that she might be turned off. It was Lord Albemarle who employed and paid the servants, and so far as Gillian knew, he had never turned off anyone; but her Aunt Margaret had assumed responsibility for managing the servants, and all among them agreed that a fate worse than death was to be summoned before her for a talk.

Having preceded Gillian to the drawing room, Lady Sutton announced the obvious, when her niece entered, gesturing to Lord Rockingham, who stood by the fireplace, and Lord Bolton, seated near it. "As you can see, my dear, the travelers have taken the time to come and wish us farewell. I think they are very kind to go out of their way."

"It is you, who are kind to receive us so early in the day, Lady Sutton." Rockingham's dimple flashed. "I vow in town neither you nor Miss Edwards would even be awake yet."

"Fie on you, my lord," Gillian said with a laugh. "I never slept past noon in town, and certainly would not in the country. Everything seems at its freshest and best in the morning."

"I vow it is a contention for which you are living proof, Miss Edwards," Rockingham replied, causing Gillian a faint blush that prompted him to smile even more deeply. "Indeed, I find I've so little desire to leave that I must console myself with the thought that the time between now and Cousin Hetty's ball will go quickly."

"Particularly," Emily chirped from the couch, "as you have heard from Lord Greville that the shooting in Cornwall is especially good this year."

Rockingham was not delighted to have his young cousin point out that he was leaving Gillian in order to engage in one of his favorite pastimes. Gillian had noticed before that the viscount not only could boast of extraordinarily long, curling eyelashes, but that he knew how to make use of those lashes. When he was not well pleased but did not care to broadcast his mood, he allowed them to veil his eyes as he did then, when he glanced to Emily.

"Lord Greville did write to say so, yes, Cousin, but I should never prefer a pheasant to Miss Edwards's company."

Emily, however, was not daunted by the relative she had known since he was in short pants, even when his tone was a shade on the cool side. "You gentlemen protest as much, Cousin Lionel, and one pheasant may not weigh a great deal against a lady's company, but when it comes to pheasant in the plural? What then?"

Gillian intervened between the two. "Then the eating is excellent."

Everyone laughed, and restored to good humor, Rockingham pushed away from the fireplace. "As little as we relish leaving your good company, ladies, I fear Lord Bolton and I must bid you farewell now, for if we do not, we shall be three days on the road rather than two, and one cannot always be confident of finding a good inn west of the Tamar."

"That is too true," Lord Bolton opined, rising languidly from his chair. "All civilization seems to stop at that rather muddy river."

Gillian thought to herself that if Lord Bolton considered himself civilized, he did little to recommend civilization, but it was not a new thought and she did not dwell on it, particularly as Rockingham was bowing over her aunt's hand saying something that caught Gillian off guard, though she ought to have been prepared for it.

"My mother has written to advise me, Lady Sutton, that she means to invite you and your niece, and Lord Albemarle, too, of course, to join us at Chevely for Christmas. My sister and her husband and children will be there, and I am confident we shall have a very festive time. But please do not give me your reply yet! I know you have much to consider, not least of all Lord Albemarle's partiality for Somerset. I meant only to give you a fair warning." Lord Rockingham smiled persuasively, flashing his dimple. "And the time to persuade Lord Albemarle, for it would make us all very happy, if you were to come."

"We are honored, indeed, merely to know that you and

Lady Becquith have thought of us, Lord Rockingham," Lady Sutton replied graciously. "And you may be certain that we will give your invitation the most serious consideration."

That old feeling of panic rose in Gillian, for it was almost as if Rockingham had offered for her, and Lady Sutton had accepted his proposal. And all again without anyone even looking to her.

Nor was she being fanciful. Only a little later, when she and Emily and Emily's abigail were bouncing along in the Wade family's landau toward Chicksgrove, Emily expressed sentiments that were, if not exactly the same as Gillian's, then much the same.

"Cousin Lionel means to offer for you at Christmas, Gilly!" Emily cried excitedly as the landau bowled down the drive. Her abigail, a small, elderly woman who doted upon Gillian almost as much as she did her own mistress, exclaimed in surprise, and Emily nodded vigorously in her direction. "It is true Smithkins! I am certain of it. Why else should he invite Gilly for Christmas, if he did not wish first for Lady Becquith to meet her and then to ask for her, for of course, Lady Becquith will approve of Gilly!"

Evidently Smith, called Smithkins by the girls, followed Emily's logic, for she beamed at Gillian. "My congratulations, Miss Gillian. Lord Rockingham is ever so elegant."

"Just wait and see!" Emily attempted a superior look, but ruined it by grinning. "Cousin Lionel will be on his knees come Christmas! Cranston!" she leaned forward to call to her father's coachman. "Can we not go a trifle faster? We are eager to get to the Beswick's for a celebratory luncheon!"

As everyone around Chicksgrove knew, Emily had inherited her father's love of swift travel, and no sooner did she cry out the request, than Cranston, the coachman, whipped up the horses.

Smith gave an anxious cry, and in a quavering voice remarked that the road was rather slick from the rain they'd had, but Emily only laughed.

Unfortunately Cranston would have been well-advised to listen to the timorous abigail and not to his lighthearted mistress. The road was not slick. It was too muddy, but when he rounded a corner and found several of Mr. Thompson's sheep milling about aimlessly in the middle of the road, there was not sufficient traction beneath the landau's wheels to avoid the sheep smoothly. When Cranston jerked on the reins, the horses swerved to the right, but the right rear wheel of the landau slipped disastrously in the mud, and the vehicle abruptly overturned.

Emily screamed, as did Smith, but in the end, they were unharmed except for a few bruises, and the fright they suffered. They had been riding on the seat that faced forward, where they were protected by the sides to which the convertible top of the landau was attached. Gillian, however, aware that riding backward made Smithkins ill, had kindly taken the seat that faced the rear of the vehicle, where there was no protective side. When the landau toppled, she was thrown out onto the rocky shoulder of the road, hitting it with such force that she lost consciousness.

Chapter 11

Pain wrenched Gillian from the blackness. It overwhelmed her, clouding her perception of where she was or why. In the distance, she heard someone crying. She thought it was Emily and struggled to open her eyes.

Bending over her was Clare, but of course, he could not be there. "Emily?" she tried to say but nothing came out. She forgot Emily and even her vision of Clare in the next moment, for she was lifted and such pain lanced her, she screamed and then mercifully, again lost consciousness.

When next Gillian opened her eyes, she did so slowly. She had no notion how much time had passed, but she did vaguely, apprehensively, recall the pain that had seemed to shatter her before, and she was wary of it. Her shoulder throbbed, as did her left side, she found, testing the various parts of her body. And her head. It ached, and seemed to be bound.

She had no desire to move and touch her head, though. Her body felt too leaden, every limb heavy and somehow distant, but after a little she began to register what her eyes saw. And her gaze steadied. Her own bed had no canopy, yet over her head was a heavy, brocade canopy. Carefully, wary of pain, Gillian swiveled her eyes, searching the room. A completely foreign dark wood paneling covered the lower half of the walls and the plaster covering the ceiling was not plain like that in her room at Moreham, but highly ornamented, the plaster ribbing forming graceful quatrefoils.

At the realization that she did not know the room, panic rose in her. Where was she and why? Thinking hard, Gillian remembered Emily. . . . They had been in the landau with Smithkins. They'd had an accident. She shut her eyes, only to relive that awful moment when she had felt herself thrown into the air, whereupon a frightened moan escaped her.

"Gillian!"

Gillian jerked her head so sharply, she set off a dizzying wave of pain.

"Oh, my dear girl! You are awake!"

"Aunt Margaret?" Half afraid to open her eyes, Gillian peered out from under her lashes. Her aunt was, indeed, bending over her. "Aunt Margaret?" she repeated.

"My dear child! Oh, Gillian, you have worried us so."

"Where am I, Aunt Margaret?" Nothing, not even her aunt's distraught manner, was as disorienting as not knowing where she was. For a moment, just at the beginning, Gillian had even wondered if she were not in heaven.

Her aunt sat down carefully on the side of the unfamiliar bed. It was high enough from the floor that Lady Sutton had to half lift herself onto it. "Does my sitting by you cause you pain?"

Just in time, Gillian remembered not to shake her head. "No," she said, and realized her voice sounded oddly raspy and weak. "Not at all."

Her aunt lifted her hand, squeezing it tightly. "Do you remember the Wade's landau overturning, Gillian?"

"Yes. I was thrown out, I think?"

"You were, my dear, and suffered injury." Lady Sutton blinked rapidly, as if her eyes had filled with tears. To see her aunt so close to crying alarmed Gillian, and she tried to move to prove to herself that she was not permanently injured. What she proved, however, was that movement caused a burning pain to spread throughout her left side. "You must lie still, Gillian!" Lady Sutton cried with such dismay that Gillian grew more alarmed. Surely, she thought, she must be horribly mangled for her aunt to carry on so.

A door opened. Gillian heard the click of the handle. "Margaret! Did I hear you speaking to her?"

It was her uncle, and when his ruddy, craggy face came into her view, Gillian's eyes filled with tears. "Uncle Arthur?"

"You've joined us again, lass! Praise be to God!"

He was bending over her, trying to smile, though his thick brows were drawn almost together over his nose, and his eyes were suspiciously bright.

"Am I badly hurt?" She addressed her uncle, for of her two guardians, he would answer her the most frankly.

Guessing somehow what alarmed her most, he said firmly, "Time will heal all your injuries, lass, but, aye you did hurt yourself badly."

When Gillian felt her aunt pat her hand, she looked to Lady Sutton. "Will you tell me why I hurt so much?"

But Lady Sutton was too distraught, and at the weakly voiced question clapped her hand over her mouth. "You are alarming Gilly without reason, Margaret!" Lord Albemarle exclaimed gruffly. "Jove! She is not in mortal danger. She has only broken several ribs, sprained her shoulder, and . . ."

"Only?" Lady Sutton's lips trembled over the word. "Gillian cannot move without such pain that she cries out, and she has been lost to us for a day! I thought she might never awaken again."

A sob escaped Lady Sutton, whereupon Lord Albemarle, to Gillian's infinite surprise, wrapped a stout arm around his sister's shoulders. "I know, my dear, I know," he soothed a bit bluffly, "and you have sat here by her all that time, even sleeping in that chair." The proof of the extent of her aunt's devotion to her brought tears to Gillian's eyes, but when she squeezed her aunt's hand, she got a different result than she had intended, for Lady Sutton began to cry quietly but unmistakably into her handkerchief. Lord Albemarle patted her shoulder a trifle awkwardly, and looking to Gillian explained, "We have been very anxious, my dear, because we could not rouse you. You hit your head very hard, you see, and if that were not enough, your breathing was so shallow, especially at first, that Dr. Hogwood feared one of your broken ribs might have pierced a lung. Had it, you likely would not have lived."

"But that did not happen?" Gillian asked.

Her uncle shook his head. "No, it would seem your lungs are intact, for you have not coughed up any blood, but the devil of it is, Gilly, you will be in danger of causing yourself such harm until your ribs knit a little."

"How long will that take?"

Lord Albemarle looked unhappy. "Hogwood cannot say with certainty. You are young and your ribs need not heal completely, only begin to knit, but in all, you shall have to lie flat and unmoving in this bed for close to a fortnight he expects. As to when you can leave the bed and walk about . . . Hogwood says we shall have to wait and see."

Perversely, though she had not wanted to lift a finger before, at the news that she was not to be allowed even to turn on her side, Gillian felt restless and tried at least to lift the arm that felt so heavy. Nothing happened, however, except that she caused her shoulder to throb enough that she moaned.

"Lie still, Gilly," Lord Albemarle chided but softly. "You also sprained your shoulder in the accident. Hogwood has bandaged it, and to spare you the pain moving your arm would cause, has bound your arm to your side as well. Do you feel the bandages around your ribs? There are a good many of them."

There had been so many unfamiliar sensations, Gillian had not remarked until then the heavy bandages girding her middle. "I feel as if I am wearing a corset." She tried to smile, for she could tell her uncle was almost as distraught as her aunt, though he made a better job of hiding his anxiety, but her effort must have been wobbly, for he gave a pained groan. "It is not so bad," she assured both her guardians. "Truly, but I am tired." Weights seemed to have settled upon her eyes, yet she fought them. There was something she wanted to know. "Where am I, Uncle Arthur?"

"You are at Beechfield Hall." Despite her efforts, Gillian's eyes had drifted shut, but at that, they opened, for she had no difficulty placing Beechfield Hall in her mind, or naming its owner. "The landau overturned at the gates."

Clare. Had she seen him? She remembered foggily that perhaps she had and again battled the downward drift of her eyelids. "Did Lord Clare come?" she asked, her mind feeling as fuzzy as her voice sounded.

As if from a very great distance, she heard her aunt say, "Yes, my dear. He came upon the accident by chance, and as you were so badly injured, he judged it best to bring you to Beechfield on a litter rather than risk taking you all the way to Moreham in a carriage. Dr. Hogwood says the decision may have saved your life, but you need not worry, Gillian. I am staying with you."

In her mind at least, Gillian smiled. Clare had not gone, after all.

The next time Gillian awoke, the room was dark but for the glow of a single candle near her bed. She knew where she was, however. Clare had come to her aid yet again, bringing her to Beechfield.

She hurt, though. Somehow, she had expected she would feel much better the next time she awoke. Evidently she would not heal in mere hours, or was it days she had been asleep? She had no way of knowing, nor did she care greatly. One uncomfortable sensation had overwhelmed all the others. Her mouth and throat were almost painfully dry. Exploring her lips with her tongue to little avail, she decided to turn her head and look for help. The constriction she had felt before around her head resolved itself into a bandage, as she felt it rub against her pillow. Her uncle had mentioned a blow to her head, and as she searched the shadows for her aunt, Gillian wondered in passing, lacking the energy for real anxiety, where she had taken the blow and whether she would bear a scar.

Gillian saw a heavy, comfortable chair had been pulled close to the bed, but it was empty. Tilting her head further, she looked beyond the chair to the door. Just out of the pool of light cast by the candle, she saw a man. He was leaning back against the wall with his arms over his chest and one heel resting on the wall behind him.

"Uncle Arthur?"

At first she thought she had not made herself heard, for her voice had emerged as no more than a whispering croak, and the man did not respond. She licked her lips, failing miserably in her effort to wet them, but it didn't matter. The man abruptly levered himself away from the wall, and even before he neared the soft pool of light shed by the candle, she recognized him.

Clare. Gillian's heart raced, and she tried to smile, though her lips were so dry, she feared the result was more likely a grimace. "Hello," she whispered.

"Good evening." His voice was too quiet to read, and she could see little of his expression, for he lingered near the edge of the light. "Your aunt and uncle are sleeping, resting from the vigil they kept with you all yesterday and much of today. Maude . . ." He paused, cocking his head a fraction. "Do you remember her?"

Gillian forgot herself and began to nod in answer, only to wince in pain. Clare took a step, inadvertent she thought, toward the bed. "What is the matter? Have you hurt yourself?"

He sounded gruff, and she could not guess whether he was concerned for her or put out at having to bother with her. "I feel the least pain when I keep my head still," she said, closing her eyes to gather her strength.

"I should go then."

"No!" Gillian winced again. She had spoken too urgently, setting off a new throbbing in her head. Still, she made herself continue. "Please? I am thirsty."

He hesitated again, but not long. Even to Gillian her voice had sounded hoarse with dryness. He moved to the table beside her, and she listened as he poured water into a glass. When he set the pitcher down, as she was lying too flat to drink, Gillian attempted to lift herself up on her elbow. Immediately pain flamed through her left side, and she collapsed back on the pillow, whereupon Clare, cursing softly, took matters into his own hands, literally. Scooping his arm behind her pillow, he lifted her slowly. "Does that hurt?"

It did, but she wanted to drink too much to deter him. "No," she said, but the catch in her voice made him swear again. Looking up, she saw he was scowling. "It is no more than I can bear," she amended. "Particularly if the reward is water."

Without wasting more time, he put the glass to her lips, and she drank greedily. Finally finished, she lifted her mouth away, and Clare gently lowered her back to the thin pillow Dr. Hogwood had allowed her.

"Thank you." Gillian had closed her eyes to savor the wetness in her mouth, but opened them and found her lips had become pliable enough to curve in a full smile. "Mere water though it was, it tasted as good as an elixir."

Clare responded with an inarticulate grunt that might have meant anything or nothing. The planes of his face seemed more sharply drawn than she recalled, but perhaps it was only the frown he wore as he regarded her. Self-conscious suddenly, Gillian was reminded of the bandage wrapped around her head and lifted her hand to touch it.

"I must look frightful," she said when she realized how wide it was. Her brow was nearly hidden behind it.

He did not attempt to flatter her. "You have looked better. But it is true as well that your appearance has improved considerably."

She realized that his expression was not so concerned or anxious as it was grim. His mouth was drawn in a tight, nearly straight line.

"Aunt Margaret says I have you to thank for sparing me what might have been a fatal trip to Moreham."

His eyes seemed to go darker than the shadows in the room. "Whether thanks are in order, I cannot say. I did bring you to Beechfield, but when I lifted you onto the litter, I caused you such hurt that you screamed and lost consciousness." She remembered, sharply, and flinched. "Jesus!" he swore, the lilt in his voice as unmistakable as the raw regret. Her eyes flew open, meeting his. Almost as if he could not help himself, Clare slowly extended a long finger and then brushed it down her cheek. "I am sorry."

"You could not have left me there," she told him softly.

He did not answer, only continued to regard her in rather brooding silence. In the quiet, Gillian wondered if she could ask why he had returned to Chicksgrove. Perhaps he had planned to do so all along. But the door to the room opened, and Clare turned away from the bed. "Ah, Maude," he said as a pair of feet tripped lightly across the room. "Your mistress awoke and desired water. I'll have a maid bring more for the night."

"Yes, your lordship! I beg your pardon for takin' so long! There was this . . ."

"There is no need for apology," he cut abruptly into whatever excuse Maude had meant to give. From experience, Gillian knew Maude's excuses could be amazingly baroque, and she wondered if Clare had learned as much in only a day. His face gave her no clue, betraying neither humor nor impatience, when he looked back to bid her adieu. "Good night, Miss Edwards. I hope you rest well."

By then even her smile felt weary at the edges. "The truth is I should have to fight not to sleep. But thank you again, my lord, for everything."

With a single, curt nod, he was gone, and Maude bustled forward to replace Clare in Gillian's vision. "I beg pardon for bein' away, Miss Gilly, but I had to answer a call of nature, if you get my meanin', and then, when I was returnin', I met Roger. He's second underfootman, and ever so handsome. Though not half so handsome as his lordship! Merciful heaven, he's a gentleman and a half, he is. You could have knocked me over with a feather when I met him in the hall, and he said he would stay with you. Truth to tell, I did hope you might wake. I thought you'd prefer his company to mine. I know I would!"

Even as her eyes drifted shut, Gillian's mouth lifted. Maude was a chatterbox with an overfond eye for the men, but she was no fool when it came to it.

Chapter 12

Jason turned the corner on the stairway, tracing without feeling the tiny hunting scene intricately carved upon the post beneath his hand. Beechfield's oak staircase was praised in every guidebook to England's country homes, or so Jason had been informed by Lely's counselor, Bexton, his lofty butler, and even Darnley. He did not doubt them. He admired it himself, but that night his mind was not upon the scenes of country life the woodcrafter had depicted on the twenty oak posts that so magnificently supported the stairs.

Albemarle had dined with him that evening. The baron was not staying at Beechfield any longer, but he rode over each evening to spend an hour or so with his niece, and twice had stayed on for dinner with his host. In Jason's opinion, it had not even occurred to the baron that he might wish to sup off a tray in his niece's room. Albemarle liked his food too well to take it off his lap. And he liked his sister too little to sacrifice his comforts to dine with her.

A faint smile lifted a corner of Jason's mouth. He sympathized with the baron there. The night of the accident, after the creaking ancient who was doctor to the parish had commended Jason for having the sense to keep his patient flat, Lady Sutton had unbent so far as to thank him for his efforts on behalf of her niece. But even emotional as she'd been at that moment, there had been a constraint in her manner that conveyed as clearly as words how much she wished almost anyone other

than the Marquess of Clare had come to her precious niece's
aid.

He shrugged at the vagaries of fate, for it had been the
purest chance that Lady Sutton had not gotten her wish. He
had not intended to return to Beechfield so soon.

Oversby had made the suggestion the evening he and Darnley returned from the hunt that they all take themselves off to
a milling-match that was to be held in Devon. The Red Scot, a
favorite bruiser of Oversby's, was the defender; the Mon-
mouth Goliath, a new, apparently large fellow, the challenger,
and Jason had leapt at the chance to be away. He felt restive
and knew precisely why. He had had enough of resisting
Gillian Edwards. He needed a new scene, or he would end up
taking her when he encountered her next on the island, or in
the woods, or wherever he would encounter her, and he no
longer gave the slightest consideration to not meeting up with
her. Whether by his design, hers, or fate's, they had met frequently enough that he might almost as well have been calling
upon her.

While the others had begun packing, Jason had set off
posthaste after Willet, the agent Albemarle had recommended.
Gray had been a fool to let him go. The agent knew his business, and Jason had felt easy at leaving him in charge, though
they'd had only two days to work together.

The drive into Devon had been amusing enough. The
women had accompanied them, of course, and when their
charms had paled, there had been pleasant countryside through
which to ride on horseback. Had they continued to travel, all
might have remained well, but in a day and a half, they
reached Little Becking, the venue of the "Great Mill," and
there had simply been too many people pressing in from all
over the country to watch a match that had taken on seemingly
biblical proportions. Oversby had sent his valet ahead to pro-
cure rooms, but even so, the man had been able to find only
two. His mood veering abruptly, Jason had decided that after

almost a fortnight, he had enough of Darnley's women at close quarters, and these quarters promised to be extremely close. Darnley had proposed going on to town, but Jason had promised to meet Caroline in Somerset, and so . . . on her account he told himself, he had left Little Becking only a few hours after he'd arrived there, returning to Beechfield in time to see a fashionable landau overturned at his gates.

Miss Wade had been sobbing in the arms of a woman he had rightly taken to be an abigail, while several feet from them, upon the side of the road, the landau's driver had knelt over a still, crumpled figure. Everything in Jason had gone still at the sight. The girl's face had been obscured, but he had recognized her carriage dress.

He curled his hand hard around the large post at the stairs' landing, but scarcely felt the bite of a carved scythe against his palm. She had not been dead, though. Before he had even pulled his stallion to a full halt, the coachman had jerked around toward his mistress and cried, tears streaming down his seamed face, "Praise God, Miss Emily! She lives!"

Emily Wade had given a wild cry and collapsed with relief, but the announcement that Gillian Edwards had not been killed off by a cruel or careless God had been a call to action for Jason. Bounding down from his horse, he had fired off orders, sending the Wade's coachman and the abigail, scurrying. Not that anyone present at the scene had questioned where Miss Edwards should be taken. It had been obvious to them all, as it would have been to Lady Sutton had she been there, that the girl lying all but still on the ground, could not withstand more than the briefest, most careful movement. And even then, she had cried out so as he had lifted her onto the litter he'd fashioned that the Wade chit had begun to sob again.

No, he did not repent bringing her the half mile from the road to Beechfield, sparing her bouncing the several miles to Moreham. Nor did he repent looking in on her two nights before, while her aunt slept. He had had to see for himself that her color was not tinged with gray any longer and that the slightest movement did not cause her to scream in agony.

She had been improved. Her complexion had no longer looked so bloodless that he feared her dead, and with bandages to support her ribs, she could tolerate being lifted for a drink of water.

He had been satisfied that she would live then, but tonight at dinner Albemarle, between discussions of the Wythy and the yield of his crops, had reported that she was fretful and not sleeping well. Was it possible that she was regressing? Of course it was. His mother had seemed to recover from a fever, only to come down with it again after a few days. On its return, the fever had killed her.

Jason took the last steps by twos. By God, he had saved her life. He had the right to look in on her to assure himself she was not failing. That was all he would do, look in, and besides the little maid would be there.

But she was not. When Jason knocked at the door, it was not the young maid Lady Sutton had brought from Moreham to sit with her niece at night who responded.

"Yes?" The voice was low but clear, its tones educated.

"It is I, Miss Edwards," Jason announced, striding into the room, frowning. "Where the deuce is your maid?"

Lying nearly flat as per Dr. Hogwood's quavered instructions, she was reading, supporting the book on her chest. "Lord Clare?" She closed the book, allowing it to slide onto her bandaged arm.

Jason strode forward into the light, scowling. "Of course it is I. Who did you expect? Surely not your maid, who is absent as often as she is here. Where is she?"

Gillian's eyebrow quirked, drawing Jason's eye. Her aunt had leant her a large, frilly dowager's cap to cover her hair, as she could not rise to wash it. With the cap reaching to the bandage that covered much of her brow, she looked a feminine veteran of a losing battle.

"Maude has gone at my request to warm some milk for me. I have not been sleeping well."

She did not look as if she had rested well. Though there was the faintest hint of rose in her cheeks just then, the color looked out of place, for her face was still pale, and beneath her eyes there were dark circles.

"And the milk helps you to sleep?" Jason questioned the obvious, but he was diverted by a hint of coolness in her manner. He'd have thought she would be delighted by company, particularly new company, and particularly his company. That she was intrigued by him, he knew too well.

"No, actually, it does not help me to sleep. But fetching the milk gives Maude something to do other than chatter endlessly in my ear about the merits of your second underfootman."

So. Her ill humor was not directed only at him. "I see." Jason crossed his arms over his chest, feeling a spark of humor flicker to life in him. It was the first real amusement he had felt since he had seen her lying still by the roadside. "And in the meantime you read? I commend you for passing the time so intelligently, Miss Edwards."

Intelligent Miss Edwards's response to his praise was to push almost violently at the book that lay on her useless arm, sending it tumbling off her. "If I never see another book in my life, I shall not be sorry! They are all about what other people do, how they walk here and there, or run, even. Imagine that! But what of you, my lord?" she went on, a vicious rip to her voice now. "What of your activities? You need not be reticent! Uncle Arthur reported the weather has been cool but sunny. Did you hunt on Saturday as he did? Or perhaps you have been fishing on the island now that I am not available to intrude upon you?"

"No, I have neither been hunting nor fishing, Miss Edwards, though I confess I have, as part of my duties as a landowner, gone riding."

"So! You have gotten out-of-doors! You have moved about.

I am delighted for you, though I cannot but imagine such activity tame by your standards. You must regret having sent your doxies away."

The moment she said it hot color surged into her cheeks, and she turned her face away so abruptly Jason was not surprised to see her flinch. He was able to see that grimace, as well as the color in her cheeks, as Gillian could not hide her face from him. Dr. Hogwood had bade her lie not only flat but still as possible. At night, her uncle had said, Maude was obliged to bind her in place, lest she turn over in her sleep and stab herself with an unhealed rib.

"Forgive me, my lord," she said in a tight voice. "I . . . I am not myself."

Jason wondered how she had learned about Darnley's traveling companions, but did not consider it an opportune time to inquire. Fighting another impulse to smile, his eyes upon her rosy cheeks, he gave a negligent lift of his shoulders. "I think you are bored, Miss Edwards," he said, careful to speak in even and forbearing tones.

The effect of his effort, however, was not what he had expected. She faced him again, almost as abruptly as she had turned away, and the flash in her eyes was all the more obvious for the way the white bandage and dowager's cap set off her misty-gray eyes. "And why should I not be bored, my lord?" she snapped, the abashment of only a moment before evidently long forgotten. "My entertainment has been to lie without moving for four entire days, while Aunt Margaret speaks of little but Lor . . . oh! Listen to me! I vow I am going mad." She squeezed her eyes shut. "Aunt Margaret has once again given up her bed and comfortable pursuits to come to my aid, and what do I do, but repay her by complaining when her back is turned."

"And a very straight back it is, too," Jason teased, allowing himself the pleasure.

But he had misjudged the volatility of her mood. When

Gillian opened those great gray eyes, he saw there were tears shimmering in them.

"It is also a doting back," he added, but thrust his hands deep into his pockets, else he knew he would touch her. "I do not believe your aunt would fault you for a word you have said, though she would certainly fault me for being on hand to listen. You have a right to be restive, Miss Edwards. I shudder to think what my temper would be, had I been lying flat for four days."

His speech soothed her a little. But not a great deal. Though her eyes were neither flashing angrily any longer nor glistening with tears, there was a degree of accusation in the clear, gray gaze she fixed on him. "I am glad for your understanding, my lord. However . . . understanding is an intangible thing providing little respite for boredom. Now you've looked in on me and voiced your sympathies, you will go away quite satisfied, leaving me to lie here for the next fortnight."

Gillian was not only a decade younger than Jason, but had also been spared the opportunity he had had to hone his assurance and will against the sharp edges of English schoolboy prejudice and ignorance.

He gave her a hard look. "You shall have to find other company to entertain you, yes, Miss Edwards. Your aunt has not invited me to visit you even when she is on hand to chaperon, and as to my coming tonight, I have only looked in on you, because your uncle said something that concerned me. Now that I've had my fears reassured, I shall certainly go shortly." When she bit her lip, he swore beneath his breath. "If I were found here," Jason went on, striving for patience, "you would be compromised beyond redemption."

"And is that not my concern?" she demanded, though her voice had weakened to a rasp. "It is my reputation of which you are so careful! And who is to discover us, if you sit with me for a few minutes each evening? Maude? She would never breathe a word to my aunt. They are born adversaries. Besides which, poor Aunt Margaret is sleeping soundly as a stone.

That is how dreadfully wearing I have been. Please! Entertain me for a little. Nothing will come of it, I know!"

What Jason knew was that Gillian knew not whereof she spoke. But then he had framed his objection to staying with her in terms of society, and Gillian was actually more right there than not. Her aunt likely never would learn of his visit, but even were Lady Sutton to storm into the room in the next instant, nothing would come of her discovery of him but for some sharp, likely ugly words. Certainly Lady Sutton would never demand that he marry Gillian to right whatever harm she might imagine his visit to her niece's bed chamber unchaperoned might have caused.

He'd not be trapped into marriage, but if society could not hurt Gillian, he knew he could. She was too attracted to him, and clearly the less time they spent together furthering her impossible attraction the better. As for his attraction to her . . . it did not quite count, for hurt as she was, he did not want her with anything like the urgency he had felt that day of the hunt.

"Oh, never mi—"

Jason knew his reasoning was impeccable, even laudable. Yet, her shoulders had sagged, and the light had gone out of her eyes, and the devil take all laudable, conformable reasoning, she must lie flat on her back for a fortnight. Abruptly, in mid-word, he cut Gillian off. "You have persuaded me, Miss Edwards. I will stay and divert you until your maid comes. With the door open, I suppose I cannot cause you irreparable harm."

Rather wryly, Jason noted that if he had thought his indulgence would bring a blinding smile to her face, he was doomed to disappointment. Her eyes flared with surprise, but after he had made himself comfortable, choosing a seat on the end of the bed so that she would not have to twist her neck to face him, he found her watching him with an expression that was unexpectedly solemn.

"I feel a fool," she said, a moment after their eyes met.

"Do you?" He shrugged, giving her a crooked smile as he

leaned back against the bedpost and stretched out his legs in her general direction. "I cannot see why. You are not the only woman who has begged for my company, after all."

Idly Jason wondered if he had not said as much to provoke her into sending him away as not. If so, Miss Gillian Edwards did not prove obliging. It was then, of all times, that she smiled, a little at least. "I do not doubt it," she said.

Jason was a man of considerable experience with women, and he knew without vanity that he was attractive to them. Over the years, they had told him so in many ways. But never simply, without expectation of return of some sort, whether a bedding or a bauble or even so little as a wink. Yet Gillian's smile could not have been termed coy by the wildest imagination. Like her words, it lacked all artifice, and like her plain, straightforward remark, it lit a slow burn in him and at the same time, quite separately, tightened something in his chest.

He gave her a mock bow, before, he hoped, she read either response in his expression. "Thank you, Miss Edwards. And now what particular topic of conversation might entertain you? My ride today, perhaps?"

"No." She smiled again more broadly, recognizing his teasing. "Tell me about Ireland. Do you have family there, still?"

As ever when an Englishman or Englishwoman, mentioned Ireland, he stiffened inwardly. Outwardly he only gave her a guarded glance from under his lashes. "Some, yes."

The girl with the thoroughly English gray eyes regarded him with unmistakable sympathy. It was, however, the shrewdness he also saw in those English eyes that kept up his guard. "Shall I guess who they are? Or are they too barbaric to discuss with a proper English girl in the dead of the night while seated upon her bed?"

He was chuckling before he realized she had breached his defenses. "You are a minx, Miss Edwards," he said then, wryly.

She tried to shrug nonchalantly but only managed a strange,

crab-like movement due to her sprained shoulder and its heavy binding. "Lud," she exclaimed, wincing even as her mouth lifted in a self-deprecating smile. "I vow I am a slowtop, for I cannot seem to get it through my head that I will suffer if I move without thinking. But distract me, my lord, and tell me about your family in Ireland, now that you know I do not consider myself superior simply because I am so very English."

"There is only my cousin, Liam, actually, and his wife, Mary, and their three children."

"And did you know Liam as a child?"

"Yes. We grew up together, doing all the usual things boys do."

"Did Liam live near you then?"

"Before Liam was born, his father's estate was seized by the English for unspecified crimes against the crown." Gillian gave a startled exclamation, but Jason shrugged off her sympathy. "Such thievery happens every day in Ireland, Miss Edwards. At least the O'Neils had the wit to find a refuge. My uncle managed Conmarra for my father, who only visited on occasion."

"It was not a love match then? Between your parents?"

Jason's gaze hardened. If she thought the private details of his life were open for her diversion, she would soon be disillusioned, but then she touched him, reaching out to the closest part of him available to her, the calf of his leg. "I am prying," she admitted with chagrin, the pads of her fingertips warm even through his trousers. "Forgive me. I have little to do but lie here and wonder about all manner of things, but that is no excuse."

It wasn't, of course. Yet, he heard himself say, even before she withdrew her fingertips, "It was a match of necessity, actually. My father's tenants were not pleased to have a thoroughly English Devereux succeed the more Irish than English branch that had held sway over Conmarra for a pair of centuries, and so my uncle offered to manage them, and the estate, if, among other things, my father would marry his sister.

As he did not consider marriage a particularly binding arrangement, for the husband anyway, and she is reputed to have been a beautiful girl, I do not think my father was reluctant to agree to the arrangement, but more importantly, he needed every penny Conmarra could possibly yield in order to live in the style he favored."

Jason spoke offhandedly, as if it did not matter that his father had milked the estate dry, and shrugging was about to change the subject entirely, when Gillian said quietly, "Is that why you intend to send much of the rent from Beechfield to Ireland? Because you would repair your father's depredations on the estate?"

When Jason stared, struck dumb for once in his life, she colored. "Oh, lud, that blow to my head did, indeed, addle my wits! Of course, Uncle Arthur would not have told you he learned that from Mr. Willet. But you must not blame Mr. Willet, my lord! Uncle Arthur has a positive talent for drawing information out of people. I think it is because he is so affable and appears to be naught but a bluff countryman, when in truth he is shrewd as the devil. Indeed, he admitted plying poor Mr. Willet with brandy."

"Mine, I don't doubt," Jason remarked, but he could not make his tone as sour as he wished. She had lightly touched his leg again, on Mr. Willet's behalf of course, and besides, every word she had said about her uncle he knew, after only two dinners with the baron, to be absolutely true. Albemarle was surprisingly shrewd, and he did have a talent for eliciting information . . . not unlike his niece.

"You have forgiven Mr. Willet, I think?" she asked, studying him. "Though he should not have said anything, it is also true that he did not reveal anything to your detriment. Uncle Arthur very much approved the amount you are putting back into Beechfield."

At that second revelation, she grinned so saucily, Jason

could only cast his eyes to the canopy above them. "Is there anything you do not know about me?"

Her grin only deepened. "Almost everything, but all I shall ask is . . . let me see . . . did you have a dog, when you were a boy?"

He couldn't but chuckle at the way she had played him. "I did. Aaron was a great beast, but a constant companion to Liam and me."

"Aaron, my lord? That is no name for a dog."

"You have little right to criticize the names others give their animals, Miss Edwards, having named your Irish dog after an Indian city."

"Your point is well-taken, my lord. I stand quite corrected." Her grin deepened, lighting her face, not to mention her eyes. "What sort of dog was Aaron?"

"Aaron was a dog of many sorts."

"Ah, a mutt!" She laughed.

Jason shook his head dolefully. "I am relieved Aaron cannot hear you disparage him so, Miss Edwards. He was very useful."

She sprang for the bait with good humor. "What did he do?"

"He ate my greens, when I was unfortunate enough to be given any, and he growled menacingly upon command. Liam and I made sure to give the signal for a growl whenever our tutor set us to do sums."

"How accommodating of Aaron, to be sure. But did your mother not lose patience with him?"

"Frequently," Jason said so readily that Gillian laughed again. "She often wished him to perdition, but she could not send him there. I was very devoted to him."

"If not to his training."

"He was excellently trained!" Jason protested with mock affront. "I assure you, Aaron never growled but on command, when he sounded unnervingly vicious."

"And so you never learned your sums?" she asked, sounding half taken with the idea.

But Jason shook his head. "Alas, my mother learned of the trick and banished poor Aaron to the stables when the tutor appeared."

"What happened to Aaron?"

"He grew old, and I went away to school."

"In England?"

"Yes. At Eton."

"Was it awful?"

No one had ever asked quite so baldly before. Jason found himself giving her a dry smile, and though he generally made light of his school years, he said before he thought better of it, "Yes, in a word, it was, though I did meet Darnley there and one or two other ramshackle sorts I could like."

"Did you get into scrapes at Eton?"

It was Jason's turn to grin. "I fear I did. It seems Aaron and I had more than a little in common." When she begged him to tell her of one of his scrapes, he recounted the most innocent one he could recall, making a great tale of a night when he and Darnley had made an assault on the locked buttery at Eton. "And so, though we nearly broke our legs, we did come away with two lemon custards," he said, finishing. Gillian had listened to every word, but by the end, she'd had to fight to keep her eyes open, and so, when she opened her mouth to ask something else, Jason shook his head. "No more tonight, Miss Edwards. You need your rest."

"Will you come tomorrow?"

He ought to have made it clear from the beginning that his visit could not be repeated. Now she looked sleepy and soft and a little bit happy, and he couldn't bring himself to disappoint her outright. "Perhaps. We'll see. Until then, sweet dreams, Miss Edwards."

She gave a disarming sigh as her eyes drifted closed again. "Thank you, my lord. Sweet rest to you, too."

Chapter 13

"An' Roger says even Bexton's warmed to his lordship. The starchy old thing didn't care by half for some o' the company that came with his lordship's friends, but I oughtn't to be tellin' you about them, Miss Gilly, seein' as how they wasn't what you might call ladies. That was the rub, o'course, with old Bexton, but his lordship treats the servants right, and hasn't laid a hand on one o' the maids—more's the pity I say! But Bexton approves o' that and o' the way his lordship is lookin' after the land. Bexton hadn't much likin' for Murdock, the agent, ye see, and when his lordship turned the man off, why, Bexton was half won over to him then, but now that he's helped you an' . . ."

"Maude?"

The little maid looked up from the sock she had been darning all the while she chattered about Clare and his servants' opinion of him. "Yes, Miss Gilly?"

"Would you fetch me the glass lying on the dressing table?"

"The glass?" Maude repeated, though she glanced to the long-handled silver mirror Lady Sutton had given Gillian for her fourteenth birthday.

"Yes," Gillian said, declining to explain why she might wish to look at her reflection in a mirror when it was ten o'clock at night and her only regular visitor, her uncle, had left Beechfield hours before.

Maude did not seem eager to perform the duty, and Gillian

understood when she saw herself. "I look like a wounded toad-stool," she moaned, pushing ineffectually at the large billowy dowager's cap her aunt had leant her, causing it to list so that she ended by looking like a deflated wounded toadstool.

Maude briskly brushed Gillian's hand aside and with quick fingers righted the cap. " 'Tis the best of her ladyship's caps, Miss Gilly. The others make ye look like a pitiful old thing, but this one gives ye the look o', I dunno." She stood back to judge the results of her efforts. "Aye, I do! Ye look like a rich servin' maid."

Maude gave a chirping laugh, and Gillian mustered a smile, grateful for the little maid's attempt to cheer her, even if it had not quite succeeded. After looking at herself, she understood at least one reason that Clare had not come to see her again. She was a sight to offend anyone's eyes, particularly a man as accustomed to women of beauty as Clare was.

"Thank you, Maude. You may return the glass to the table, but would you fetch me some milk?"

"I'll fetch you anything, Miss Gilly, so long as 'tisn't laudanum you want."

Gillian grimaced. Lady Sutton had persuaded her to take laudanum two days before to help her sleep better, but the opium-alcohol mixture had had the opposite effect on Gillian, giving her a light fever fraught with strange, unsettling dreams.

"No laudanum ever again, Maude! Oh, and will you leave the door open?" she asked as Maude started to leave.

The freckle-faced girl glanced back to Gillian, a shrewd twinkle in her merry eyes. "Aye, that I will, Miss Gilly, and if a certain gentleman is on his way to his room and looks in on ye, well then, no harm done, I say! Perhaps he's not so pretty as t'other lordship, but to my mind, he's the more manly one."

Maude was gone with a saucy swish of her skirts, leaving Gillian to think, among other things, how little control she had of the girl. But why reprimand her for speaking the truth? Gillian, herself, had been struck by how like a boy Rockingham seemed at times. While Clare . . . was entirely a man. So much a man, he had no interest in a green girl's sickroom.

She bit her lip, looking up at the canopy that had become as familiar to her as the back of her hand, but she could not make the longing to see him recede. Perhaps he knew. Perhaps he did not come for fear of deepening her interest in him, her attraction. Perhaps he reasoned that he'd hurt her the more when they parted.

Gillian closed her eyes against the too-familiar canopy. They were all suppositions: he did not come because her looks offended him; or because a sickroom put him off; or because he did not find her amusing enough; or because she found him too amusing not to mention attractive.

She would never know, because he would not come. Why she had asked Maude to leave her door open she couldn't think. Did she mean to call when he passed her hallway, yelling at him like a fishwife? " 'Ey, you there, yer lordship! Where do ye think yer goin', creepin' by my room all quiet like? Get yerself in 'ere!"

Gillian had not said a word aloud, but the coarse language rang so distinctly in her head that she chuckled, despite her low spirits.

"You are laughing to yourself, Miss Edwards. Is that a bad or a good sign?"

Gillian jerked her head. She felt only a twinge of pain now when she moved inadvertently, but it was enough to take her by surprise. And blast him for that, she thought grumpily, as well as for coming when she was behaving as if she were mad.

Yet perhaps she was mad. He had only to come into her sight, and she not only forgot any resentment, but her heart seemed to trip over itself. If he had been dressed in evening clothes before, she had been too weak and distracted to notice. She was, evidently, stronger now. Seeing him in black coat

and trousers, she understood why the style Brummell had set
had achieved such favor. Perhaps because of his own dark hair
and eyes, perhaps merely because of the way he carried his
well-made frame, the reserved black appeared the essence of
elegance on Clare. He wore the usual white waistcoat as well,
but as to his cravat . . . she saw with a start that he had untied
it at some point in the evening and left the ends to dangle casually onto his chest.

He looked an utter rake, elegantly dressed and yet un-
dressed at the same time.

"Your uncle said you had had a difficult bout with laudanum. Has it made you laugh to yourself?"

Standing with his hands in his pockets, regarding her
steadily, Clare did not appear prepared to entertain her lightheartedly for a half hour. "I think it is boredom that has turned
my brain so that I am laughing at nothing, my lord. But, yes, I
did have an untoward response to the laudanum." Gillian held
his gaze, ignoring a rush of self-consciousness. There was
nothing she could do about her looks, but she could know
something of where she stood with him. "Will you tell me if
you mean to visit me only when Uncle Arthur has given you
some cause for concern about me? I believe the last time you
came, he had reported I was not sleeping well."

Gillian had gotten no better at reading his dark gaze, and
that was all Clare gave her in response, a level, penetrating
look that she feared plumbed her thoughts with ease. Yet she
did not allow herself to flinch away from his perusal of her.
Why should he not know how desperately she longed for company? And if he read that she longed for his company most of
all . . . he would surely leave. She shut her eyes.

After a moment, Gillian heard Clare move then heard him
sit down on the arm of the wing chair in which her aunt sat to
read to her. When he did not speak, she realized further that he
was waiting for her to open her eyes. It was a game he would
win, of course. She'd not outlast him. Even then she had to

fight to keep her lids closed, and as to telling him to be gone . . . did he know how little chance there was of that?

For an awful moment Gillian thought she might cry. Before she could do anything so self-pitying, however, she flung her eyes open and put every ounce of strength she had into meeting his gaze directly. He was not amused by having outwaited her. He was regarding her as consideringly as before, though perhaps a bit more grimly.

"In two weeks or so, you will leave Beechfield, Miss Edwards, after which, we will not see each other again. It has been my intent all along to put the estate up for sale and return to London."

She had her answer. Perhaps he was put off by her bandages and inexperience and did not care for a sickroom, either, but all that was still conjecture. The one certainty was that he did feel wary of her attraction to him.

A strange ache, a mixture of longing and tenderness, and even a touch of humor, made her bite her lip. There he was, looking the essence of a rake, so much so, indeed, she could scarcely keep her eyes off of him, and yet, rogue that he presumably was, what did he do with a young lady prostrate in bed before him? He concerned himself, and seriously, judging by the look of him, with the hurt he might do her heart.

"You informed me early on that you were not a candidate for domestication, my lord. I have not forgotten your advisement."

It being the truth, Gillian met Clare's probing look without hesitation. He gave something between growl and a grunt. "Nor am I a candidate to receive an invitation to dine at your aunt's table."

Particularly not if he looked as thoroughly like an untamed male, as he did then. Gillian almost smiled at the thought of what her Aunt Margaret would say were she to see Clare with his cravat untied and hanging loose, revealing a V of bare chest.

"Do you understand me, Miss Edwards?"

She had been diverted for a moment by the sleekness of the skin bared to her gaze. But at Clare's question, put half impatiently, Gillian met his gaze again. "Yes, my lord. You are saying that you are a confirmed rake and Irish to boot, I think?"

For a moment, she thought she might have angered him, then suddenly he laughed aloud, and she felt her heart melt. "My congratulations, Miss Edwards. Women are not generally so succinct or straightforward."

She wanted to ask him if he really had known *so* many women, but recognized the impossibility of it. "I am pleased that you would acknowledge how my time in this bed has benefited me, my lord. As I have had little to do but read, I daresay I shall soon be a perfect conversationalist."

"And what have you been reading today?" he asked, picking up a book she had let fall to the bed before she had asked Maude to fetch her mirror. Clare's brow lifted as he read the title. "Shelley? Does your aunt know what you've chosen, Miss Edwards?"

"I am reading his poetry, my lord, not his biography."

"And what, pray, do you know of Shelley's life, Miss Edwards?"

At the new, teasing gleam in his eyes, Gillian caught her breath, but she managed, after a moment, to give him a mock-knowing look. "Girls shut away in schools have little to do but talk. I know quite a bit about Mr. Shelley's scandalous life."

"I don't believe you." His fine mouth turning up at one corner, Clare lounged back against the wing of the chair, seeming perfectly comfortable. "Tell me one scandalous *on-dit* you know about Mr. Shelley."

Unfortunately, though the girls at Miss Millington's had rolled their eyes and said Mr. Shelley and his friends were a fast set, no one had been specific about what any in the set had done. Still, Gillian's mouth curved. "He visited a young, unmarried girl in her bedroom after dinner."

Clare's response to her deliberate provocation came quickly enough. "You shock me, Miss Edwards. But I wonder if you know the worst?" Gillian shook her head, watching his eyes. The gleam in them danced now, making her smile. "The girl had a sprained shoulder and several broken ribs."

Gillian clapped her hand to throat as if in shock. "The poor dear! She must have been helpless before him."

"Don't," he warned, his eyebrow lifting abruptly, "look so hopeful, Miss Edwards."

Despite everything, up to and including the way they flirted with the truth, Gillian began to laugh. And Clare looked, surprisingly, pleased.

"I am glad to hear you laugh, Miss Edwards, though I must say"—he paused a moment to study her—"that all in all you look a great deal, as opposed to merely somewhat, better tonight."

Gillian had not learned much in the way of coquetry from Lady Sutton. At Clare's remark, she flicked the lace of the puffy cap and replied tartly, "I do not see how! In my opinion, I look like a freakish species of toadstool with this cap on my head."

Perhaps she had exaggerated but only to make her point. The last thing Gillian had expected to do was to cause Clare to throw back his head and laugh aloud, but she found, when he did, that she liked watching him laugh with abandon; liked, too, very much having been the one to amuse him so.

"You see!" she was emboldened to continue. "You are mad with laughter, because it is true. Aunt Margaret has not allowed me visitors because first, she thought me too weak from my injuries and then she thought me too weak from the laudanum, but I confess I shrink from the thought of visitors, for fear I will become a figure of fun to everyone in the neighborhood."

Clare glanced wryly from Gillian to the table beside the bed, where a stack of notes a hand high stood. "So little does everyone in the neighborhood think of you, Miss Edwards, that all of them have put themselves to the trouble of writing to you. Indeed, your uncle swears you have received notes from people he has never heard of, though he thought he knew everyone about Chicksgrove."

"As he does, of course, but by their land, not necessarily their names," Gillian chuckled fondly. "I've only to say what a man grew last year in his fields, or what crops he lost to rain or drought for Uncle Arthur's brow to lift in recognition."

"You seem to have recovered from the laudanum. Is that true? Your uncle said your response to a single dose was unpleasant."

Gillian fought a shiver. "Yes," she said. "I have recovered."

Clare frowned at her. "You are not very convincing, Miss Edwards. My mention of the laudanum has made you look pinched. Your uncle said you were plagued with unhappy dreams. Have they reoccurred?"

"No." She hesitated a moment then added almost against her will, "I have not slept deeply enough to dream."

"You have not allowed yourself to dream you mean?"

He was still frowning in concern, but Gillian feared she would bore him soon, and made herself smile. "I will sleep eventually I am sure."

"No doubt, but you needn't wait so long." Clare took her hand, startling her, but he ignored the faint rose that blossomed on her cheeks. "Tell me what sort of dreams you had."

The warmth of his clasp seemed to have spread throughout her body, though most particularly to her cheeks. Still, Gillian hesitated. "You cannot wish to hear my unpleasant dreams, my lord, though I thank you for asking."

"If I had not wanted to hear them, I'd not have asked," Clare informed her, but with reasonable patience. "And I have heard it said that if you tell your dreams, you'll not be plagued by them again."

Gillian thought he was only being kind, yet she had feared sleeping. Her breath caught in her throat as she recalled the worst of the dreams, and holding Clare's hand, she said abruptly, "I do not remember them all, but in the worst, I was alone again, as I was after my parents' death; except in these dreams, I could not even reach Uncle Arthur and Aunt Margaret, though I tried and tried."

Perhaps her distress showed on her face, perhaps it was only that Clare could understand, but he tightened his hold on her hand. "I cannot imagine much worse for a child than to be orphaned except being orphaned in a foreign land, distant from all family. Had you ever met your aunt and uncle?"

"No. I had never been to England, and as you might imagine, they had never made the journey out to India. I did not know how they would receive me until I arrived on Uncle Arthur's doorstep with Mrs. Wright. My knees were knocking."

She had a fleeting grimace for the little girl who had stood so fearfully on Moreham's steps, but then, thinking of what had come next, Gillian began to smile. Understanding, Clare smiled back at her. "Your bravery was rewarded was it not? Rather than the wicked guardians you naturally feared, you got Albemarle and Lady Sutton."

Gillian nodded. "Aunt Margaret may seem a stickler, but I . . . I am the child she never had, you see, and it was she who tucked me in every night and bandaged all my scrapes."

"What? She never read you a lecture?"

Clare's dark eyes were twinkling, and Gillian laughed. "Many, but all to my benefit I am sure, and besides, she read Uncle Arthur so many more I could never feel put upon."

It was Clare's turn to laugh. "I have noticed a certain antipathy between the two except in regards to you, Miss Edwards, when they are of one devoted mind. Your uncle has told me all about you as a child. For example, I know that you rode like 'a cavalryman' from the moment your uncle put you on a horse. And it was a horse, not a pony, because he did not have a pony on hand."

Playing on the word, Clare rubbed the center of Gillian's palm with his finger, making her breath catch on a laugh. Perhaps he had not realized what he did, but at her breathless laugh, he gently let go of her.

"I can see you have had some scintillating dinner conversation with Uncle Arthur," Gillian said, but she knew she rushed her words. It was difficult to speak naturally, when she had to exert an enormous effort not to betray how much she regretted the loss of his touch.

"I cannot say at all that I object to Lord Albemarle's conversation. His heart is in the right place, after all."

Gillian's own heart leapt at that, but she could not possibly have played the coquette and asked him archly what he meant. Even had she had the courage, she'd not have had the clarity of mind, for she could not seem to think at all, beyond looking into his dark eyes and marveling at how liquid they seemed in the candlelight.

"Though I do not believe you will, if you should have any more ugly dreams, Miss Edwards, you may send Maude to awaken me."

"You would come?"

Clare nodded. "I would. You needn't be frightened by false dreams. You need your rest too much."

Impulsively, Gillian reached out and clasped her hand over his. "You are being very kind to me, my lord."

Before she had even finished speaking, Clare drew back, sliding his hand out from under hers, and rising from the bed. "You are ill and in my house, Miss Edwards. I feel a responsibility for you. The better you rest, the sooner you will mend."

"And be gone?"

He looked at her a long moment, then said guardedly, "As we have already established, Miss Edwards, you cannot remain here at Beechfield forever."

Chapter 14

The first day Dr. Hogwood allowed Gillian to sit up in bed, Emily Wade came to visit, entering the sickroom in a whirl of muslin skirts, fresh air, and good cheer. And vast, if excited, disappointment, to which subject she went as soon as she had embraced her friend rather fervently and dried her eyes of the tears that pricked them.

"Oh, these tears are so absurd! Of course you are well, Gilly! It is not on your account that I cry, you understand, but on another altogether! I was truly cast down when Lady Sutton remarked to Mama and me that she has not invited Lord Clare to visit you! Lud, and I thought you would know all about him by this time!"

Emily made rather noisy use of her handkerchief, while Gillian smiled, not at all fooled about the real cause of her friend's tears. But Gillian was relieved as well as touched. There would be no questions as to whether she had seen or spoken with Clare, and spared the questions, she would not be obliged to lie to her friend.

"Did you think Aunt Margaret would ask Lord Clare to visit me, when she did not allow even you to come, Em?"

"No, I suppose not," Emily allowed on a sigh. "Yet I cannot help being disappointed! If nothing else, we could compare our impressions. Gilly, you will call me a fanciful fool, but to me there is something quite untamed about him. You should have seen him that dreadful afternoon! He was like a force of nature when he leapt off his horse and charged forward to take care of you. No one thought even for a moment of gainsaying a word he said. Particularly not I! I confess, I was weeping uselessly. Oh, Gilly, I thought . . . well, never mind what I thought." Emily tossed her head, consigning to the rubbish heap the fears she had had that Gillian might die or live permanently maimed. "The point is that I could not seem to do anything but act the watering pot, until he strode up to me with a ruthless look on his face and took my chin in his hand. Yes, Gilly! He did, and none too gently, either. Then he said quite carefully, but still with that awful urgency about him, 'Miss Wade, your friend is in dire need of assistance. You may help to provide it, or you may continue in this useless way. What is your choice?' I tell you, Gilly, I did not shed another tear."

Gillian sympathized. She had been daunted by Clare often enough, though not, it was true, of late.

She had not been certain he would visit her with any regularity even after she had assured him she knew better than to imagine his visits would lead to anything permanent or binding between them. But whatever reservations he might still have harbored, her plight, lying immobile, looking up hour after hour at the same stretch of canopy, had weighed the more heavily on him. Or she supposed it had, for every second night or so he had stopped in to visit with her. He had never stayed for longer than half an hour, but his visits had been the focus of Gillian's days.

They had discussed any number of things, but particularly Gillian's recollections of India. At first, Gillian had thought he was humoring her with his questions, for even her own aunt and uncle had scant interest in the far-off land where their younger brother had gone to make his fortune, but after a little, she realized from the questions Clare asked that he'd read a good deal about India, and indeed, much of the world.

She had told him one night, without naming names, of her attempt to impress her new acquaintances in England by telling them of the man she had seen killed in the bazaar. Before she had even gotten to the reception she had received from everyone but Emily, Clare had laughed and said he did not doubt she'd only succeeded in shocking her audience. "English children," he'd said, only half teasing, "can be the world's greatest prigs, excepting their elders of course."

After that it had not been so difficult somehow to ask whether the rumors that he had engaged in duels were correct. They were. He had engaged in three duels with pistols. When she asked why he had been challenged, Clare had only laughed, though he had said that the duels had occurred in his younger days when he had been, as he put it, "Somewhat wilder and rather less averse to letting a little English blood." At the thought of his opponents lying bleeding to death in the dawn's light, Gillian had gasped, prompting Clare to inform her that none of his opponents had died. "I only wanted to wreak a little vengeance, Miss Edwards, not have myself hung" had been his exact words.

The theme of wreaking some sort of vengeance upon the English had arisen again in a somewhat different context when she had asked him who managed his estate in Ireland. "It is Liam, Miss Edwards, who manages the English winnings I send to Conmarra." Pricked by curiosity, she had dared to ask if it were satisfying for him to lavish English funds on Irish soil, to which he had answered with the bland, indirect observation, "And it is Irish soil husbanded by a thorough Irishman, too."

After that Gillian had avoided the subject of Ireland, and not only because Clare seemed to become more Irish and distant from her. That last answer, particularly, had made her wonder if he ever meant to return to live in Ireland himself. Perhaps he thought it somehow just to leave his Irish soil to the ministrations of his "thoroughly" Irish cousin forever, but were she to question his future intentions, he might well think she had forgotten his caution and begun to hope for a place for herself in that future.

As to that, Gillian simply refused to question her secret hopes. There did not seem any point in delving any deeper, for nothing could have persuaded her to ask Clare to halt his visits. Without them to look forward to, she told herself she would die of boredom and determinedly left the matter there.

That day, mercifully, she had Emily to help distract her.

"I hope you do understand why I did not come before, Gilly," Emily said, after settling herself comfortably in the large chair near the bed. "Lady Sutton advised us that she thought company would not be the best thing for you as you had to lie still, but when she sent a note before luncheon today saying that Dr. Hogwood had given you permission to sit up in bed, Mama and I rushed at once to our carriage."

"I should like to see your mother rush anywhere, Em," Gillian said with a chuckle, "but I do get your point, and I am grateful you came as soon as you could."

"You look a great deal better than I thought you would, Gilly."

Despite Emily's solemn expression, Gillian gave her a wry look. "You would not have thought so had you had the pleasure of seeing me in Aunt Margaret's mobcap. I resembled nothing so much as a freakish toadstool."

"Oh, Gilly!" Emily blinked back sudden tears. "How can you have a sense of humor about such a thing? I would have been in tears. I am in tears!"

"Well, to be quite honest, I consider the cap a good deal more humorous now it is gone and my hair is washed. Lud, Em, I cannot tell you what a pleasure it is to have clean hair!"

"And did Dr. Hogwood say when you will be free of your bandages, Gilly? Or when you will be able to return to Moreham?"

"He says only that he would not wish me to be bounced around in a carriage for at least another week to ten days."

"But that cannot be! You will miss the ball."

Gillian grimaced down at her left arm, resting now in a sling in order to spare her shoulder. "I doubt I would be a very graceful dancer with my shoulder still sore and my arm all but useless, not to mention the rigid pose I must keep to endure the bandages with which Dr. Hogwood has bound my ribs. It occurred to me today as he was retying them, that he could have lived a happy life as a torturer under the Inquisition."

"Gilly! You are the outside of enough, and I know that despite your teasing, you are disappointed about our ball. I am! And Cousin Lionel! I had not stopped to think how he will take the news that you are virtually imprisoned in Lord Clare's home!"

"I should think he would be glad that I lived," Gillian said evenly.

Still diverted by her own thoughts, Emily missed the odd note in Gillian's voice, and waved her hand rather airily. "No doubt he will be, but just recall how prickly he was after Lord Clare came to your assistance during the hunt! I suppose I can scarcely blame him, however. The marquess has such presence, Cousin Lionel must feel rather diminished by comparison. I know that is not the kindest thing to say, about your future husband, but Cousin Lionel is young. In time, I am certain, he will acquire the same air of assurance as Lord Clare. It is odd, is it not," Emily continued, going off on a new tack without stopping for breath, "to think that my cousin has less assurance than Lord Clare, when Lionel is accepted everywhere and Lord Clare is not. But, I have learned something about Lord Clare that goes a bit toward explaining his commanding air. It seems Aunt Sarah knows his paternal grandmother. Yes, Gilly! And Aunt Sarah has come to help Mama with the ball, and she told us that though Lord Clare's mother was, indeed, native Irish, she came from one of the ancient ruling families in Ireland. I suppose having that blood as well as his Devereux blood, which everyone knows is as old as blood comes, it is little wonder that Lord Clare has such an air about him. Lud, Gilly, I do not believe I could sleep for excitement if I were in your place!"

Later that night, Gillian recalled Emily's words about sleeping. She knew she would not sleep easily that night, but not because she was excited. And not on account of anything to do with Clare, either, at least directly.

She had edited her account of Dr. Hogwood's visit when she had discussed it with Emily. The old doctor had also unwound the bandage about her head to examine the wound across her temple. His response had been to cluck with satisfaction, but Gillian had chanced to look over his shoulder at her aunt, and Lady Sutton, in the moment before she had controlled herself, had looked stricken.

Gillian had put that devastated look from her mind at the time. Or put it to the back of her mind. She had been too taken up with the joy of sitting up again to allow herself to dwell on it, and then Emily had come, distracting her completely.

But Emily and her mother had eventually left Beechfield taking with them all their lighthearted gossip and their gay hopes that Gillian would soon be back at Moreham Park. Now it was night, and undistracted, her thoughts had eventually turned to the wound. Gillian had never thought of herself as a vain creature, yet she found that she simply had to see for herself just how disfiguring the scar was.

It would have been a simple matter to ask Maude to fetch her the long-handled mirror again, but she shrank from the thought of having anyone else present while she examined herself. She felt too vain and silly worrying over something so superficial as her looks when she was lucky to have her life. Nor did she much want to face another expression of dismay, or worse, one of pity, before she had prepared herself for it.

Accordingly she dismissed Maude as soon as the little maid came to her, saying that as she could sit up and reach the bellpull by the bed, she did not need anyone to sit in the room with her. Maude did argue, but not long. Likely she thought her mistress expected a visit from Clare, but in fact, Gillian did not think Clare would come to her that night. She was certain he would think she had had company enough and wait until the next night or the next to come to her.

The moment Maude left, Gillian threw back the bedclothes. It seemed as if she had been waiting for days to examine herself. It was not, however, half so easy to walk as she had expected. The first time she put her weight on them, her legs buckled, and she had to grab the bedpost to prevent herself from falling and reinjuring her ribs.

She must have something on which to lean, she realized, and that something presented itself in the form of Delhi. Her uncle had brought him that day, and the dog heaved himself up from the fireplace the moment she stirred. Leaning half her weight on Delhi, she managed to shuffle slowly across the room to the vanity table, but Gillian had not only miscalculated the strength in her legs, she had overestimated her stamina as well. Collapsing upon the stool before the vanity table, she found she hadn't the energy even to lift her arms to unwind the bandage. Afraid she might swoon if she remained sitting without support, she decided to return to the bed and inspect herself there. Tucking the mirror under her arm, she once again leaned her weight on Delhi and crept inch by inch back across the room. Nearly halfway, her legs began to shake so uncontrollably, Gillian realized she would fall. Casting around wildly, she saw the chairs by the fireplace. They were closer than the bed, so she thought she could make them. Biting her lip so hard she drew blood, she did with the very last remnants of her strength and will.

She had not quite regained her breath when she heard a familiar knock at her door. There was nothing to do but respond, for if she did not, he would look in simply to assure himself she was well.

When Clare strode into the room, perhaps because Emily

had likened him to an element of nature that afternoon, Gillian was struck afresh by how the Marquess of Clare seemed to charge the very air around him. And set off every bell of excitement—though perhaps they should have been bells of alarm—there was in her head.

His forceful gaze went directly to the chair where she sat, as if he had noted the change in the direction of her voice from the door. "What in the devil are you doing there?"

She took a final deep breath and willed her voice to steadiness. "I am sitting in this chair, because if I had remained in that bed another moment, I would have screamed."

More aware of the thick bandage around her head than she had ever been, Gillian gazed up into Clare's dark eyes, wondering if he were wondering what horror lay beneath the bandage.

"I wonder," he began, causing her heart to lurch sickeningly inside her, "if I misunderstood your uncle when he said Dr. Hogwood had given you permission to sit up in bed . . . only?"

"Dr. Hogwood is an ancient, conservative gentleman," Gillian replied, half enjoying the game now. "And though he is a kind gentleman and quite competent, I decided to stretch the permission he gave me to include sitting up in a chair. It is not so different from sitting up in bed except that my knees may be bent for a change."

"All true but, of course, for the walk required to reach the chair."

Her uncle had left his snuffbox behind upon the table next to Gillian. Clare picked it up and began to toy with it idly, but Gillian was very well aware he watched her through dark lashes, awaiting her defense.

She did not fail to give it. Firmly she observed, "I walked here with Delhi's assistance."

"Ah!" He clapped his hand shut over the snuffbox. "Of course, there was no danger that you would fall and reinjure yourself, or injure yourself in some new and threatening way, for you were supported by your faithful dog."

After a fortnight in his house, Gillian knew Clare better. She knew to look at the corners of his mouth to see if there was a betraying softening there. His eyes gave him away, too. When something amused him, the faintly etched lines at the corners of his eyes invariably deepened. She knew as well, however, that the lift of one eyebrow and a flat look in his eyes indicated at the best, exasperation.

"And why in the deuce did you not wait for Maude?" he continued, his tone now confirming he was, indeed, provoked with her.

"Maude weighs no more than a twig, my lord. I cannot think she would have been much help, and because I do not need someone hovering over me every minute now that I am able to reach the bellpull, I sent her away."

"Wonderful! Now, rather than attend to her duties, she is free to stir up my household further than she already has."

That diverted Gillian. "What do you mean?"

"I mean that she has transferred her affections from my second underfootman to one of my grooms, causing considerable havoc in the process. But Bexton will manage Maude, I am sure, and so we need only concern ourselves with you, Miss Edwards, the premature walker. I can scarcely credit that you would endanger yourself on a whim."

Before the searching gaze Clare gave her, Gillian shifted uncomfortably and sought a diversion. "You quite overwhelmed Emily Wade the day you came to my aid, my lord. She likened you to a force of nature."

He shrugged, either unimpressed or uninterested. "Did you enjoy your visitors?"

Gillian watched him stroll across to the fire and prop his shoulder casually against the mantelpiece. When he glanced back at her, lifting an eyebrow, she nodded. "Yes, I enjoyed them very much, especially when Emily gave her awed re-counting of your actions."

He turned fully about so that both shoulders rested against the mantelpiece and folded his arms over his chest. He seemed about to say something, but then his glance fell to the seat of her chair.

Gillian looked down at once, but too late. The mirror had been hidden in the folds of her robe until that nervous, un-controlled movement a moment before. Now she could see her face and, of course, the bandage that covered her fore-head. There did not seem anything to do but look back at Clare with her chin lifted and hope he would be reluctant to ask what concern had prompted her to risk an injury for her mirror.

It was a small hope, and had as long a life.

"The bandage around your head looks new. Did Hogwood not look at your head wound?"

"He did."

Gillian did not see why she should have to be effusive on every point that interested Clare. He certainly did not tell her all she wished to know about him.

"He did not show it to you, however?"

He was untamed, sophisticated, assured, and a blasted bull-dog! "No, he did not," she allowed a trifle bitterly.

Clare pushed himself away from the mantelpiece, and with-out a by your leave, proceeded to seat himself upon the arm of her chair. Gillian's eyes went wide as she looked up to fathom his intent. He did not give her the time to discern it. Before she had any notion of what he intended, he reached out and began to untie the knot that held the bandage in place.

"Oh, no!" she cried, catching his fingers in her own and holding them tight. Later Gillian would remark on the warmth of his bare skin, for he wore no gloves, and of course she did not. At that moment, however, she had to fight just to hold his gaze. The wound had become so hideous in her mind, she was certain he would be revolted were he to see it, yet to say so would be tantamount to admitting not only her fear, but how important his opinion was to her.

Clare had no intention, though, of sitting in silence and waiting for Gillian to apply her mind to conjuring some plausible reason for not looking beneath the bandage. "As you spent much of the afternoon listening to Miss Wade rattle on about your accident, you know very well that I have seen your wound at its worst." He did not bother to untangle his fingers from hers, but lifted her hand with his as he traced the wound beneath the bandage. "I assure you it was not then, nor could it possibly have become in some mysterious way by now, a wound that would detract from your rare beauty."

Gillian bit her lip, trying somehow to master the enormous lump that all but closed her throat. His remark about her rare beauty, she dismissed as hyperbole. But his attempt to reassure her made her want to weep. "I feel a self-pitying fool," she said after a moment. Her voice sounded raspy, and she cleared her throat. "I have my life, thanks to you, and today I even regained some freedom of movement, yet what do I fasten upon? Aunt Margaret's expression when Dr. Hogwood removed the bandage. She put her hand to her throat and looked quite horrified."

"And so you thought to see for yourself," Clare said, his tone so reasonable that Gillian nodded. "Good then, let us get on with it."

"But . . . !"

When he only regarded her with one eyebrow lifted, waiting to hear her basis for further objection, Gillian found she could not tell him she did not want him to see. Biting her lip, she shrugged off the rest. And with a brisk nod, Clare slipped his fingers from hers and began to undo the bandage.

She had told herself she would not, but when the bandage lay in a heap in her lap, Gillian looked up swiftly to gauge

Clare's expression. Once she might have thought his look un-readable, but now she could detect a softening in his eyes. It gave her the courage to lift her mirror.

The wound was a thin line curving from one side of her temple back into her hairline. Pink in the middle, it was clearly outlined by a series of neat but exceedingly prominent black stitches. Nothing about it was attractive, but neither was it truly hideous. Feeling quite as if a great weight had been lifted from her shoulders, Gillian chuckled. "Lud, but you were right, my lord! My vanity warped my judgment. The wound is not nearly so bad as I feared. I merely look as if I have been temporarily hemmed."

When Clare made no reply, she looked over the mirror at him and quite forgot her healing wound. There was an alto-gether new expression in his eyes. She'd have said it was a fiercely tender look he gave her, but the words were too con-tradictory to be sensible.

"What is it?" she whispered finally when the silence be-tween them became too intense to bear.

"You," he said after a moment and in a rough voice. "You, Gillian."

Sitting on the arm of her chair, Clare had not so far to lean down to bring his mouth to hers, and yet Gillian, staring, watching him lower his mouth to hers, had more than ample opportunity to protest—as she should have done. She knew what she intended when he flicked his intent gaze to her mouth. Yet she never thought to stop him.

She wanted Clare's kiss, had yearned for it a long, long time, and with her heart thudding heavily against her chest, her lips parted in anticipation.

Then, his hands framing her face, he was kissing her, his mouth and his hands sweeping her up into a whirl of nearly unbearable, sweet, warm, aching pleasure.

Gillian did not even realize she had closed her eyes until

Clare lifted his mouth from hers, and her eyes flew open to meet his.

"There," he said, his voice low and husky. "Now you may be absolutely certain just how unattractive you are." And then, deliberately holding her eyes, he lowered his head again, only this time, he kissed the scar with its neat black stitches.

Chapter 15

His knock was brief and authoritative. Lady Sutton's spine stiffened infinitesimally. Inclining her head, she sent her maid scurrying to open the door to the sitting room she had come to think of as hers, though it was, of course, his.

"You wished to see me, Lady Sutton?"

He was frowning rather sharply, and she saw that he carried his riding crop still, indicating he had responded immediately to the request for his presence she had relayed through Bexton. Perhaps not so oddly, the assurance "Gillian has suffered no harm" came to Lady Sutton's mind, but she did not blurt reassurances to anyone, and most particularly not to Irish rakes, no matter how compelling they were. Or perhaps, particularly if they were so striking.

"Yes, Lord Clare, and it was good of you to come so promptly. Tell me, do you play chess?"

His gaze sharpened upon her, but Lady Sutton remarked that she had not taken the marquess too much off his stride. After the half moment's pause, during which he studied her, he inclined his head. "I do."

"Well, then," she said, taking a breath though she held his dark, rather piercing gaze unwaveringly, "I wish to invite you to play a game with my niece." Lady Sutton supposed Clare had every right to narrow his eyes then. In the three weeks they'd been at Beechfield, it was the first overture she had made to him. Reminding herself he was the only resource upon whom she had to call, she stiffened her spine again and continued, "Dr. Hogwood had not been certain before, but he declared positively this morning that Gillian is not strong enough yet to attend the Wades' ball on Friday. There was never any question of her dancing, of course, but we had hoped that she might go for the company, and I believe you can understand that she might be a trifle blue-deviled."

"Yes, of course," Clare said, giving Lady Sutton to believe he would accept her invitation, but he surprised her. "I understood, however, that Mrs. Wright was to come and visit today. Bexton said something of it."

Lady Sutton's mouth pursed in an expression of irritation. "Mrs. Wright sent a note this morning saying she has unfortunately twisted her ankle, but if you haven't the time, my lord . . ."

Her ploy, slightly to her discomfort, produced a knowing gleam in Clare's eyes, but it was, nonetheless, effective. "Not at all, my lady. I was merely concerned for Mrs. Wright. What time would be best for you and Miss Edwards?"

"In about an hour, perhaps? I am grateful, my lord. I know the young people gathering at the Wades will be able to visit Gillian as soon as the damage that dim-witted yeoman did to the middle bridge is repaired, but in the meantime, she is as I said, a trifle blue-deviled. Will you take some tea with us as well?"

Lady Sutton added that last as much to divert attention from the unfortunate subject she had had no reason to mention as to learn Clare's likes in regards to tea. She'd have sent word to Bexton about the tea anyway, but as she watched Clare leave her room to change from his riding clothes and call for a chess set, she admitted to herself that she had felt an overpowering need to justify Lord Rockingham's absence, though why she should have felt the need in regards to Lord Clare she could not have said. Perhaps she had been addressing herself more than the marquess. True, the principal bridge between Roundley House and Beechfield, the middle bridge, could not be used, as one of Albemarle's yeoman working on the project of clearing the Wythy had heaped his wagon with so many tree limbs from the river that the bridge had collapsed beneath the weight. Albemarle had very nearly been seized by apoplexy and not only because the limbs must now be recollected. As a result of the accident, the half hour required to drive from Beechfield to Roundley House had been doubled. Still, Lady Sutton thought the viscount might have subjected himself to the extra effort at least once. Of course, a young man of Rockingham's high principles might not care to associate with a man as notorious as Clare, but with his high-mindedness, he punished her niece.

And Gillian had felt the lack of his company, Lady Sutton believed, for her niece's spirits had changed over the course of the last several days. When Dr. Hogwood had first allowed her to sit up, she had been quite excited, indeed almost distractedly so, but as time had passed with no visit from Rockingham, she had become increasingly subdued. That morning she had reacted to the news of Mrs. Wright's mishap with a concern for the older woman's ankle, but with only a shrug for the company she would miss.

That faint, emotionless shrug had settled Lady Sutton's mind. Above all things, she did not want her niece to brood, for brooding, she firmly believed, would retard the process of Gillian's mending.

Hearing her aunt's footstep in the hallway, Gillian lifted the book that had been lying forgotten in her lap. If Lady Sutton found her staring out the window again, she'd be put to the trouble of making more excuses for Rockingham's absence.

They knew the viscount had returned to Roundley House. Rockingham had sent a note in which he had said he was sorry to hear of her accident, and hoped she would recover speedily, but he had begged her to understand he could not visit just then. With the middle bridge impassable, he would be obliged to be away from his sister and his cousins and their guests too long. He would pay her a visit either after the ball when there were fewer guests to entertain, he had said, or when she returned to Moreham Park.

His note had provided the one amusing moment in the last several days. She knew very well that it was not the hour's drive that put Rockingham off. The viscount simply did not want to visit her while she was staying in Clare's home. Lud, he might have had to greet the marquess courteously, and horror of horrors, thank him for his efforts on Gillian's behalf. With a slight shrug, Gillian dismissed Lord Rockingham from her thoughts. It was not his absence that upset her at all.

Clare had not visited her again since he had kissed her.

Gillian closed her eyes in that brief time before her aunt opened the door. She could almost taste his mouth afresh, feel his lips, tender at first and then harder and demanding on hers. All over again, her senses quickened and her heart raced. It had felt so right. Even the soft kiss to her scar. She had not worn her bandage since, much to her aunt's dismay.

Yet, he had not come again. She did not know why. He had not come to tell her. She could only speculate, something she had spent hours doing. And her conclusion? That he had kissed her to reassure her about her looks, no more. To an experienced man the dizzying passion that had rocked her, would be nothing, or if not precisely nothing, then commonplace. He'd have experienced something like it innumerable times with as many women. Yet, experienced as he was, he'd have sensed her response, and knowing her as he did, he would know it meant that despite all his cautions, she had fallen in love with him.

Damn him! Dr. Hogwood had removed the bandage from Gillian's shoulder and even some of the binding from her ribs, and so she had the freedom of movement to ball both hands into fists and drum the arms of her chair. Did he not realize how wretched it was for her to be so ignorant of his thoughts?

Would he hold himself away until the day she left Beechfield, when he would, perforce, be obliged to bid her a stiff, formal farewell in front of her aunt? She had thought he had come to care for her more than that.

"Gillian?"

Clare, blast him, had made her forget her aunt. Immediately she forced the vestige of a smile. "Yes, Aunt Margaret?"

"I have a surprise for you, my dear." Gillian could see the bit of color edging her aunt's cheeks, and never having seen such a display of agitation, waited with unexpected curiosity for what her aunt would say next. Even so, she was not prepared by half. "I have invited Lord Clare to engage you in a game of chess."

Gillian stared witlessly. Of all the possibilities she had considered, it had not once occurred to her that her aunt would be the one to return the wolf to the lamb's bedchamber.

"Lord Clare is coming this afternoon?"

"I know how unexpected this announcement must be, my dear, but it is my judgment that you are in need of new company to stimulate your mind. Without it, I fear you will remain in this listless mood, which can only retard your recovery."

Gillian said something about wishing her mood had not unsettled her aunt. And she said something about how thoughtful her aunt was, but, in truth, Gillian never knew precisely what she had said.

Too many thoughts spun through her head for her to fix on one. Clare was coming in a few minutes to her room. How could she manage to act naturally with her aunt present? How could he? What would have been natural even without her aunt? Did he want to come? Had he been dismayed by her response to his kiss?

She was not, and she noted it, worried about her looks. He had told her how she looked to him that night. He had kissed her. Hard. On the mouth, leaving her lips swollen and aching for more.

Gillian had settled nothing in her mind, when Bexton showed Clare into her room. As if they were once again in Mrs. Wright's parlor, and she encountering him for the first time, Gillian found she could not bring herself to meet his eyes. She was too afraid she would read that he thought her a troublesome, too-forward, green girl.

Beyond a sweeping glance to confirm that the man speaking to her aunt was, indeed, Clare, Gillian kept her eyes fixed upon Lady Sutton. And when her aunt brought Clare to the table, where the chess pieces had already been set out upon the board, Gillian flicked her gaze in the general direction of his face, and gave a stiff, forced smile, but no more.

She could not have done more, for she had taken in the strong, chiseled lines of his face and realized how familiar he had become to her. She knew his face as well as she knew her aunt's. And she knew *him* that well or almost. She had spent more time alone with him than with any man, but for her uncle. And she liked what she had come to know of the Marquess of Clare as much as she liked what she could see.

He sat down across from her, and suddenly, on a hope, she lifted her eyes to his. Her disappointment was instantaneous and made her heart sink like a stone. She might have been a stranger to him from the look in his eyes.

"Lady Sutton has suggested that you would enjoy a game of chess, Miss Edwards."

And Lady Sutton was looking on. Gillian clenched her fist in her lap lest her eyes reveal everything from her hopeless interest in him to her pain. She was too young. She was too inexperienced. She could not behave as if nothing had happened. And yet she must.

"Yes," she said, her voice a little low perhaps, but not trembling at least. "I am afraid I have grown a bit bored with my own company, and my aunt was not only astute enough to diagnosis my condition promptly but kind enough to seek a remedy."

"Go on with you, my dear." Lady Sutton smiled at Gillian from the chair she had had strategically placed halfway between the table and the window, so that she could embroider even as she kept watch over the pair playing chess. "A fool could have seen that you might benefit from some new company."

Benefit? From Clare's company? But even as she put the despairing question to herself, Gillian was asking herself, whose company she'd have preferred. Rockingham's? Mrs. Wright's? Even Emily's?

Her smile firming by slow degrees, she turned back to Clare, and this time when their eyes met, she saw a gleam flash at the back of his eyes. On the instant, excitement charged through her. Whatever his reason for not coming to visit might be, it was not that she lacked appeal for him.

"Shall we begin, my lord?" she asked immeasurably more confident suddenly.

"You may do the honors, Miss Edwards, as you are my guest."

It was, of course, the reply any gentleman would make to a lady, but Gillian suspected that the very offhandedness of it indicated as well that Clare did not believe she would be any match for him. Therefore, as she contemplated her first move, the slightest smile teased the corners of her mouth. Clare had never played against Lord Albemarle. Had he, he might not have been so casual about giving her an advantage.

She moved a pawn in a standard opening gambit. Clare's response was not so standard, but it was nothing she had not seen before. Gillian moved another pawn.

Silence settled over the room, but after a time Gillian found she was not content with silence. If she had hesitated to meet Clare's dark eyes earlier, she was not reluctant now. That gleam she'd seen in his eye had emboldened her. And besides, there was a favor he could do for her, a favor she saw as recompense for his having left her in suspense as to whether he would visit again and why he had not.

"I had a note from Emily Wade only yesterday," she began as she moved her bishop into an exposed position. "They are in quite a ferment at Roundley on account of the ball."

From the corner of her eye, Gillian saw her aunt glance at her, but Clare did not look up from the board. Evidently he was weighing why on earth she would so blithely risk a bishop.

Gillian waited until he had advanced his knight in a move that could, eventually, lead to his taking her exposed bishop. "Emily said they have invited over a hundred guests."

Still, Clare did not respond, but Gillian excused him, for she was in the process of using a pawn to capture the knight he had moved into her trap. Surprise flared in his eyes as she removed his ebony piece from the board. He had not expected her to deal him a blow. She smiled limpidly.

"Do you intend to go, my lord?"

"Where is that, Miss Edwards?" he asked, his attention quite on the game.

"To the Wades' ball, my lord."

Clare did not answer at once, but Gillian recalled how often Lord Albemarle had advised her that patience rewarded its practitioner. Seeing that Clare threatened her rook with a pawn, she brought up reinforcements before she glanced up at him again.

He was watching her now. Lounging in his chair, his fingers steepled together, he observed her, not the game. It was not a slavishly admiring look he gave her, though. Clare was regarding her thoughtfully, as if he wondered why she wished to know his plans in regards to the ball.

She lifted her eyebrows to remind him of the question he had not answered. And he nodded slowly, even, she thought, reluctantly. "Yes, I have accepted the Wades' kind invitation." Again her aunt glanced at them, the movement an abrupt one of surprise, but Clare did not seem to notice. Gillian had gestured to the board to remind him it was his move, and he had seen that she was in a position to take his bishop on her next move.

Her flank was unprotected, however. He detected the weakness and moved a rook to threaten her piece.

"I see that Dr. Hogwood has removed the bandage from your shoulder, Miss Edwards, but even so, Lady Sutton told me earlier that he does not wish you to tax yourself by attending the ball."

Gillian nodded her head but did not reply otherwise as she studied the board, trying to determine what move would best suit her strategy then.

"I am sorry."

Gillian looked up. "Sorry? Oh, on account of the ball." She smiled, and gestured to the game. "It is your move now, my lord, but you needn't be sorry. I think I shall enjoy having the entire house and its staff to myself for once. That is if I can persuade Aunt Margaret to go and enjoy herself."

Clare glanced sharply at her. He had not lifted his head entirely, for he had been studying the board, but even with his lids half lowered, she could plainly see real suspicion dawn in his dark eyes. Gillian wanted to giggle, perhaps because what she wanted of him was so much to ask, but her aunt was already speaking.

"Gillian! We have discussed this matter sufficiently, and there is absolutely no reason to burden Lord Clare with it."

"I do not mean to gainsay you, Aunt Margaret." Although she was addressing her aunt, Gillian noted from the corner of her eye that Clare's mouth quirked faintly but undeniably. "I merely wished to assure myself that Lord Clare could, if you wished it, provide you escort to the Wades'."

"Really, Gillian! Lord Clare will think we are in collusion against him. I do not mean to attend the Wades' ball."

"Allow me to assure you, Lady Sutton, that I could not

think so ill of you." For her, Clare had a smile that was easy, even charming, and rather surprisingly effective. Gillian watched in some astonishment as her aunt's brow cleared. "I think your niece has merely seized upon an opportunity presented to her. From the game she is playing, I would say she has a decided tendency toward opportunism."

"I don't doubt you will be astonished to learn it, Lord Clare, but Albemarle taught her," Lady Sutton replied, diverted, perhaps by the smile. "For a man who at times seems to lack even a passing acquaintance with common sense, my brother does have some understanding of strategy."

"As do you, I believe, my lady," Clare said, taking Lady Sutton as much by surprise as he did Gillian. "You did not forewarn me of Miss Edwards's abilities, ma'am."

Lady Sutton did not exactly smile. She only looked well pleased. "I did want her to have a game, you see, and gentlemen can be so reluctant to face, ah, challenge from a female."

Gillian looked up swiftly from under her lashes, but she need not have worried how Clare would respond to that innocent, but decidedly leading remark. He said merely and quite unexceptionally, "I am confident the challenge will be salutary, my lady."

Apparently it was not unhealthful, anyway, for they continued to play, and Clare took first one of Gillian's rooks and a little later a knight not to mention several pawns. She glanced at him through her lashes as he placed her ivory knight with the other pieces he had won. He had not extended an invitation to Lady Sutton to accompany him to the Wades', but Gillian did not see what more she could do, short of asking him outright to persuade him to extend the invitation.

Distracted, she moved a bishop foolishly and lost it.

While Gillian studied the board and chided herself for allowing her concentration to waver, Clare glanced to her aunt. "Indeed, Lady Sutton, I wish you to know that I would be honored to have you keep me company to the Wades' that evening. I am hopeful the middle bridge will be restored by then. Lord Albemarle's men and mine are working on it."

"Ah!" The sharp cry from Gillian had nothing to do with the invitation for which she had hoped, but everything to do with their game. She had not seen until then the threat Clare would pose to her queen in only two moves. But seeing it, she saw as well that he had extended himself on the gamble.

When she moved, saying check, Clare chuckled. "Truly, Miss Edwards, I had not sought to distract you a moment ago, but I did hope you would not see that particular play." Moving his king to safety, he glanced at her. "You really are very good."

Her aunt could not see the warmth dancing in his eyes. Gillian did, though, and tore her gaze away at once, lest she blush. "I do not mean to press you, Aunt Margaret, to accept Lord Clare's very gracious invitation, but if you miss the excitement of the Wades' ball on my account, I shall feel far worse than if you leave me alone. Just put yourself in my position, and you will understand. Were you unable to attend, you would still command me to go. Besides," she coaxed, "you will be able to entertain me for days with all that goes on."

"But I cannot simply abandon you to gad about the countryside, my dear!"

Gillian couldn't but smile at the thought of her starchy aunt gadding anywhere. "Think of your going as leaving me in peace, then. I will have an entire evening free of any strictures about how much I am moving or how sharply."

"Gillian! I only mean you good."

"As I do you," Gillian returned, grinning at her aunt with more affection than any stranger might have suspected Lady Sutton might like. But she did. She was smiling almost helplessly at her niece. "Please?" Gillian pushed. "Lord Clare would not have invited you had he not wished to take you with him."

"I shall think on it," Lady Sutton conceded at last before

turning to Clare to say, "I do thank you, my lord, for your invitation. I hope you will not mind if I give you my answer tomorrow?"

"Not at all, Lady Sutton. Please take all the time you wish to decide what you prefer to do. Though, if you truly do not wish to go, I would advise you not to listen to your niece. She is most persuasive."

Chapter 16

"Do you know how gratified I am that you are here tonight, Jason?" Lady Caroline Castlemont gave Clare a coy look through her justly famous lashes. "I was not at all certain you would deign to attend an entertainment so tame as this."

"You thought I would snub Hugh after the difficulty you and he must have had to persuade Mrs. Wade to extend me an invitation?" Jason smiled down at Lady Castlemont, but his gaze did not linger upon her. He had an excuse in the crowd upon the dance floor. They danced the waltz, as Lady Castlemont had prevailed upon Mrs. Wade to allow the dance for the particular reason that she wished to dance it in Jason's arms, and half to her surprise, and certainly to Mrs. Wade's, some ten to fifteen others couples had come out onto the floor as well, daring the disapproval of the matrons, who still shook their heads, though the dance had been allowed at Almack's.

"Ah, here comes Lord Albemarle." Jason gracefully and efficiently swept Lady Castlemont out of the baron's way. Lord Albemarle had persuaded Mrs. Wade's elder sister, Mrs. Sally Warren, to be his partner, announcing within Jason's hearing that his "Gilly girl" had taught him the dance, and he meant to do her proud.

Lady Castlemont wrinkled her patrician nose as the baron just missed colliding with them. "What a country bumbler he is, all noise and no style."

"I take it you have not engaged Albemarle in a chess

match," Jason remarked, only to curse himself. He was having difficulty enough keeping his mind upon Caroline without carelessly prompting himself to remember Gillian Edwards.

"Ah, yes, I forgot you would have had opportunity to come to know Albemarle rather well. Has he stayed at Beechfield, too?"

Jason was not at all surprised by the cool edge to Lady Castlemont's tone. Her claws were the principal reason he had come to the ball. He intended to make certain that she would not turn them upon Gillian when he broke the news that he could not tryst with her after all.

"No, Albermarle only comes for dinner. Lady Sutton is the one who has stayed."

At the amusedly pained look Jason gave her, Lady Castlemont laughed, mollified. "My condolences, Jason. I know you have found little pleasure in that dragon's company."

No, only in her niece's.

He executed a series of turns but could not escape Gillian. On the last turn, indeed, he ended near Lady Sutton, gossiping happily with five or six ladies of her age. With her erect spine and her sharp, powerful nose, she was the most imposing lady among them.

Yet imposing as she undoubtedly was, Lady Sutton sat there only because her slip of a niece had adroitly maneuvered them both. The beautiful Sassenach with the incandescent smile and the shrewd mind, who had played him to a draw in that chess game; who had not asked anything for herself, either, only asked, in so many words that he escort her aunt to the ball. Lady Sutton might have ridden with Albemarle, of course, but she would never have left Beechfield unless she could account for Jason's every move. Had they come separately, all the gossips would have had a splendid time speculating upon whether Gillian had been left alone with him.

And so he had walked into the Wades' ballroom with Lady Sutton on his arm. Had the girl with the beguiling gray eyes realized what that would do for his credit? He suspected she had, which gave the game to her, for he himself had never considered what effect his escort of Lady Sutton would have. Everyone present had been forced to consider why Lady Sutton had come with him, and remembering what he had done for Gillian—a tale that seemed to have grown out of all proportion to reality, thanks to Miss Wade he very much suspected—he had been welcomed almost as if he were one of their own, and a heroic one of their own at that.

Jason smiled slightly. He scarcely knew how to conduct himself as a minor hero. Perhaps he should puff himself out and bow grandly. To hear he had done that would put a twinkle in her gray eyes. He had put rubies around women's throats, diamonds on their wrists, and emeralds in their ears, but he had come so far that all he wanted was to put a laughing gleam in the eyes of a young woman.

Yet he had robbed the twinkle from her eyes the last time he had seen her, the night following their chess match. He had gone to her room, knowing well he should not, but telling himself he wanted to be certain she really would not mind being all alone on the night of the ball. It had been the merest excuse, of course. He had simply wanted to see her, but when he had gotten to her room and stood in her doorway watching her before she became aware of him, it had been all he could do not to stride into that room and sweep her into his arms and kiss her thoroughly again. And again. He wanted her, more every day it seemed. She had not understood why he refused to go beyond her door. Her eyes had been dark with entreaty, so dark, so uncertain, too, that he had put his finger on the pulse throbbing at the base of her throat. She had not been aware of it, but she'd flushed, knowing it betrayed how she, in her turn, wanted him.

Devil it! He was no saint. Perhaps he did have a greater capacity for fidelity than he had ever realized. Certainly he had no desire for the thoroughly desirable and experienced woman in his arms, then, but that said nothing as to whether he could forever control his desire for Gillian. Where in the bloody hell had Rockingham, her rightful swain, been all that week? Why had he neglected her? Had he been nursing the sulks because she had gotten herself injured and taken to another man's home? He had been sulking all that evening. Great God, did the pup not see what he had in her? Did he not see that he was the one with the entrée, the one to give her the life she should live? And more, did the fair-haired darling not see that he was tempting Jason beyond all belief with those petulant, moody stares? How would it be possible to give her into the keeping of such a callow fool? If he thought on the question too long, if he should come to believe that Rockingham would subject her to schoolboy sulks all her life . . . devil it! He felt a wild recklessness keening through his veins.

"Jason?"

Saved by the call of the siren, Jason tried to smile at the thought. He could not manage more than a faint lopsided near grimace, but at least his thoughts had been diverted. Knights in shining armor had disappeared with the Dark Ages. He must control that recklessness in him that cared naught for consequences. He had business at hand. Delicate business, too, disappointing Caroline. It would take all his skill to manage that gracefully.

"Will I lose all credit in your eyes, Caro, if I admit I am a trifle distracted because I have never danced the waltz with so many people about?"

The excuse worked even more handsomely than Jason had expected. Her eyes took on a sultry look as she smiled more seductively than amusedly. "I am not surprised to learn you like to dance in private, Jason. And I admit, the idea intrigues me. Just think how little we need wear. Only tell me when, and I shall come for an exhibition."

"It is a tantalizing prospect, Caro, but you seem to have forgotten I have guests at Beechfield, or do you not care if Lady Sutton meets you at the door?"

From her expression, Jason realized that Lady Castlemont had either forgotten his guests, or had expected them to disappear at her convenience. Her lower lip began to puff out, never a good sign. "Do you mean I cannot ever come to Beechfield?"

"I do not know how much longer I shall be hosting my unexpected guests, Caro."

"But, Jason, surely there is a hunting box we could use! You are not obliged to account to Lady Sutton for your every hour. Or perhaps it is Gillian Edwards to whom you account for your time," she added, going from hot pique to cold suspicion in the twinkling of an eye.

"It is, indeed," Jason said deliberately, and seeing her start of surprise, he went on in the same mocking tone. "Lady Sutton leaves her quite alone all of the day, and so I am free to do as I will. Invention is required, as she sports bandages everywhere, but the challenge is amazingly exciting."

Lady Castlemont giggled despite herself, Jason thought. He smiled back. "A rather bizarre circumstance is it not?" he asked, meaning the words more than she could have realized. "I am sorry, Caroline. Truly. But my house is not my own until the local doctor—he is that crane-like ancient speaking with Hugh, by the by—gives Miss Edwards permission to ride in a carriage."

"She cannot even do so little?" Lady Castlemont asked, diverted for a moment.

Jason shook his head. "The crane is afraid that being jostled in a carriage might cause one of her ribs to give way and puncture a lung."

"Great God! What a horrid thought." As Caroline sounded rather more disgusted than sympathetic, it did not astonish Jason that she displayed no further interest in the girl who might well be her sister-in-law one day. "But blast it all,

Jason!" she cried, though she was mindful to do so in a low voice. "I have come so far, and I want you! Did not Lely build a hunting box?"

"Someone did, for there is a box. However, it has not been used in years. The roof has rotted and quite an amazing number of small animals have taken up residence inside."

"How dreadful!" Jason nodded, congratulating himself for calculating correctly how little Caroline would care for the thought of rodents. "But that means that I shan't see you!"

The waltz came to a close. Jason bowed rather lazily. "Not privately, no. It's the deuce of a situation, but there it is."

Having led his partner from the dance floor before the waltz was over, Lord Albemarle was able to watch Lady Caroline Castlemont toss her head as if in displeasure, and then abruptly, her mouth a tight line, angle her chin toward the refreshment table as if she were demanding that Lord Clare attend her there.

"She is quite a beauty, your cousin," he remarked to the woman beside him in a rather more discreet tone than usual.

Mrs. Warren nodded readily. "Oh, yes! Caroline is the beauty of our family. I have always thought it a great shame, she hasn't the morals to match, though I suppose it is true that Castlemont must assume some of the responsibility for the way she leads her life. As I understand it, he has given her permission to do what she will, so long as she does it discreetly."

"In our day, Sal, demanding Lord Clare's presence at her hosts' ball would not have been termed discretion."

Mrs. Warren's eyes widened in surprise. "How did you know . . . you rogue, Arthur! You have gotten me to confirm what was only a guess. You have always been too clever for me. But do you know," Mrs. Warren mused, glancing back to the pair in question, "I rather think Caro is having some difficulty with the marquess, not, mind you that I can truly blame her for trying with him. Lud, he is enough to tempt even an old woman."

When it required a moment for Mrs. Warren to summon the will to pull her gaze from Clare's ruggedly appealing face, Albemarle gave a great chuckle. "That he's an attraction for women is obvious. But what else do you know of him, Sal, this dark, Irish lord who is my new neighbor?"

Mrs. Warren shot the baron a speculative look, but one of the qualities Albermarle had always admired in her was that she knew when to voice her questions, and better, when to hold them. "Well, as it happens, I do know a bit," she allowed, at which Albemarle gave another of his robust laughs.

"Why else do you think I appealed to you, Sal? Of course you know 'a bit.'" He laughed again. "You've your ear closer to the ground than anyone I have ever known."

"You haven't known that many, Arthur, buried here in Somerset. That is why you must apply to me on the subject of Clare. And now, for laughing at me, you shall have to appease me with another glass of punch, if you wish to know more."

Lord Albemarle was glad to serve her, and they were soon cozily settled in comfortable chairs near the refreshment table, where, as Mrs. Warren remarked, they could observe Lord Clare as they gossiped about him.

"It is most unsatisfying to gossip about a person when he or she is out of sight. You do not get anything like the same zest in your *on dits*."

"Sal . . ."

Lord Albemarle said nothing more, only boomed out her pet name, and Mrs. Warren patted his hand. "Very well, Arthur. Now, let me see. I knew Clare's father. He made the rounds in London before he inherited the lands and title in Ireland. He did not have the same rather lazy, wicked, and altogether delicious presence his son possesses, but he was a handsome boy, nonetheless. When his uncle died, and he went to Ireland to take control of the property he had inherited, rumor has it that he was not at all prepared for what he encountered. It seems his Irish tenants were not well pleased to have a bona fide

Englishman replace their old, more Irish-than-the-Irish lord.
They gave him quite a bit of difficulty, but according to the
stories, he did find the leisure to take notice of the sister of a
neighbor. She was native Irish, but of an old, ruling family,
and beautiful to boot. When her brother proposed a marriage
and promised to bring Clare's tenants around as his part of the
dowry so to speak, the newly made marquess leapt to accept
the offer. What the marchioness may have felt for the marquess, I do not know. She rarely left the estate, but it is common knowledge that after he got his heir, the eighth marquess
kept one high flyer after another."

To himself Lord Albemarle remarked what a pleasure it was
to converse with a female who did not feel called upon to
speak in indecipherable euphemisms, but it was a fleeting
thought. He had still more he wanted to know, and was keenly
aware that at any moment they might be interrupted.

"And the boy? What of him?"

Lord Albemarle nodded his head toward Clare, and Mrs.
Warren glanced to the man in question. Lady Castlemont had
been led out onto the dance floor by another gentleman, but
Lord Clare, she noted with interest, was not following the
countess's movements. Leaning indolently against one of the
columns that bordered that side of the ballroom, he was listening, his head cocked rather attentively, to, of all people, ancient, quavering Dr. Hogwood.

"Clare was sent as a boy to school here in England, and
spent many of his holidays with his Devereux grandmother.
Did I mention that I know her?"

"No, but I never doubted you knew someone authoritative,
Sal!"

Mrs. Warren gave him an owlish look. "You always did
know precisely what it suited you to know, Arthur. Well, Mrs.
Devereux is so high in the instep she totters, but nonetheless
she has a great fondness for her scapegrace, half-Irish grand-
son, which only proves I suppose that women have been sus-

ceptible to him all his life. Be that as it may, when he turned eighteen or thereabouts, his father was killed in a carriage accident, and he became marquess only to find that the estate he had inherited was so deeply in debt, it could provide him next to no living. Indeed, according to his grandmother he'd have lost the property, had he not proved to have such a way with cards—according to Mrs. Devereux, it is his, as she put it, 'keen English intelligence' not his Irish luck that accounts for his good fortune at the tables. For my part, I rather imagine he benefited from some happy combination of the two, for benefit he has. The rumors that he's penniless are quite groundless. Mrs. Devereux lives very well, and all on his largesse. He's simply indifferent to the opinion of others and so has never displayed his wealth, and too, he has sent a good deal of it back to Ireland, again by his grandmother's account. He's a cousin, I think, who oversees his estate there, while he remains in England seeing to his grandmother and taking English money for his own purposes."

"Well now, 'tis an interesting tale you have told, Sal," Albemarle remarked when Mrs. Warren was done. "I take it the rest has only to do with deep gaming and less than virtuous women?"

"By the scores, so it is said."

Lord Albemarle shot her an amused look. "You sound positively wistful m'dear! Positively wistful!"

"Well, just look at him!" the elderly woman protested, demonstrating a clear memory of having been young once.

Albemarle was about to give some response, when they were distracted by the sound of a loud, petulant voice.

"I say, man! If you cannot serve up punch any more carefully than that, then you deserve to be hung!"

"I'm that sorry, m'lord! I . . ."

"Get away, I say! Jove, one cannot get proper service in the country! Hugh might as well have a dog behind the punch bowl."

Mrs. Warren winced and leaning closer to Albemarle whispered, "He has been in this foul mood since he learned of Gillian's accident and I must add, where she is recuperating. Both Hetty and Hugh have tried to explain that Lord Clare had little choice except to take her to Beechfield, but as you can see, my noble, if young, cousin has not allowed himself to be mollified. As you may imagine, none of us have much enjoyed his company this week. Even Caroline has admonished him for his pettishness, but it is Hetty's servants who have paid the highest price."

Rockingham was dabbing angrily at the glove the servant had unfortunately splashed with punch, while Hugh Wade attempted to placate him.

Lord Albemarle frowned, watching the scene. "I cannot say I much like this, Sal. If he is so concerned about Gillian's being at Clare's, why the deuce has he not gone to visit her?"

Mrs. Warren sighed. "I vow I cannot say precisely, Arthur. He has inquired about her condition, but to every suggestion that, you may be certain, Emily and Hetty made about visiting Gillian, he returned a curtly negative response."

"Enough, Hugh!" Rockingham's snappish voice carried to them again. "I am not a child! And I wish you will not treat me as one. I have already told you, I do not care to dance this evening."

Rockingham rudely shook off the hand Hugh Wade had on his arm and stalked away from the refreshment table. At once Albemarle heaved himself to his feet. "Rockingham!" He'd a loud and unquestionably distinctive voice, but still the viscount took another step or two before he bowed to the inexorable demands of courtesy and turned. Noting the impatient set to her cousin's expression, Mrs. Warren immediately rose herself, thinking it would not hurt to have a lady present when Albemarle attempted to reason with Rockingham.

She had a little way to go to reach them, for their momentum had carried the two men almost to the other side of the ballroom, and as she approached them, Mrs. Warren sensibly glanced about to see if anyone was near enough to overhear whatever might be said. Her gaze did not travel far, however. It halted on Clare. She had forgotten the marquess momentarily, but he was quite close enough to hear what he wished. Though they'd their backs to him, Rockingham and Albemarle stood only a little away from him. Clare's hard, handsome face was shuttered, and she could not read his thoughts, but Mrs. Warren did not believe there was any question that he was listening. His dark eyes were fixed upon the two men.

". . . Regret you could not come to visit Gillian this week," Albemarle was saying when Mrs. Warren turned her attention to him. "You do know she was confined to her bed for a fortnight, and even now is too weak to do more than walk from her bed to a chair?"

"I have kept myself informed as to Miss Edwards's injuries and progress, my lord," Rockingham replied in a tight tone. "Indeed, she wrote me a note herself, telling me she was still very weak. On the basis of it, I judged she needed to regain a bit more strength before she received visitors, and also I had responsibilities here, Lord Albemarle, that prevented me from visiting Miss Edwards. I have not seen my sister in nearly a year, and with the middle bridge impassable and the additional time it would take to reach . . . Miss Edwards, I thought it best all around to wait until she is at Moreham Park again. Lady Sutton believes Dr. Hogwood will give permission for her to return home in the next day or two."

"Did Margaret say, so? By Jove, that is more than I knew!" Genuinely surprised, and perhaps a little displeased not to have been told the good news, Lord Albemarle looked as if the wind had been taken from his sails. "Well, that's right and tight then. You'll visit her in a day or two at Moreham. Lud, I am the last to know, it seems! But you'll be careful with her, young man, when you see her!"

Mrs. Warren looked a trifle anxious. Albemarle was blustering now, and Rockingham, in his turn, was regarding the baron quite coolly. "How do you mean that, my lord?"

"Well, she's suffered these last weeks, and her looks show it. She's pale and there's still a suggestion of shadow under her eyes. Not to mention that blasted wound on her head. I do not know why Hogwood has not taken the damned stitches out. Beg pardon, Sal."

Mrs. Warren hid a smile at the purely mechanical sound of that request for pardon. "Of course, Arthur. I understand you are strained on Gillian's account. But I did not realize she had a cut on her head."

It did not seem as if Rockingham had known as much, either, for he was frowning rather sharply as he, too, looked to the baron. Albemarle wagged his large head. "When she hit her head on a rock, she cut herself badly. She'll wear a scar all her life."

"What?"

"Well," Albemarle, seeming to take in the consternation in the viscount's expression, pulled up short. "I do not mean to say she will be marred. It would take a good deal to do that in Gilly's case, you know as well as I, Rockingham, but a bit of scar over her temple will show I'm afraid. You see, that is what I was getting at! She says naught about her looks, but she's a female, my boy, and females worry over their looks. Do I do your sex an injustice, Sal?"

Mrs. Warren dutifully shook her head. "No, Arthur. Any woman would worry over her looks, though I must say one of Gillian's most appealing qualities has always been her seeming unconcern with her uncommon beauty."

"Well, be that as it may, and it is true, I agree," Albemarle declared, pleased, "I wish Rockingham, here, to be reassuring to her."

Mrs. Warren hoped her young cousin might be half amused by Albemarle's blustery, heavy-handed attempts to instruct him in the art of courting, but the viscount was not so amenable. "I think I know how to behave with a lady, my lord," he said in a frigid voice. "Though I must say that along with everything else to be endured, it is the outside of enough that she will be scarred as well."

Rockingham departed then. Abruptly, after the briefest of bows and without another word, he took the opportunity to join the crowd just leaving the dance floor. Albemarle looked to Mrs. Warren, his brow lifted, and as the viscount was her cousin, she simply did not allow herself to do anything but put the most generous construction possible upon his remarks.

"Well, it is the outside of enough, Arthur. Poor Gilly should not have to wear a scar after the trials she's been through."

"You think that's what the pup meant, Sal?"

She nodded, though a bit slowly. "Yes, I think so. What else could he have meant?"

"Hmm. Yes, of course. Well, at least he's been prepared for her wound. It is slight, really!"

Mrs. Warren patted the baron's arm, and assured him he had done very well, but even as she did, she glanced beyond him to see how Clare had taken the viscount's somewhat ambiguous remarks. He had heard them, it seemed, for he was even then following Rockingham's progress down the length of the ballroom. As to any further reaction on the marquess's part, however, Mrs. Warren was frustrated. Before she could note much more than that his jaw had a hard set to it, Hugh Wade distracted him, likely in the hope of getting up a card game.

Chapter 17

The question had become: how could he possibly abandon her to such a self-absorbed, petulant popinjay?

Jason stared into the fire in his study, a glass of brandy in his hand, considering his answer to the question that had dominated his thoughts since he had listened to the exchange between Rockingham and Albemarle the night before. He made no apologies for eavesdropping. Rockingham had not whispered, particularly not when he had made that intolerable remark abut Gillian's scar.

Great God, the shallow fool wanted her for an ornament and no more. One blemish, and he was disgusted. He would not care that she'd a mind, and a good one. Her duty was merely to bring the viscount envy for having won the Beauty of the Season.

Jason tossed off the remainder of the brandy. It burned down his throat, but not so hotly as the tension inside him. He had also heard Rockingham exercise his pique on the Wades' unfortunate servant. If Jason had not been certain before, he now knew the viscount's type. Rockingham had been bred to be a petty tyrant. The world must revolve around him or those near him would pay—those near him, who were inferior and helpless, his servants, for example . . . or his wife.

And if his wife were to have a difference of opinion with him? Jason could see all too well the expression Rockingham would wear were the wife he had taken as an ornament and bearer of his heir to gainsay him on something. The viscount had worn that tight, vexed, pettish look all the night before.

He would quash her lively curiosity; declare her not always reverent humor uncalled for; and her passion? Jason stared unseeing at the clear bottom of his glass. Beneath that composed exterior, passion ran deep in her. She had responded without reserve to that kiss of his. With Rockingham . . . he rose abruptly from his chair to stalk to the fire. When he got there, he stared down blindly until a log fell. Then he lashed out, kicking it, sending sparks flying up the chimney. The viscount wanted a perfect ornament, and he'd not approve anything so uncontrolled as passion in that elegant, impeccable ornament. He'd go to paid women for his passion, and all Gillian's warmth and eagerness would wither by slow degrees from neglect. Or else she'd become a Caroline in time.

Jason flung the brandy glass into the fire, whirling about as it shattered explosively.

He'd not have it. He could not, and he would do what he must.

Though Albemarle might, in time, be persuaded to accept his suit, Lady Sutton would not. True, she had come herself to tell him that Dr. Hogwood had given Gillian permission to return to Moreham the next day on the condition that the carriage be driven slowly. She had taken the opportunity to thank him graciously enough for the trouble he had gone to on her niece's behalf, for the hospitality he had shown them both, and for providing her escort to the Wades' ball. Yet, despite the very slight unbending, there had been in the way Lady Sutton regarded him an underlying element of wariness, as if she considered him a tiger or a wolf, perhaps, that had until then behaved properly, but who could say about the future?

Jason smiled grimly as he took the steps two at a time. If Lady Sutton considered him so far outside the confines of her society that she would prefer to give Gillian in marriage to a fool who would make her niece miserable, then she left Jason no choice but to act as she seemed to expect, by his own rules. And by God, he would make Gillian his.

When he stepped into the middle corridor leading to Gillian's room, Jason frowned. The door that had been open for him other nights was closed. Could something be wrong? Had she fallen and no one thought to tell him? Had he misunderstood Lady Sutton? Had she taken Gillian that day?

His fears only increased when he knocked on her door and got no answer. Thrusting it open, he strode within, his eyes sweeping from the empty bed to the fireplace. Seeing a fire burning brightly there, he felt a relief so intense, it seemed to pierce him. She was there, seated near the fire, a shawl wrapped around her robe, her head propped against the side of the chair, fast asleep.

He walked quietly across the room, content to study her for a moment. She sat normally, confirming that Dr. Hogwood had removed the bandages about her ribs, as Lady Sutton had said. Her scar gleamed white in the light, but for the black stitches that had not been removed. Yet the wound was nothing to the smooth, satin of her skin or the generous shape of her mouth, or the curling golden-brown lashes that shadowed her sleep-flushed cheeks. Her hair tumbled loose over her shoulder, gleaming like old gold in the firelight, and Jason caught the fresh scent of violets as he bent down to kiss her brow.

"Oh!" She woke at the touch of his lips.

He expected her to smile, but she did not. Indeed, her mouth, just at the edges, turned down, and when their eyes met, he saw hers were great pools in her face.

She said nothing in that moment after waking, only gazed at him with those too-large eyes, looking so grave, he took her hands in his, a desire to protect her from whatever was amiss crowding out all else. "Gilly girl? What is it?"

She gave a cry of distress. And without warning propelled herself out of the chair and forward. He caught her, pulling her to him with a care for her newly unbandaged ribs. "What is it?" he asked as she buried her face against his chest. He did not press her when she did not immediately answer. She felt too good in his arms, her breasts soft against him and her hair like satin beneath his hand.

He kissed the top of her head again, "Gilly girl? You did not take more laudanum?"

It was a measure of how far things had gone for Jason that her pet name came naturally to him. Still, he knew he had used it, and when she lifted her head from his chest, he half thought she meant to protest the familiarity.

But her eyes were too wide and too dark a gray for such a small offense. "I am to leave tomorrow. And I feared . . . I feared you did not mean to come tonight. Oh, Jason!"

She said his name on a half sob, and going on tiptoe, caught his face between her hands. He had thought he might have to persuade her to take the next, irrevocable step. But she wanted him, it seemed, as much as he wanted her.

And he did want her. When he had decided that she would fare far better in life if she wed him, despite his low standing with the sticklers in society, he had reasoned in all sincerity. But he served himself when he served her. Great God, her mouth had been all he could think of at times: willing, trembling, soft beneath his, as it was now.

She loved him. He knew it as certainly as he knew that Rockingham would never take damaged goods. Let the viscount take another then, a pattern card in his style, for after this night Gillian would not be able to marry where her aunt wished, but only where her heart lay.

Gillian groaned as Jason slipped the frog-like fasteners of her robe apart. He had built such a fire in her, stroking her, petting her, tasting her, she felt as if she might go up in flames if he did not touch her now there and there and all the places she had never thought of. He whispered all the while, calling her his love, telling her how beautiful she was, what he wanted, what he wanted her to do, making her ache, making her feel as if her entire body were crying for him. He was careful with her, mindful of her ribs and her shoulder, but she scarcely thought of them. She hurt not on account of him but for him.

She would have him, too. And though she knew it was wrong. All the night before, while everyone else danced gaily at the Wades' ball, she had sat before the fire with a cup of tea, and considered the decisions she had to make without interruption or distraction.

They were hard decisions, for she had to decide between people she loved. On the one side was her aunt, with Rockingham, and on the other, Clare. Or Jason, as she had allowed herself to say.

The pull to her aunt was great. Gillian loved her. To disappoint Lady Sutton, and do so as deeply as she would if she chose Jason over Rockingham, made her want to cry out in distress.

But could she wed Rockingham? Could she go to his bed? Could she even accept his hands on her?

No. And no! She could not do it, not even for her aunt. Truth to tell, she did not think she could have taken the final step with Rockingham even had she never met Jason. But she had encountered the Marquess of Clare, and knew his touch. Even the thought of the viscount's hands upon her made her shiver with distaste. Not that she could compare the two men in that regard really. Rockingham had never sought to kiss her or even to lay a caressing hand on her. He had touched her only to stake his claim with an immaculately gloved hand, whether on a ballroom floor or the Throckmorton's terrace.

But what of Jason? Could he overcome his aversion to legshackling? Would he rather she wed Rockingham? Would he mind seeing her in town on Rockingham's arm, knowing they had just arisen from the same bed? At the questions, Gillian buried her head in her hands. Not out of embarrassment, at all, but to try and still the joy and excitement rising in her. She had recalled how he had been that day of the hunt in the woods. "Are you betrothed to him yet?" Jason had asked, and not at all indifferently. He would not, she knew with rising certainty, care to think of her in the viscount's bed.

But he'd not ask for her, either. She had come to that conclusion a little later when her emotions had calmed. There were two reasons she thought he would hold back. First, because he feared he would make the same sort of errant husband his father evidently had. And second, he thought she would suffer for his reputation and background.

Neither objection weighed with Gillian. With the exception of her aunt, she did not care what others thought of him—or her for marrying him—and as to her aunt, she thought that surely she could bring Lady Sutton to accept him by and by.

That left only what sort of husband he would make, and there, Gillian decided she had more faith in Jason than he did in himself, for he did not seem to count his restraint with her in his own favor. She did, though, for she knew very well how easily he could have seduced her even as early, God help her, as their encounter on the island, not to mention the latest one when he had explained why he would not move beyond her bedroom door by laying his finger on her throat on the pulse throbbingly heavily for him. But he had not seduced her and then abandoned her to her own devices once he grew bored. The rake had resisted the temptation she knew she was to him. And why? Because, of course, he was a man of honor. And because he cared for her.

There was no other man for her. Gillian knew it in her soul, but how could she overcome Jason's deep reservations in regards to wedding her? Seated before her fire that quiet night, she had debated arguing those reservations with him. That reasonable course would take time, however, and Gillian had known even then that time was one thing she lacked. Dr. Hogwood had indicated he would allow her to return to Moreham soon, perhaps even as soon as two or three days after the ball.

Without time, it seemed to Gillian there was only one solution. When Jason came to visit her next, as surely he would before she left, then she would tempt him beyond bearing, and afterward, because he was an honorable man, he would make an honest woman of her despite his own reservations. And in the teeth of her aunt's.

When night fell that day after the ball, and Gillian knew for certain that she had, indeed, run out of time, for Dr. Hogwood had unwrapped her ribs and decided they were mended enough for her to be driven slowly to Moreham, she dismissed Maude early and sat down near the fire to wait.

Yet when hour followed hour and there was no sign of Jason, she began to fear he would not come. Desperately she weighed whether she'd regained sufficient strength to search for him, but knowing little of the house or where to look, she had had little choice but to wait. In the end, she might have tried to find him, but waiting, warmed by the fire, she fell into a light doze. Then she awakened suddenly to find him there, watching her sleep, his eyes seeming soft as velvet. Still affected by the fear that she might miss him somehow and lose him forever, she had not even been able to smile a welcome at him. She'd only been able to go into his arms, where she very much meant to stay.

Chapter 18

Even with the windows closed, Gillian could smell the smoke. In the early morning hours the vicarage in Chicksgrove had caught fire, and though dozens of men from across the parish had rushed to help, two homes near it had caught as well, while several others were threatened. Her uncle had gone to the village, taking with him as many laborers and servants as he could spare. Jason had done the same.

Jason. Gillian found herself at the window, though she could not possibly have seen him. She longed to see him, however, and to an unnerving degree. She was his now. She had lain with him.

Her hands tightened on the comb she held in her hands. It was difficult for her still to lift her arms to comb her own hair, but she had been able to . . . lie with Jason. Dear God, he had made it so easy! And so shockingly wonderful. A heat rushed through her at the memory of what he had done to her; what she had done . . . willingly.

It would be all right. She had taken him into her bed for a good reason. He would marry her now, something he wanted. She believed that, if she also believed he'd have held back from marrying her for reasons she considered unfounded.

Thinking of one of those reasons, that she might no longer be welcomed in as many *tonnish* ballrooms, Gillian abruptly turned away from the hazy view. She did not give a fig about the fashionable affairs of the *ton*. Not a single fig. She would take Jason over Almack's any day. Only now, this morning, without him there, she wished she had spoken to him a little more the night before. But what, she asked herself for the thousandth time, could she have said? "I want to lie with you to assure that you will marry me, though you have never spoken a word of love to me or mentioned marriage other than with derision."

He had spoken words of love there in her bed. Gillian's expression softened, and her cheeks heated all over again. He had called her his love. Over and over. His beautiful love, too. He had not said he loved her, but she would not quibble. It was the same thing. He had not, however, left her before he had murmured anything about asking for her hand. Really there was little reason to wonder at his omission! They had . . . they had made love twice. She blushed the harder, though there was no one in her room to read her scandalous thoughts. Her aunt was below consulting Bexton as to whether there was anyone left at Beechfield to drive the marquess's carriage and return them to Moreham. Gillian had not argued when her aunt had left the room, but she had no intention of leaving Beechfield before she saw Jason. To her aunt she would say that they owed him the courtesy of staying to give him thanks for all he had done. After they gave that thanks, though, she meant to find some excuse to be alone with him. She needed reassurance.

He had kissed her good-bye, when he had left her bed sometime before dawn. She had tried to rouse herself, but she had scarcely been able to do more than return his kiss, and even that she had done with her eyes falling closed again. He had laughed with lazy tenderness at her sleepiness, and had made her smile with her eyes quite closed. Little surprise, then, that he had not leaned down to ask her to marry him. She'd likely only have snuggled deeper into her covers.

Gillian bit her lip. There was no point in regretting what had, in all truth, been a delicious languor. With Jason's kiss still warm on her brow and her lips, she had slipped back into a sleep as warm and beckoning as a pillow of the softest goose down. And he would return. She had only to be patient, not to mention proud that he would stir himself to help mere cottagers in the village. Idly she wondered if Rockingham had gone to Chicksgrove. She thought Mr. Wade would have done so, though he had a houseful of guests still.

Not so idly, Gillian's eyes strayed to the bed. It was properly made up and did not look even to have been slept in, much less to have been the scene of her . . . she flinched when the word "debauchment" came to her mind. It had not been that! It had been her wedding night, or as good as. Though . . . had it been her wedding night, she would not have awakened with a start of panic, recalling everything the moment she opened her eyes and fearing that one of the maids bringing her morning cocoa might see the telltale signs of her loss of innocence. Scrambling out of bed as quickly as she could given her sore ribs, she had looked down at the sheets, uncertain what she meant to do with them, only to find that Jason had had more thought for the morning than she. She had never noticed during the night that he had left her robe beneath her, and so it was the robe, more easily hidden than a sheet, that had been stained. She ought to have felt grateful that he would think to protect her from servants' gossip, but somehow she had felt more deflated than glad. Had he announced that morning to the world that he was marrying her, servants' gossip would not have mattered much.

To her. She must recall that Clare had lived with gossip and raised eyebrows most of his life. That he would want to protect her from the sting of censure meant he cared for her—not that he was a practiced rake, accustomed to seducing innocents.

She needed distraction, Gillian thought with some rue. Something to occupy her so that she did not count every moment that passed or entertain unwarranted fears or mark every twinge of soreness between her thighs.

At the sound of Emily's voice in the corridor, Gillian looked heavenward. Surely God was watching over her, despite everything, for had she tried, she could not have conjured up any more desirable distraction than her friend.

"Gillian, look at you!" Emily beamed as she swept through the door. Glancing behind her friend, Gillian saw it was a maid who had shown her upstairs, not Lady Sutton, and she was glad, for their conversation was ever more interesting when they were alone. "You are out of bed! And I vow," Emily went on grasping Gillian by the arms, and examining her with a wide smile, "that you would start a rage for stitched wounds should you go out in public. La! How is that I would look a bedraggled object of pity if I showed my wound before the stitches were removed, and yet you . . . you look beautiful as ever!"

"It is your generous eyes that make the difference, Em. And Maude's determination. She spent hours, or so it seemed at the time, arranging my hair to hide as much as possible of the scar, but in truth, I am sick to death of my injuries. Tell me instead of the ball, and you smell of smoke. Have you been to Chicksgrove?"

"I have, Gilly! I could not resist when Papa went with some of the men. I have never seen a great fire. And lud, I vow I hope I never do again!" Emily's smile turned upside down. "The vicarage is no more than a shell. The Beswicks lost everything they own, as did the Mumfords in the house next to them, and the Morrises did not fare a great deal better. But at least, that is the worst of it. Some other houses were damaged, a few rather badly, but no one else is without a home."

Emily rattled on a little while, talking of the fire and the plight of people both girls had known all their lives. "But!" Emily exclaimed after a little while, her eyes lighting, "I have not told you the most interesting part by a yard! Gilly, you will never guess who accompanied me into Chicksgrove and is there even now."

Perhaps it was only because she was so unsettled in her mind that Gillian should have felt a prickle of unease. Certainly she had never before felt prescient. "Did Rockingham go with you?" she asked, though somehow she knew it was not the viscount who had put that dancing light in her friend's eyes.

And, indeed, Gillian's mention of Rockingham caused Emily's eagerness to falter somewhat. "Gilly, I have a message from Cousin Lionel. As I left, he asked if I meant to come and see you today, for I had told him yesterday I planned to do so, and he has sent a message. He understands you are to return to Moreham Park today, and he wishes to call on you tomorrow. Today, I am afraid, Aunt Sarah and one or two of the other ladies still with us have engaged Cousin Lionel to escort them to Durston. They wished to escape the smoke, you see. It is much thicker at Roundley House than here, as the breeze is blowing in that direction. He hoped you would not feel neglected. He . . . well, after all, he has been here nearly a week and has not called upon you!"

A visit from the viscount was almost the last thing Gillian wanted at that moment, but still she managed to say evenly enough, "I cannot say I would feel the same were I in his place, but I think I understand that Rockingham would not wish to call upon me so long as I am residing in Lord Clare's home."

Emily studied her friend a moment, for though she was a chatterbox, she was no fool. But seeing the faint shadows beneath Gillian's eyes and the evidence of tension about her friend's mouth, she judged Gillian was not strong enough yet to discuss what Emily considered a nearly unforgivable failure on her cousin's part.

Her thoughts turning to light entertainment, a sparkle lit her eyes again. "But speaking of Lord Clare!" she cried, leaning forward eagerly. "You have not guessed who accompanied me into Chicksgrove, but I shall not put you to the trouble, Gilly, for in truth, I doubt you could guess. Cousin Caroline went with me! And, given my hints, I vow you can guess why!"

For Gillian, it was as if her throat closed. Dread clutched it so that all she could do was shake her head.

"To see Lord Clare!" Emily pronounced as if she had brought the most splendid news. "Gilly, they are lovers! La, would not Mama sink into the ground to hear me say such a thing, and Lady Sutton . . ." The young girl irrepressibly rolled her eyes. "She would fall into a faint, I am sure! But as neither Mama nor your aunt are here, I shall tell you all I know. I did think it odd that Mama should have sent Lord Clare an invitation to our ball. Did that not surprise you? Of course it did," Emily rattled on, answering her own question. "Mama has all but proclaimed him notorious, yet she invited him to her ball. You may be sure I asked her why, but she would say nothing beyond some nonsense about his being our neighbor. I suspected that was not the half of it, and learned at the ball how right I was! Gilly, I must say first that he was the most compelling gentleman present that evening. You will not have seen him in evening dress, and so I shall tell you that he looked at once so elegant and so . . . masculine that I found it almost impossible to take my eyes from him. La! I longed to be able to dance with him, as, of course, did all the other young ladies, but he did not even glance our way. Indeed, he only danced with one woman, and he danced with her twice!" Emily pounced upon the word, for to dance twice with the same partner was to indicate some particular interest.

The dread that had closed Gillian's throat swelled, filling not only her throat now, but her chest as well, squeezing her lungs so that she could not breathe. As Emily gossiped on about how beautiful Lady Castlemont had looked and what a handsome pair Jason and the countess had made, Gillian felt sick.

"I'd not have thought a man of his height could move with

such grace, even though he's such an air of assurance! And, of course, Cousin Caroline was the most beautiful woman present. Had you been able to attend, I imagine the honor would have gone to you, though, even then . . . she is so very womanly, if you understand what I mean."

Gillian did understand, and not only because she had encountered Lady Castlemont at any number of affairs during the Season. Giving the tutoring Jason had given her the night before, she could understand at least a little better than Emily why a bosom as white and as full as Lady Castlemont's would attract a man's attention. And hold it.

For Emily's benefit, Gillian knew she must make some response, but her lips were too stiff to form words. All she could manage was a stifled murmur that could be taken for assent.

Emily, luckily or not, needed no more. "Well," she went on, "both times they danced, they danced the waltz! Yes!" She nodded vigorously when Gillian gave a start of surprise. "At Cousin Caroline's insistence, Mama allowed the waltz to be danced in our house. I do wish you had been there, Gilly! It was quite unforgettable. But, to return to my story, once when they danced, I overheard Aunt Sarah say to Mama, 'Well, I suppose there is no longer any mystery as to the identity of Caroline's latest attachment.' As you may imagine, Gilly, my ears pricked, and though I am shamed to admit it, I stepped behind a potted palm to prevent them catching sight of me. And though eavesdroppers are supposed to be punished, I was rewarded, for Mama not only nodded at that but actually said that there had not been any mystery in her mind for some time, as Cousin Caroline had written almost a month ago to beg her to invite Clare to the ball. Can you imagine, Gilly? I had not known Cousin Caroline was so wicked, but apparently she is, for Aunt Sarah, who is the greatest wag, as you know, said in that dry way of hers, 'Well, this time, at least, I can commend her choice.' Of course, Mama was scandalized, but Aunt Sarah only laughed and glancing pointedly at the ladies seated near them said, 'Just look at the way nearly every female in the room is following the marquess's progress about the dance floor. All our eyes are fairly hanging on him. Lud, Hetty, I'd say he is Ireland's revenge on the English. And if I were a few years younger and had even half of Caroline's looks, I vow I might try to sample his version of his revenge, myself.' Can you believe she would say such a thing, Gilly? I could have been knocked over with a feather, but that was not the end of it. Mama—my mother, Gilly—actually laughed at that, then went on to remark that she feared Cousin Caroline might be suffering from frustration, for with you and Lady Sutton here at Beechfield, Caroline could not meet Clare! Really, I did not know whether to be more shocked by the revelations about Cousin Caroline's conduct, or Mama's response! But is it not a delicious *on-dit*? Imagine Cousin Caroline carrying on so with Lord Clare! Lud, it is so shocking! And poor Lord Castlemont. He really is an unprepossessing man, but I wonder if he knows, and if he does, what does he think? It must be quite awful for him."

Gillian could not guess about Lord Castlemont. She knew only that she felt as if she had been turned to stone but for one place on the left side of her chest where her heart was. The ache there was so intense, she was afraid to move. Emily was saying something, but Gillian could not hear, for the jumbled phrases repeating themselves loudly in her mind.

Ireland's revenge on the English. Poor Lord Castlemont. Caroline's latest attachment. ". . . With you and Lady Sutton here at Beechfield, Caroline could not meet Clare."

Nor could Jason meet Lady Castlemont. But *he* had not suffered frustration. He had had a little fool to seduce.

"Gilly! Gilly, are you all right? You look so pale! Have I bored you into a swoon?"

Drawing upon some core of pride she had not even known she possessed, Gillian summoned the strength to smile and if the effort was wan, it did not matter, for she said with perfect truth, "I think I overdid it a bit yesterday, Em. I have not re-gained all my strength, but I will. Oh! Em, I just thought of it, but how did you get here from Chicksgrove?"

"I came with your uncle, for the fire is all but extinguished, and I left our carriage at Cousin Caroline's disposal. She went off with Clare, you see, and I did not know how or when she planned to return to Roundley House. It is my intention to ac-company you to Moreham Park. We should be leaving at any time. Your aunt and uncle are arranging your removal now."

It was the last straw. Lady Castlemont had left Chicksgrove with Jason. Perhaps he had a hunting box in which to entertain her.

Gillian stared at Emily unseeing a moment, then she stood very carefully. "Perhaps you could help me downstairs, Em. I should like to leave for Moreham Park as soon as it is possi-ble."

Chapter 19

"What a fire, eh, Clare? Jove, I thought we might lose the entire village, and I am grateful to you for going down, lad! There are many who would not have put themselves out, if they had come here as recently as you have. I doubt you even knew by sight the mother and father of that child you snatched from the flames." Lord Albemarle heaved himself from his chair and did his unexpected guest the honor of pouring him another brandy, though it was only early afternoon. "Here's to you, sir!" The baron lifted his glass and drank deeply before he resumed his seat and made an expansive gesture with the glass. "But perhaps I only weary you by repeating what you must have heard at least a dozen times yesterday. The poor Morris pair were nearly prostrate with gratitude to you, and only just behind them in singing your praises was Lady Castlemont."

Jason's mouth tightened so briefly, Albemarle was not even certain he had seen the indication that the countess's praises had been less than welcomed, but the baron found he was not surprised when his guest shrugged, saying dismissively, "I did what any man would have in the same situation."

Albemarle's heavy features sobered. "You believe in fairies, if you believe that, Clare! The roof to that house was falling in, but I'll not be tedious on the matter except to add that it was good of you to offer the Beswicks that house on your property. As you said, it is only a tenants' house and not half so fine as they are accustomed to, but it sports a roof, and that's more than they had before you made the offer."

"The house was standing empty. They will be doing me the favor of keeping it up."

At the spare reply, Albemarle studied his unexpected guest with increasing interest. He'd have sworn Clare was paying more attention to the brandy in the glass he swirled than he was to the words he spoke, and yet why had he come if not to discuss the fire? Time would have to tell he thought, half smiling to himself, for of a certainty Clare would not be moved before he wished to be. He seemed relaxed enough, lounging back in his chair, his long legs stretched before him and crossed at the ankles, but despite the relaxed pose, Albemarle had the sense that he was coiled tightly as . . . some large, dangerous cat waiting to pounce.

The baron was amusing himself by imagining Sally Warren's response, should she have heard that fanciful notion, when Clare glanced up at him, pinning him with a gaze that was intense enough, Albemarle decided, he could be compared to a dangerous cat.

Then Clare gave him a lopsided, rather ragged smile, and Albemarle wondered if he were not slipping into senility. Dangerous cat? The man now looked as boyish as such a man could look.

"This is proving to be more difficult than I had expected, Albemarle, but then . . . I suppose I should just get on with it. At least I'll no longer have to ponder how to go on. You see . . . I know this is going to come as some surprise, sir, but . . . Great God! I have never been in this position before, nor ever expected to be." He gave an oddly choked laugh, then shaking his head, turned an almost grimly determined look on Lord Albemarle. "To put it simply, sir, I wish to ask for your niece's hand. My interest in her will seem shockingly sudden to you, but I assure you, Albemarle, that I have been in her company enough to know that she is lovely, intelligent, spirited, and all I . . . well, in truth, all I never knew I did want in a wife. I will be able to care for her well enough," Jason went on, little trace now in his manner of his earlier uncertainty. "I am a great deal wealthier than most suspect, nor would I take her away to Ireland to live. I have found Somerset to be very hospitable, and I have always intended my land in Ireland to go to my cousin and his children. I know I am not received by the highest sticklers, but I think that might change, given how well regarded Miss Edwards is. However, should I not be forgiven either my mother's family or my reputation, I do not think Miss Edwards would be seriously dismayed. Though she is as sociable as the next woman, she seems genuinely to prefer country life and the companionship of good, close friends to the massive affairs that pass for entertainment in town. And so there you have my reason for calling on you today, sir. I hold your niece in the highest regard, and would do everything in my power to make her happy."

"Well, lad, you have, indeed, taken me by surprise!" Lord Albemarle boomed the obvious, while he studied the Irishman. By repute, Clare was a disreputable rake. Yet only the day before the baron had seen him charge into a burning house to rescue a child, and he knew from Hogwood that Clare had all but saved Gillian's life. There could be no higher recommendation for Albemarle than that, particularly as he had half decided that Clare's rival for Gillian would be inclined to meet any difficulty with nothing more intelligent than a sulk. "Have you spoken to Gilly?"

"No, sir, I have not." Jason had not spoken to her verbally, and he was careful to keep from his expression any suggestion that he had communicated with Gillian Edwards in any way other than words. He did not wish to play that card unless he must.

At the negative response, Albemarle's thick eyebrows shot skyward. "Doin' it by the book are you, lad? Now that does come as a surprise."

Jason could not but smile then, but the baron's responding smile faded after a moment. "You know Rockingham's been sniffing after her," he remarked, seemingly as much to himself as Jason, for he did not await an answer. "Can't say I am keen on the boy myself, but Margaret is. Family's great guns in town, and m'sister fancies the thought of Gillian gracefully presiding over the *ton*. Still"—Albemarle pursed his lips thoughtfully—"I cannot but suspect a man who tongue-lashes another's servant and at a ball, yet. Nor was I well pleased by his reluctance to visit Gilly. If he were so concerned with where she was, why did he not storm into Beechfield and stake his claim? A man would, and a man wouldn't give a fig if she had a small . . . "

Abruptly Albemarle swung his large head about to regard Jason with a keen look. "You must have seen her wound when you played chess with her, and yet it doesn't seem to have put you off." Jason started to make some answer about beauty being more than skin deep, but the baron had evidently not been asking for his opinion. "It's another reservation altogether that I have about you, Clare," he continued. The baron's use of his title name, as much as the announcement of a reservation, caused Jason to brace himself inwardly at least. "From what I understand your father was not a faithful husband. I make no judgment upon him, you understand. But I want better for Gilly, and who's to say you'll be any different than your father? You've not been up to now, by all accounts."

Jason met the baron's eyes without resentment. He'd wanted better for Gilly than his father, too. "I have not taken vows up to now, either," he reminded Gillian's guardian levelly. "But, more important, I am the product of two parents. My father, as you say, loved easily and often. My mother, on the other hand, did not. She fell in love late, and was never interested in any other man than my father, though God knows, he gave her reason aplenty to look elsewhere. For my part, I have never loved until now."

There. He had said it. And Albemarle looked almost as surprised by the admission as Jason was that he had made it. Still, and Jason would forever count it in the baron's favor, his host did not require a second phrasing of the sentiment to believe. After a startled, if keen look, Albemarle merely nodded sharply. " 'Tis the answer I wished to hear, lad. Well, the best I can do for you is to set the choice before her. I don't mean to force her into anything. You understand that?"

Jason had absolutely no doubt as to what Gillian's answer would be. She had already given it. A smile he could not control flashed out. "Yes, quite. Will you put the choice to her soon, sir?"

Albemarle allowed himself a hearty, satisfying chuckle. "As if you would not run upstairs and do it for me, if I did not. But I'm pleased to see you can at least show the requisite respect for the elderly, and be assured, I shall go at once."

Lord Albemarle found Gillian in the library, but before he greeted her, he scanned the room for Lady Sutton, and breathed a sigh of relief when he did not see her there. He wished to be certain of Gillian's mind before he took on his sister.

"Gilly?"

"Yes, Uncle Arthur? My, but you look very serious." Gillian concentrated upon forcing her mouth into the smile her uncle would expect from her.

"Well, I've a serious matter to discuss with you, Gilly girl. It isn't every day a gentleman asks for your hand."

Gillian stared. "What? Lord Rockingham has come asking for my hand. I thought . . . I thought he intended to wait until Christmas."

"And what answer would you make the viscount?" Lord Albemarle asked, shamelessly taking advantage of her misapprehension.

Rockingham! Gillian clasped her hands together tightly.

Could she marry him now she had learned what a bounder Clare was? No! She did not want him. And dear heaven, she was used goods anyway.

Seeing Gillian's distress and feeling responsible, Albemarle reached out at once to soothe her. "Now, now, Gilly girl." He patted her shoulder awkwardly, afraid he might touch some bruise. "I did not intend to upset you, only wanted to know if you were eager for the boy. But as I can see you are not, I will tell you that it is not Rockingham below at all, but Clare."

Had her uncle slapped her, Gillian could not have been more stunned. Jason was below. He cared for her aft . . . no! She must not let herself be gulled again. Her thoughts seemed to fly as she considered his motives. He did not know she knew of Lady Castlemont. Marrying Gillian, he might think he would gain entry into the *ton* and thereby meet Lady Castlemont, and any other paramour, the more easily. Or . . . would marrying Gillian not be a perfect Irish revenge upon the English? He could betray his English wife, while cuckolding an English peer.

"Clare? Clare has come to ask for my hand?" Gillian was distantly aware that she did not have control of her voice, but she could not seem to stop herself. "He came to you without any warning to me? Of course he did! He's as arrogant as he is faithless!"

"Gilly! Gilly girl!" Lord Albemarle regarded her with a dismay for which Gillian held Jason ultimately responsible. "Clare says he loves you, and he seemed . . . well, confident of your response."

"Because he is an arrogant . . . arrogant Irishman!" she cried, unable to think of anything worse at the moment. "He does not love me. I doubt he could love anyone but himself. And you may tell him to take his offer of marriage to Ireland for all I care, so long as he is gone, and I never have to see him again!"

Dismayed by Gillian's overwrought response, Lord Albemarle attempted not to reason with her so much as to get to the cause. But he quite failed. His niece met his every attempt at a probe with increasing heat that revealed nothing except the depth of her antipathy toward the marquess. Finally, unhappily, Albemarle conceded defeat and returned to his study to inform Clare that his offer of marriage had been rejected.

The marquess was quite as startled as Lord Albemarle had expected. There was a moment's pregnant silence, then an explosive, disbelieving, "What?"

But Albemarle was more concerned for his niece than for his neighbor's sensibilities. "What's between you, Clare? I guessed there was more than a chess game and that help you gave her with Davy Jennings to prompt you to ask for her, but I was willing to overlook any other—chance—meetings you might have had, yet damn it, man, she refused you in a fury. What made her so wild?"

Clare regarded his host with eyes that caused Albemarle, no coward by any means, to give thanks he was an old man. Had he been younger, he thought Clare might have torn him apart merely for suggesting that he had done anything to turn Gillian into the distraught fury he'd left upstairs.

And as to an answer, the marquess said only harshly, "I have not the slightest idea what made her wild. I should like an answer myself. And now, good day."

Albemarle sagged down into a chair, ignoring an impulse to call the marquess back and force the two young people together in order to get to the bottom of the emotion between them. He knew he could not force Clare to anything.

In the library, Gillian sat as silent as her uncle did in his study. Staring unseeing into the fire, she listened for some sound of Clare's going. Clare, the treacherous rake, the user of innocents, the wretched . . .

The door to the library flew open with a force that brought Gillian up out of her chair and turned her around all in one motion. It was Clare. The very air around him seemed to vibrate with his anger, and the force of his gaze was such that it wiped away any irrelevant questions such as how had he found her or where her uncle might be.

"What in the devil prompted that answer to your uncle? Are you miffed that I did not ignore the fire raging through Chicksgrove to ask for you yesterday?"

"What in the devil prompted that question you put to my uncle?" Gillian ripped back at him, her eyes blazing. Now that she saw him she was so angry with him for deceiving her, for playing her for a fool, that she'd have liked to claw his eyes out, and was not even the least shocked by the violence she felt. "Did true love prompt you, my lord? Perhaps for your mistress! I am surprised you could tear yourself away from her this long! Get back to her, you Irish black-heart!"

A muscle flexed along Clare's lean jaw. And it was a moment before he spoke very low and very carefully. "I do not have a mistress, and you will have this one chance only to listen to me."

She wanted to listen. The desire to listen to him, to have him tell her that he loved her, that he did not care twopence for Lady Castlemont was great enough to cause Gillian to clap her hand to her heart, as if she were afraid the struggle not to be seduced by him a second time might break it. And her response, when she made it, was all the sharper, shriller, and more uncontrolled. "Get out! Get your lying Irish tongue . . ."

But he was gone, having wheeled about on the first command and departed her life without another word.

Chapter 20

"Aunt Margaret, may I speak with you a moment?"

"Of course, my dear."

Lady Sutton sat gravely, waiting for her niece to take a seat. She knew nothing of Clare's proposal. Gillian and Albemarle between them had agreed there was no reason to tell her, but the elder woman knew something was amiss. Gillian had been pale and withdrawn since they had left Beechfield.

"I've had a note from Lord Rockingham." Gillian paused, turning the note over in her fingers, but could find no reprieve in the cream-colored rectangle from the blow she would deal her aunt. "He is coming to call this afternoon."

"Oh?"

Gillian heard the unease in the single syllable, and thought perhaps her aunt had guessed what she would say. Unhappily she found it no easier to go on. "When he comes, Aunt Margaret, I wish to decline his invitation to go to Chevely for Christmas." Lady Sutton took a sharp, deep breath. Gillian was not certain whether she was shocked or giving herself time to think what to say. But there was nothing she could say. Gillian could not have married Rockingham even had she wanted. He would never take her now that she was used goods. To spare her aunt the effort of argument, she said with quiet force, "I cannot marry the viscount. I am deeply sorry, Aunt Margaret, for I know how my decision will disappoint you."

Gillian ground her teeth into the soft flesh of her lower lip, holding back the tears that stung her eyes. Were Lady Sutton to learn the whole . . . but Gillian shut off the thought. Her aunt would never learn the whole. Gillian was determined on it, and she must control her tears, for disappointing her aunt in regards to Rockingham would never have driven her to sob as she was on the very brink of doing.

But her aunt could read the unnatural shine in her eyes well enough. "My dear, Gillian! Please do not cry on my account, for you must know that I desire your happiness above everything!"

"Oh, Aunt Margaret!" The tears welled over then, and when Lady Sutton held out her hands, Gillian took them, holding them tightly. "You are so good to me, I . . ."

"Gillian! I love you, my dear. And if the thought of marrying Lord Rockingham reduces you to this unhappy state, then . . . I cannot but regret ever promoting his suit."

"You are determined to make me cry!" Gillian freed one hand to swipe at the fresh tears on her cheeks. "And I'll not hear that you regret anything. He was a reasonable choice, quite the best catch of the Season in everyone's eyes, only I . . . I find him pleasant company, Aunt Margaret, but I want to feel more for my husband."

Lady Sutton fussed over her niece a moment, using a delicate, prettily embroidered handkerchief to dry her eyes. Then, when Gillian was steadier, she took both her niece's hands again and asked carefully, "Gillian, will you tell me something? Has Lord Clare influenced your feelings in regard to Lord Rockingham?"

Gillian caught her breath against the sharp thrust of pain the mention of Clare brought her, and quickly shook her head. "I am afraid I was uncertain about Lord Rockingham from the first, Aunt Margaret. Not that I took him into dislike. He was a familiar face in town and good company, but I never felt quite as ease with him. Nor am I even now entirely certain of the depth of his affection for me. Oh, I know he admires my looks, and was greatly pleased by my success in town, but he has never asked my thoughts on any subject of importance. Indeed, I am not convinced he would be pleased to know I do think, and too, I am sorry to say I do not much respect his choice of friends."

When Gillian paused, Lady Sutton nodded. "You mean Lord Bolton, I think, and I cannot but admit that I do not have much liking for that young man, either. As they had become friends at school, I hoped that one day the viscount would outgrow him."

"Perhaps he will, but . . . no, I feel quite mean-spirited! And I do not wish to dwell upon the viscount's supposed shortcomings. I only want you to understand that I have not made this decision lightly. I thought my misgivings might fade with time, but they have only grown stronger. Aunt Margaret, I am so sorry to disappoint you . . ."

"Now, child! I should be far more disappointed if I saw you in an unhappy marriage on my account. And I will confess to you, Gillian, that I have had my own doubts. When Rockingham did not come to Beechfield to visit you, I was most disappointed. It seemed very small of him to deny you his company because, as I suppose, he did not wish to enter the home of a man he seems to consider a rival. But is he, Gillian? Is Clare a rival for your affections?"

"I shall not wed Clare, Aunt Margaret."

"You have been subdued since we left Beechfield," Lady Sutton pressed, though she did so gently.

Gillian bowed her head and reminded herself that above all, she wanted to spare her aunt as much pain as she could. "I have been weighing this decision about Rockingham, you see."

"Oh, my dear, I wish you had confided in me! I would have told you then as I do now that I would never want you to wed anyone for whom you could not come to care a great, great deal."

Gillian could not speak for the lump in her throat. She did not deserve that statement of unstinting loyalty and support. Not one word of it, for she had betrayed her aunt as deeply as it was possible to betray a person who loved and trusted her.

After the interview with her aunt, her meeting with Rockingham was almost nothing for Gillian. When she had told him that after due consideration and with thanks for his kindness in extending the invitation to Chevely that she must decline his invitation, he said, "I see," stiffly enough that she knew he did see. He did not press his suit or demand an explanation for her supposed change of heart, though he did say, half petulantly, half defensively, that he regretted his duties as a guest had detained him at Roundley House. "You must have been quite bored confined to your room," he added, but spoiled the moment by darting her a quick look that seemed to search for some betraying sign that she had been entertained by her host.

She'd have respected the viscount more if he had asked straight out about Clare, but feeling glad in all to be done with Rockingham, she merely said "I was bored at times, yes, but Aunt Margaret was with me and Em came to visit often. Where do you go from Somerset, my lord?"

And that was that. She had turned off two gentlemen in as many days. One she cared little about, but the other . . . She had thought he had come to care for her. She had even thought he had come to love her. Oh, what an absurdly green, green girl she was! True, he had not given her a slip on the shoulder straightaway. There was some honor in him, but when she had gone into his arms that last night, she had put his thin honor and what restraint he possessed to too great a test.

Or perhaps it was Lady Castlemont that had worn his restraint thin. Perhaps the sight of her at the ball had whetted his appetite for a woman so much that any woman would have done.

The thought was like a dagger, Gillian could not seem to turn aside. Over and over she tortured herself with what might have gone on between Clare and his mistress. And she called herself worse than a fool for having willfully decided he was not what he himself had warned her he was: no candidate for domestication. Oh, God, but she was glad to be quit of him, and his travesty of a proposal of marriage. As if she would ever have shared her husband!

At times, Gillian longed for nothing more than to strike out at Jason, to hurt him as he hurt her, while at others she wanted only to keen her misery and shame. She cried in the night, her pillow clutched to her, but during the day, she had to stuff all the ache and hurt and fury away, for she had her aunt and her uncle and even Emily and Mary Beswick to see. As a result, a merciful numbness set in after a time.

The season had changed since her accident. The trees had lost their leaves, and the gardens were bare and brown. Walking with Delhi, scuffing at the few ragged leaves the gardeners had overlooked, Gillian felt as dead as the world around her. There scarcely seemed a point to living, and as to the future, she could not bring herself to care about it.

The future, however, came to her, in a negative sense. Gillian had not dared to allow herself to think of the possibility that she might be with child. It was too dreadful to contemplate that she might bear the proof of her shame and stupidity for all the world to see, yet beneath the deadened surface of her feelings, there remained a tenseness. All the odder then, that when her monthly flow did start, she should sink to the floor of her room to bury her face in her hands.

It was well and truly over. Any possibility that she might be forced to go to Jason was void. She had not known that she half longed for it, had not realized even that she wanted to carry his child. There could not have been a more foolish wish, and Gillian knew it, but all the possibilities, all the "what ifs" that she'd not allowed herself to entertain came rushing in on her. Perhaps in time she could have brought him to love her had she accepted his offer of marriage. Perhaps, if she had given him a chance, he could have learned to be faithful. Perhaps Emily had seen amiss. Perhaps that final straw, Jason and Lady Castlemont leaving Chicksgrove together, had been something else. Perhaps . . . perhaps she ought not to have been afraid to give him a hearing, when he had said he had no mistress. God knew, she was young. She had hated just the thought that he'd had mistresses in the past, but then to put a face to what had been an abstract notion, and such a beautiful, sophisticated face . . . had she gone a little mad?

For the first time, Gillian wondered where Jason was. Had he gone somewhere with Lady Castlemont? Was the countess at Beechfield? Was he there alone? And if he were alone, what would that mean? Half angrily Gillian tamped down a sudden, painful surge of hope. She would not be devastated a second time, but she could invite Emily to take luncheon and ask in some discreet way, what her friend knew. Surely there could be no harm in knowing, and if . . . but she would consider what to do after she knew more.

Gillian had just sat down to pen a note to Emily when her uncle's butler, Padgett, came to advise her that she had a visitor, a gentleman whose card announced him to be a solicitor. Astonished, Gillian inquired if Padgett was certain the man had asked for her, to which Padgett replied, in the kindly way that was his, that he was quite sure. As her aunt was taking a nap, and her uncle had gone to Durston to look at a hunter for sale there, Gillian went alone to meet the man.

Mr. Gordon, a tall, slightly stooped man of middle age, was a trifle disconcerted to learn her uncle was away from home. "Well, I suppose it is of no matter," he said after a moment's consideration. "I was instructed to bring this letter to the both of you, Miss Edwards, and remain to answer any questions you might have, but as the letter concerns you alone, I can see no harm in allowing you to read it without Lord Albemarle. If your uncle has questions later, he may write to me."

Accepting the single sheet of thick vellum he held out to her, Gillian was aware of a tightening in her stomach, but she did not ask Mr. Gordon whom he represented. She saw that he was served tea and biscuits, then retired to the next room to learn in privacy what and who had brought the solicitor to her.

Gillian displayed a good deal of foresight when she did not snatch the letter and read it at once, as she had wanted to do. Had she, she'd have gaped witlessly in front of a stranger.

Written in a clerk's neat, even hand, the letter announced that the property of Beechfield in the county of Somerset had been given to Miss Gillian Edwards for her use for the remainder of her life. If she had children, the property was to go at her death to the eldest, but if there were no children, the property was to return to the Marquess of Clare or his heir. At the bottom, on the designated line, there was a bold, scrawling, legal signature: Jason Devereux, Marquess of Clare.

Gillian looked up swiftly from it, sucking in her cheeks, trying to stave off the by-then familiar rush of sharp pain. The reminder of Jason was too strong, however. It overwhelmed her pitiful defenses, washing through her, leaving her with her head bowed. He had touched the very page she held. He had dictated its terms and signed his name.

She stared at the neatly penned words dancing before her eyes, and finally they resolved themselves into something almost sensible. Dear God, he had given her Beechfield! And she knew why. Jason had faced the possible consequence of that night they'd shared as she had not. And he had sought to cushion the blow. If she did carry his child, no man would marry her, unless she brought something valuable to the marriage. There were ten thousand fertile acres at Beechfield, inducement enough for a third or fourth son with little interest in either the army or the church to accept another man's child as his own. She could also, if she wished, remain independent. He had given her the freedom of choice, all the while providing for the child she only might be carrying.

Could he not care for her and do such a thing? Had his only concern been for the child she might carry? It was to her he had deeded Beechfield. Beechfield!

Mr. Gordon waited for her in the next room. If he could not answer those questions, he could perhaps answer another. And if he had speculated as to why a man would make her such a gift, Gillian did not allow herself to dwell on the thought. She had more pressing concerns than the opinion of a man she would never see again.

But Mr. Gordon smiled quite naturally when she returned to the drawing room. "That was quite refreshing, Miss Edwards," he said gesturing to the tea tray. "Thank you and now, there is one more matter to discuss before I answer any questions you may have." He extracted a paper from a thin leather case he had carried with him. "If it meets your approval, I shall see that this is what is published in regards to the property in question. As you can see, it announces that the ownership of Beechfield Hall and the surrounding estate has been transferred from Lord Clare to your uncle. Because Lord Albemarle is your guardian, there is no need to mention your name, nor is there any obligation to state publicly what may or may not have been paid for the property."

Gillian felt tears prick her eyes. He had to have some care for her, at least. He had to have, for not only had he made himself a good deal poorer to take care of her, he had done it in such a way as to spare her any possibility of gossip. It would be thought that her uncle had bought the property, something Lord Albemarle had even been heard to say he wished to do in the days when Lord Lely had still owned the property but left its management to the agent, Murdock.

"I see, Mr. Gordon. Thank you for bringing all of this personally. If my uncle has any questions, I am sure he will get in touch with you. But before you go, can you tell me where Lord Clare is? I . . ."

She could not think what to say, she wanted so much more than to merely thank Jason. Mercifully Mr. Gordon did not require a detailed reason for her interest in the marquess's whereabouts. "Indeed, Miss Edwards. I can tell you that his lordship has returned to his estate in Ireland."

Gillian saw the solicitor to the door, then tried to summon calm as she waited for her uncle to return from Durston. She did not look forward to telling him of Mr. Gordon's visit. Her uncle knew Clare quite well enough to be certain that the marquess was not so quixotic as to make her a gift of a large estate without a very good reason. And he knew, as well, that Clare had asked for her.

In the end, Gillian could not face him as he read the letter. After she handed it to him, she went to the window, and so when Lord Albemarle spoke as shrewdly as Gillian had guessed he would, he addressed her back. "Gilly girl," he said quietly, "are you carrying Clare's child?"

Her hands clasped together so tightly that her fingers were white, Gillian bowed her head. "No, Uncle Arthur."

There was a pause, but she could not have turned to face him to save her life. Then he asked quite gently, "Might he have reason to believe you are?"

She stared at her clenched fingers through tears his tone had brought on. "Yes."

Another moment of silence ensued. Gillian felt as if she could not draw breath, and then abruptly she swung about. "Do you despise me, Uncle Arthur? It was my doing not his, really, and if you cannot have me . . ."

Lord Albemarle never allowed her finish. Surging to his feet, he held out his arms, and Gillian ran into them. Her uncle murmured a great many soothing things, many of which only caused Gillian to cry the harder, but finally she sobbed herself limp, and they sat down together on a small couch before the fire that warmed the study.

"Gilly girl," he began a bit hesitantly, while she was mopping her eyes with the large handkerchief he had produced for her. "You need not answer if you do not wish to do so, but I think you will understand that I cannot but wonder why you did not accept Clare's proposal of marriage. I know that you would not have . . . gone to him, if you did not care for him deeply, and Clare did tell me that he loved you."

Gillian studied the rumpled mess she had made of her uncle's handkerchief, then finally in a small, almost weary voice she said, "I could not share him, Uncle Arthur. He went with his mistress the day after . . . while I was still in his home."

Lord Albemarle frowned. "With Lady Castlemont?"

Gillian was shocked into looking up. "You knew?"

"Mrs. Warren and I were good friends as children, and it was she who passed on the rumor to me. But I wonder, Gilly, who told you that Clare went with Lady Castlemont?"

A bit wryly, Gillian thought she need never again worry about shocking her uncle. "Emily. She saw them leave Chicksgrove together the day of the fire."

He nodded as if she had confirmed his guess. "Did you lay the charge before Clare, then?"

Gillian thought back to the few words she had said, and gave a small shake of her head. "I accused him, but . . . I would not listen to his defense. I"—she wadded the handkerchief into a very tight ball, pressing it between her palms—"I was afraid I would believe anything he told me."

"And now, what do you believe?" Lord Albemarle asked, gesturing to the letter in his hand.

Gillian sat back on the couch, staring at the letter a long moment, then slowly lifted her eyes to her uncle. "That I ought to have given him a hearing, and will do so now, if he will allow me to change my mind."

Chapter 21

The formal gardens at Conmarra were not so different from the gardens at Moreham. Gillian found the main walk easily enough and set off down it with her shoulders squared. She was glad of the sun shining above, though. She needed its warmth. She felt cold with anxiety. Dear God, why had she not written?

She had been asking herself that question since she had set out for Ireland, even though she had answered it once before for her aunt. That had come after Gillian had told Lady Sutton of the gift Clare had made her. She had been frank with her aunt to a point. Lady Sutton might not know that Gillian had given herself to Clare, but she knew now that Gillian had fallen in love with him. Lady Sutton had not been so astonished by the news as her niece had expected. She said she had noted an emotional response in Gillian whenever his name was mentioned, and had guessed there was deep feeling between them.

Gillian took a deep breath against the sudden sting of tears. She was extraordinarily lucky in the guardians she had. They had stood staunchly by her, despite how shoddily she had dealt with them. Indeed, they'd stood so staunchly by her, they had both insisted on accompanying her to Ireland, after she had explained to her aunt that having denied Clare a hearing on the charges she had made against him, she feared if she wrote to him he would write in reply that she need not bother to come.

Lady Sutton had remarked in return that a man who gives a woman an estate of ten thousand acres must surely have enough regard for that woman to come to her were she to write and tell him she would listen to whatever he had to say, late though she might be with the invitation. But Gillian knew, as Lady Sutton did not, that Clare might only have been thinking of his child when he had made her owner of Beechfield, and in her mind could too clearly hear Jason warning, *"You will have this one opportunity only to listen to me."* No, by letter he might have denied her a second chance to hear him out, but if she went to him, she had to believe he would not toss her out bodily.

The butler, an Irishman with a pointed, angled nose remarkably similar to that of Bexton's, his counterpart at Beechfield, had told her that his lordship was in the woods that lay only a short walk through the gardens and across a part of the park. He and "the family," as the butler had put it, were gathering holly with which to deck the hall for Christmas.

Gillian wished mightily that Jason were alone. She had tried to think of some strategy to get him away from his family without revealing her presence, but she had not been able to think of any way to persuade the dignified butler to abet her schemes. She had, however, felt up to informing the butler, she would find the marquess herself, for a servant could be sent back to advise her his lordship was unavailable.

True, Jason had told Uncle Arthur that he loved her, but he had not told her, and he had ridden off from Chicksgrove in company with Lady Castlemont that afternoon. Gillian clasped her gloved hands together a little more tightly. He had not remained in England at Lady Castlemont's side, however. She must cling to *that* fact still, for it had carried her across the Irish Sea and now down an Irish stone path.

She continued to put one foot before the other briskly enough, until she descended the steps of the terrace that separated the gardens from the soft, rolling lawn of the park. Then, turning to her left as per her instructions, she went suddenly still. The butler had said the woods were only a short walk across the park. She had simply not imagined how short a walk. The woods were only thirty yards from where she stood.

And a group of people was emerging from them. Already one, a woman holding a little girl's hand, had seen her. Gillian could not make her feet move another step. A tallish man with a boy on his shoulder saw her next, arrested there at the bottom of the steps. His eyes never left her as he turned to call something over his shoulder. Gillian's gaze skipped nervously beyond him, but it was a young brown head she saw. She was placing him as Liam O'Neil's eldest son, when a man stepped up beside him. The boy made a gesture toward her, but already Gillian's eyes had locked with Jason's.

He had been smiling, laughing perhaps about the amount of holly they had gathered, but when their eyes met, his expression froze. She should never have come. She should have written and had him tell her he had no time for a weakhearted, overly cosseted Sassenach child-girl who went mad at the first sign of difficulty. The very thought that he might see her as a coward, however, made Gillian lift her chin and all but stab the air with it. She had no thought for the others, had no thought for how grim she might have looked, or how defiant. She stood waiting, her hands clasped before her eyes fastened on Jason, as he approached her, eating up the short distance between them with his long, easy strides.

His expression never softened. The closer he came, indeed, the tighter the set of his jaw seemed to become. And his eyes . . . looked hard as onyx and as impenetrable.

Then he was before her, tall enough to fill all her vision, and handsome enough to make her glad he did. Her throat seemed to close.

"Come," he said, half turning from her even as he reached her. "There is a summer house by the lake where we may have some privacy."

Gillian inclined her head, unable to speak for the thickness in her throat. Surely those would not have been his first words to her had he loved her. Even had he been angry. But he did not seem that. His tone had been guarded and firm, not harsh, and his expression matched, she saw, darting a swift glance at his taut jaw. It was the expression a man might wear before he dispatched a merely unpleasant duty.

The park sloped down to a natural lake. Even in winter it was a pretty site, bounded by woods on one side and gently rolling land on the others. Gillian took in nothing of it. Her every sense was attuned to the man beside her. Before she had come, she had thought her life would be dull and gray without him. Now she saw him, she knew it would be worse. If he did not care for her in truth, she was not certain she could bear the knowledge.

The summer house was damp, but there was a stack of wood by a large fireplace, and Jason took the time to start a blaze. Gillian stood in the middle of the large, airy, chilly room watching him and trying to fight a feeling of reality. He could not want her. He was too distant. She clenched her teeth to keep from whirling away on a sob.

When the fire caught, sending a rush of heat even as far as Gillian, Jason slowly stood and turned. She realized then that he had been putting off the moment when they must speak, and it was only a stray, useless glimmer of pride that allowed her to meet his eyes.

She could read nothing in his expression and was unprepared for his first words. "Are you increasing?"

No hello, or even, forgive the chill in the room, though she had traveled a long way. Her chin rose again. "And if I were?"

"I would marry you," he said with as little warmth as hesitation.

So. He would do the honorable thing, if absolutely forced to it. "And if I were not?"

There was a flash in his eyes, come and gone too quickly to read. "Are you?"

A question for a question for a question and so on. Gillian had had enough. Her eyes flashed. She had crossed a sea for him. Had bounced over miserable roads, had subjected her uncle to abysmal seasickness, and Jason did not even take the time to say he was surprised to see her.

"I am only increasing in nervousness!"

"You are not with child?"

Hadn't she just said so? Dear God, did he want her only if she were carrying his child? Did he not care for her at all?

"I am not with child, no!"

Oddly some of the tension in his stance seemed to evaporate. He had never taken his eyes off her from the moment he had turned about, but now they seemed to probe more intently. "Then, why have you come?"

He seemed to be searching her soul with those black eyes, but in truth, Jason did not look any friendlier. Gillian decided to say no more than that she was a fair person who regretted not giving him a hearing. She would not commit herself further than that. Her pride might be all she had left at the end of the encounter.

"Why have I come?" she echoed, wanting time, though she had decided her course. It was impossible not to want to draw out the moment. It might be the last one she would have alone with Jason. And he was there so close and so familiar. Her eyes lingered on the sharp, clear-cut lines of his face. Lud, but his nose was so straight, it was little wonder he was autocratic, and his chin and jaw so firm and chiseled, there could be, again, no mistaking, his will. But his mouth . . . she remembered suddenly all he had done to her with his mouth.

Color surged into her face, and she felt the heat of it just as she saw him flick his gaze to her cheeks. "Why?" she repeated, wanting to distract him, but managing only to bring his dark, penetrating eyes back to hers. They caught her as fast and sure as they always had been able to do. "Because . . . because I have been wretched without you!" The words came from nowhere, and yet she could no more have caught them back than she could have given him up without any fight. "I love you! But," she rushed on, making herself say it all before she fell into his arms and agreed to anything—or he thrust her away. "I'll not share you! I could not. Ever!"

She sounded like a schoolgirl. Oh, oh, dear God. Gillian swept her eyes shut. He would send her away, and there was nothing she could do. She had spoken the truth.

Then his hand was on her arm, and he was hauling her to him. Gillian's eyes flew open. Jason was smiling. Brilliantly.

"Well?" she demanded, when he did not seem inclined to do more than smile down in that way at her.

"Well," he said, still smiling that brilliant smile that made her heart fly, "it took you a deuced long time to get here, Gilly girl. I had nearly given up on you."

"What?" she half shouted, pushing away from him.

But Jason had no intention of letting her go. He pulled her back tightly against him. "Beechfield was a declaration, Gillian." He was still half smiling, but there was an intensity beneath the humor. "You were so angry that wretched day, I judged that I would have to take my chances with a grand gesture if I was to get you to listen to me without humbling my pride entirely."

"And so you had me humble mine?"

She did not ask it angrily. Jason's eyes had dipped to the ribbon of her bonnet, and after trailing his hands up her arms and over her shoulders, he began to untie Gillian's bow, causing her heart to pound too hard for anything so unpleasant as anger.

That morning, pressed for time, and too anxious to sit still, Gillian had had Maude braid her hair and pin the braid atop her head. When the braid fell loose over her shoulder, Jason tossed the bonnet onto a nearby chair and untying the ribbon around the end of the thick tawny plait, began to undo all of Maude's work.

"You called me a black-hearted Irishman and a liar," he reminded her, glancing up from his project.

Gillian caught his arm, squeezing it urgently, though she scarcely realized what she did. "Jason, I have come all this way to apologize for what I said to you that day! I was jealous, terribly, terribly jealous. I thought . . . Emily had overheard some talk about Lady Castlemont being your mistress and then she saw her cousin ride away from Chicksgrove with you."

"Lady Castlemont followed me from Chicksgrove," Jason corrected, still working on her braid. "We had had an understanding before I went down to Somerset. That is quite true, but by the time she arrived for the Wades' ball . . . everything had changed." Jason spread her hair across her shoulders and as if he had dreamed of doing it for a very long time, he slowly ran his fingers through its silky weight, bringing his hands at last to the back of her head. Cupping the curve there, he tilted her face up to him. There was no humor at all softening his expression now. He seemed intent on drinking in the sight of her. "You had come into my life, Gilly girl, and turned it upside down. I had always thought I would be the sort of husband my father was, but when I saw Lady Castlemont at the Wades' ball, I understood I would be like my mother not my father. I have never had less interest in a woman. I did not want her to turn any disappointment she might feel in regards to me against you, however. She is the sort who could, and I did not speak plainly enough to her that night. Hence, she followed me out of Chicksgrove, whereupon we had a scene on a public lane that was not only unpleasant, it was so prolonged, I missed you before you left Beechfield. You cannot imagine, I think, what it was like to return to that house and find all trace of you gone." His hands tightened on her. "I could not have lived there without you. That was the message I wished to convey, or part of it, when I gave you the estate, but Gillian, none of that goes to the apology I owe you."

"Me?" Gillian looked at him, startled.

Jason nodded, looking so grim suddenly that Gillian pressed her hands reassuringly against his chest. "I ought never have taken you to my bed that night even though I feared that Lady Sutton would deny you to me and hand you over to Rockingham if I did not make you irrevocably mine."

"Like a pirate," Gillian murmured half to herself as she dipped her head to kiss his chest just where his cravat disappeared beneath his coat.

But Jason had heard her, and shook her shoulders a little. "More like a fool, a reckless fool!" he exclaimed in disgust. "That is how I acted. Had I gone to Albemarle, he'd have supported my suit, as he did two days later, and I would have saved us both this few weeks, for you would never have been so wild over the Castlemont nonsense, had you not felt as vulnerable as you must have felt after what we had done."

Gillian felt the blush rise on her cheeks and laid her forehead on his chest to hide her response to the memory of all they had done. He smelled good, but even more, Jason felt so right and familiar, she wanted to cry for joy at being where she was.

"I did feel vulnerable," she admitted quietly after a minute. Then she lifted her head to look him directly in the eye. "But the responsibility for what we did is equally mine." When Jason started to protest, she laid a finger across his lips. "Yes, Jason," she insisted, though he promptly kissed her finger. "Listen, please, for I've my own apologies. Unbeknownst to you, I had decided to seduce you." At his lifted brow, she smiled but only briefly. "It is true. Our minds, it seems were on like courses, though we did not know it. I had reasoned that though you wanted me, you would never ask for me unless I left you no choice but to make me your wife. I ought, of course, to have talked to you, but somehow it seemed we'd no time for talking and that I would lose you if I did not act. Yet I do not regret anything, though you are right to say these last weeks have been miserable, for I have learned a valuable lesson. And that is to trust the man I love. I daresay we shall encounter other women who have been your mistress." Gillian gave him a rueful smile. "I won't pretend that I will encounter them easily. But I will always give you a hearing, Jason, before I allow a rumor to undo me again. It is, I think, a valuable lesson."

Jason growled, which might have meant many things, but as the growl was followed by a fierce, hard, long kiss, it seemed to mean he approved of the lesson she'd learned.

"God, Gilly," Jason whispered forcefully sometime later, his lips only scant inches above hers, "I wanted nothing more than to gallop back to Moreham the next day and shake you until you believed in me, but I could not force you to listen to me. You had to find it in yourself to believe in me and in the two of us. The only flaw in my plan was that you might have conceived that night, and if you had, I would never know whether you came to me only on account of the child."

"Now I understand why you demanded if I were increasing in much the same tone as you might have used to ask if I had murdered Willet, our agent." Gillian put undue emphasis on that "our" and she grinned up at Jason, her brimming heart in her smile. "What an extravagant gesture giving me Beechfield was, Jason! I wanted to weep."

"I did not want to make you weep, only bring you to me." He pulled her close and kissed her as if he could not resist. "Ah, Gilly, Gilly, I have missed you. I was afraid for the first time in my life, afraid you might not come."

It was Gillian's turn to give Jason a blazing smile as she twined her arms around his neck. "When I discovered I was not carrying your child, and that there would really be no link between us unless I acted, I moved heaven and earth to get here, which I must tell you means I have brought Aunt Margaret and Uncle Arthur with me."

"Lady Sutton?" Jason echoed in unfeigned astonishment.

Gillian laughed. "I think she was won over when she learned you had given me Beechfield while Rockingham had not even bothered to call on me when I was recovering."

"And what of the viscount?"

Gillian smiled up into Jason's suddenly intent face. "He was never a consideration after I met you. We had our parting of the ways the day after you came to Moreham."

"And so you are quite free to marry me?"

His smile made her heart melt, but still she asked, "Jason, do you really want me? I can be so foolish!"

"Evidently it is a brand of foolishness for which I am a fool." He grinned down at her a long moment, then his smile faded. "I love you, Gilly. Unreservedly and forever. And I want you for my wife. Will you have me?"

"Unreservedly and forever," she said in the same grave, intent tone. "I love you, my own, and life seemed a paltry gray thing without you."

"God above, but I have waited a seeming eternity to hear you say that, my love."

Jason swept her into a tight embrace, which Gillian returned for some minutes before she leaned back just a little to look up at him. Her face seemed to glow with her happiness. "Will you not kiss me, Jason? It is an English custom to kiss the bride, you see."

"Is it now?" A grin broke out on his face. "Well, what a happy combination we are, my love, for you see, while it may be an English custom to kiss the bride, it is an Irish one to kiss her a very, very long time."